French Kissing

"I'd also like to know why you lied to me?" Gray said. His eyes were a hard, dark green.

She wanted to sink through the floor. "I didn't exactly lie."

"You led me to believe you were at college. An adult. God, Marcy, do you realise the position you've put me in?"

Marcy wished she could cover her face and make it all go away. But her arms were hugging her bag.

"I didn't think it mattered. It wasn't like it was illegal or anything. I had no idea you were going to be teaching at Springdale."

They hadn't ever really discussed his job, which was odd when you thought about it. Or maybe not. Marcy had shifted out of the subject of college and careers as much as possible, to avoid revealing her own situation.

"Going into a bar was illegal. Buying alcohol for you was illegal. Taking you back to my place..."

"...was not illegal." She finished for him.

"That hardly matters now, does it? I could lose my job at the very least."

"I'm sorry." She really was. "I just liked being with you so much." I liked you, she thought. I still do.

Something softened in Gray's eyes when she said this.

His voice was husky. "I liked being with you too." Then he became stern again. "But that's it, Marcy, I'm your teacher now. Nothing more can happen. And no one can ever find out what did."

FRENCH KISSING

by

Noël Cades

First Printing, 2016

ISBN: 0-9945811-0-6
ISBN-13: 978-0-9945811-0-5

This book is dedicated to kalez, awk, averywrites, tevak, sushigoldberg, penguination, hamlet, nat_designer, ricree, naj, woodchuck, lukas, plasmid, milk drinker and not forgetting the brilliantly talented poad, ampersand and jotbot

1. Crashing down

Marcy was looking forward to the perfect, uncomplicated senior year... but Fate had other plans.

Right now life seemed like a dream: the hottest boyfriend, the best girlfriend and her parents had just bought her the coolest car. Okay, so it was fifteen years old and a little battered and rusty in places, but was hers. It represented freedom. The chance to go wherever she wanted, whenever she wanted.

So long as she respected curfew, of course.

And got good grades.

And visited her Great Aunt Esme every Sunday afternoon.

There were quite a few conditions on this freedom, all things considered. Otherwise the keys got confiscated and it was back to being driven around by her parents again.

But still, nothing could dampen Marcy's spirits. It was the last week of summer break and she should have felt sad about the vacation ending. Instead she was excited about her final year of high school. It was the last year she would get to spend with all her friends before many of them moved away to college in different parts of the country.

Marcy had been working at a local coffee shop over the summer, and she was driving there now. Katy Perry was playing on the radio and she sang along, feeling her life was absolutely, flawlessly perfect.

Except that everything was about to come crashing down around her.

Quite literally.

Her shift started off OK. Ben, the cute gay guy who managed the café, was in a good mood. Things were busy enough for the time to pass quickly, but there wasn't such an overwhelming rush that customers got rude and demanding.

"You'll have to let me know what hours you're available for when term starts. You're a good worker, Marcy, I'd hate to lose you," Ben said.

Coming from Ben this was high praise. He was usually very flippant and fake-critical about her work.

"I'll have a lot of study, but maybe a couple of shifts a week?" she suggested, and went to serve a super-hot customer who had just come up to the counter. Marcy wasn't looking at guys for herself, but her best friend Addy was single, and it never hurt to play matchmaker.

He had black hair and green eyes. Definitely a college guy, maybe even a graduate. Probably not Addy's kind of guy unfortunately, as she preferred blond surfer types.

"What can I get you today?" she asked him. He ordered a coffee and went off to a table.

"He's new around here," Ben said when the customer had gone. "He's not a face I'd forget. Or a butt," he added, eyeing the customer from the back.

"No looking and no touching!" Marcy joked. "You're as hitched as I am." Ben lived with his boyfriend Jason and the two of them were rock solid, despite Ben's flirtatiousness.

When Marcy had her break she phoned Josh, her boyfriend. They had been going out since Valentine's Day. He had been on a trip with his parents the last two weeks, so they were belatedly celebrating their six months anniversary that evening.

"Hey, how was the trip? We still on for tonight?"

Marcy was expecting a "yes" and a "missed you" and a "can't wait to see you". She wasn't expecting an awkward pause, and what followed.

"Marcy, there's something I need to tell you..."

After she got off the phone she was too numb to cry. Too shocked to even react. Ben could tell something was up but he didn't press her.

Josh had met someone else. In just two weeks. Her Josh. Her perfect, wonderful, loving boyfriend. How could he do this to her?

The only slight, saving grace, the only thing that made this bearable at all, was that the girl didn't go to their high school.

Marcy finished her shift in a blur, hardly noticing or caring that the cute customer left her a great tip or caught her eye and smiled at her. She was The Rejected. She was unloved and unwanted and discarded. The sun had gone out of the sky. That was the day's first disaster.

As planned, Addy came to meet her at the end of her shift. They were heading to the mall to pick out an outfit for Marcy's supposed anniversary dinner that night. Except that clearly wasn't going to happen now.

"Oh no, you've had bad news haven't you?" Addy didn't need to be psychic, Marcy looked as miserable as hell.

"It's Josh." Marcy told her what had happened.

"Oh God, that makes me feel even worse," Addy said.

"Worse? Don't tell me you have bad news too?"

"Mom got a job. In New York. It was all really last minute, a position suddenly came up. I know she's wanted this promotion for ages, I just never thought it would happen now. Or be in New York."

"But what about school?"

"I'll have to transfer to a high school there. I wanted to ask her to let me stay here and board with your family, but you know she needs me. Since Dad died…"

Addy didn't need to say any more. Marcy understood.

"It's ok. I'll miss you like crazy though. More than that asshole Josh anyway." Marcy's grief was already turning into anger. Addy's leaving was such an awful prospect that it even overshadowed Josh's betrayal. Marcy had known Addy since she was five, she was her oldest and best friend.

"I'll miss you too. You'll have to come and visit. Fly up for some Christmas shopping," Addy said. December seemed like a century away, but it was something.

"You'll be all Gossip Girl by then with brand new friends. All New York sophisticated."

"Never." They hugged, half laughing, half crying. "So do you still want to go to the mall?" Addy asked.

"No. If it's okay with you I think I'll go home and cry. Lick my wounds a little."

"And take down all of that jerk Josh's photos. You know I never liked him," Addy said. "Let me know if you want to do something later tonight."

So that was strike two. Bye bye boyfriend, bye bye best friend, within just a couple of hours.

Despite it all, Marcy felt strangely calm as she drove out of the parking lot. Either calm or numb, it didn't matter, but at least she was in a fit state to drive.

Unfortunately the truck driver behind her wasn't. As she waited at the intersection, he rear ended her car, forcing it to collide with the vehicle in front.

This was undeniably The Worst Day of Marcy's life. Ever.

Sick and shaken from the jolt - thank God for seat belts or her head would be through the smashed up windscreen - she managed to get out of her car.

"Are you okay?" It was the driver of the car in front. He looked familiar.

"Yes, I think so. I'm so sorry… your car…" Marcy stared at the dented metal, crumpled by her car. Her beloved car. She hadn't even looked at the damage to her own vehicle.

"It's okay, it wasn't your fault."

It was a busy road and Marcy could already hear the sirens of a police car that had been travelling the other way and turned around to investigate.

She looked again at the driver. Oh God! It was him, the dark haired customer from the café. She hadn't noticed how tall he was from behind the counter. Or how incredibly good looking.

After the police had left, all the necessary details had been taken and the tow truck company called, Marcy was left wondering how to get home. Her windscreen was completely smashed in, her car was undriveable.

"Can I give you a lift somewhere? I should still be able to drive my car, the windscreen and headlights are intact."

Normally she wouldn't accept lifts from strange guys, but surely bad things only come in threes? Marcy simply couldn't imagine how Fate could throw her any more rocks that day.

"Sure, that would be really nice of you."

Marcy slid into the front passenger seat as he got back into the driver's seat. She found herself noticing how long and muscular his thighs seemed beneath his jeans. I'm as bad as Ben, she thought, and I'm supposed to be practically bereaved.

"I'm Gray by the way."

"Marcy." She looked at his profile, he really was spectacularly good looking. Definitely older than the average guys she and Addy hung out with.

"So have you always lived here?" he asked.

"I was born here, never lived anywhere else. And you?"

"I'm new in town as they say," he told her. "Just got a job here, I arrived yesterday. I don't know a soul. Except you." He looked over at her as he said this, his green eyes meeting hers. She felt her stomach give a jolt.

"Well if you need a tour guide..." She didn't want to sound like she was super keen. But he was so hot, so well-defined. Those clear cut features, that angular jaw, his broad, muscular shoulders. He made even Josh, whom Marcy had always considered good looking, seem kind of soft and indistinct.

He smiled at her. It was devastating. "I might take you up on that."

They swapped numbers when he dropped her home. She went inside, not sure if her heart should be singing or shattered.

2. Gray calls

The next morning, Marcy came out of the shower to find a text on her phone.

It's Gray. Car Crash Guy. Wondered if you're free to meet? Coffee shop 11am?

He messaged in nearly full sentences which was unusual but nice. It made him seem older and a little more formal, but Marcy liked it.

She had nothing else on that day. Checking that her parents could give her a lift in, she texted him back to accept.

And now for something to wear. This should have been the easiest thing in the world but today Marcy practically pulled her entire wardrobe onto the floor. In the end she picked out some short shorts that showed off the full length of her thighs and a white tank top, since it was a hot day. She slid on her sandals and threw her phone and money into the cute purse she'd got for her last birthday.

Looking in the mirror she scowled at herself and then tried to put on a sexy smile. She was having a good hair day at least, her usually auburn hair had streaks of strawberry blonde thanks to the summer sun and was framing her face in just the right way. Her dark blue eyes showed no signs of having cried for hours the night before.

If truth be told she hadn't cried that much at all. A least not as much as she had feared she would. Pulling down her photos of Josh and all their other relationships mementoes had only made her weep a bit.

Addy had come over and they had held the relationship funeral together. Everything had been buried in a shoebox that was now in the attic. Then they'd drowned their sorrows with ice cream and chick flicks, and vowed to swear off men for life and become nuns.

Marcy figured even the strictest Mother Superior would break her vows for a guy as hot as Gray was. She rang Addy before heading out.

"The convent will have to wait. I have a date with a super hot guy in half a hour."

"Already! Not that guy whose car your wrecked?" Marcy had told her about the crash and getting a lift home.

"The truck wrecked his car, not me," Marcy pointed out.

"Well have fun rebounding! And call me later and tell me everything, every last juicy detail." Addy said.

With a few butterflies in her stomach, Marcy walked into the coffee shop after her parents dropped her off. Fortunately the nearest drop off point was out of view of the café. She felt like a little kid getting driven around by her parents, though she supposed having a smashed up car was a reasonable excuse.

It was a brilliantly sunny day, warm with cloudless blue skies, making it hard to believe that summer was nearing its end. If only it could be the start of summer again, Marcy thought. She wasn't ready for the leaves to start changing colour and the nights to draw in.

Gray was already there, at a table. It was a little strange to Marcy meeting a new date in her place of work. Sort of familiar yet unfamiliar. She saw Ben giving her a knowing smile from behind the counter and felt herself blush.

Gray was even better looking than she had remembered. He seemed to get more stunning every time she met him, and it made the butterflies even worse. He must be an actor or model or something, Marcy thought. His features were clean cut and flawless, like a Greek god. His dark hair fell over his forehead in a way that made her itch to push it back so she could gaze into his eyes. His lips were so perfectly formed, masculine but sensuous... she wondered what it would be like if he kissed her...

Get a grip girl! she scolded herself, aware that she was probably gawping like an idiot.

He didn't seem to notice anything wrong. He broke out into a dazzling smile when he saw her and stood up. "Hey Marcy! Great to see you again."

It was funny how seeing him made everything else fade into the distant past. Yesterday morning felt like it happened years ago. She should be heartbroken, but she'd turned a whole new page.

"So how's your car?" she asked him.

"In the shop. I got a rental car while it's being fixed. You?"

"I got a lift," she told him. She didn't want to mention that it was from her parents.

"Great. So did you want to get a drink here or shall we set off?" he asked.

"Where are we going?"

"That's up to you. I thought you might give me an insider's tour of the town. I'm assuming this is the best place to get coffee?"

"Ben would like to think so." They both laughed. Ben, hearing his name, looked over and scowled. "We're going to head off," Marcy told him. "I'll see you tomorrow."

It was amazing how natural and right the "we" sounded. Somehow she felt like she was on a team with him, even though she barely knew him. Maybe it was some kind of survivor's bonding, after the shared trauma of the accident.

"What do you get up to around here?" Gray asked her as he pulled out of the parking lot.

"School mainly, or from next week anyway."

"What's your major?"

Oh God! He thought she was a college student! Marcy felt way too awkward to tell him that she was only at high school.

"Still undecided, but maybe English literature or creative writing." This was kind of true. It was what she was thinking of doing when she finally got to college. "You'd like to be a writer?" he asked.

"Maybe. But plays, not novels." Marcy's dream was to be a playwright. She had fallen in love with theatre when they'd taken a class trip to see Othello some years ago. She found it more intimate and more magical than any movie she had ever seen. "What about you?"

14

"I majored in French. My mother's French, so it was kind of an easy choice for me," Gray told her.

"From Canada?"

"No, she's from France. Paris, France. My eldest sister was born there. My father worked for the US embassy."

"So do you all speak fluently?" she asked.

"Pretty much, but it gets rusty. We all speak English over here. It's only when we visit my grandmother that we have to speak French," he said.

Marcy suggested they visit the lake since it was such a beautiful day. "You can hire boats there."

3. At the lake

"It's beautiful here," Gray said, looking out over the water.

The sky above them was that intense blue that you get between summer and autumn. Willows trailed their leaves along the edge of the lake and water birds floated past.

They were in a rowboat, drifting on the surface and enjoying the breezes over the water that eased the heat of the day. Gray had picked up some beers and they were having a relaxed time of it.

Marcy found it really easy to be with him. Even though she hardly knew him, she just felt comfortable with him.

Comfortable but also a bit on edge. Because she felt hugely attracted to him, and she couldn't tell if this was a date-date or a friends-date.

After all, he had said he was new in town. Maybe he just wanted to be shown around?

She was looking for some kind of sign that he found her attractive. It was hard work stopping herself staring at him as he was so much better looking that anyone else she had been out with. He left Josh in the dust.

"You said you wanted to be a playwright. Do you do any theatre?" Gray asked her.

"God no. I'd be hopeless." A neighbour was always trying to encourage her to join a local musical theatre group, but Marcy had been too busy and too shy.

"I don't mean acting necessarily. General production, directing, backstage stuff. The general scene," he said.

"Some things like that at school - at high school," she told him, implying it was long in the past. "Do you act?"

"Just some amateur productions in college. For fun, really. I thought I'd see if there were any theatre companies around here."

He was going to be busy, Marcy thought. He'd already told her about various sports he did: trekking, cycling and swimming.

"The only one I know of is all old ladies. Or at least people my parents' age. They mainly do musicals."

Gray laughed. "Maybe they need younger blood."

"I can ask for you." Mrs Helberg would be all over him, Marcy thought. She'd probably put on West Side Story and cast Gray as Tony and herself as Maria. That might even be worth watching.

"So what else goes on around here. Bars, clubs? What's good?"

He must really think she was twenty-one, or near there. She knew where the supposedly cool places were but neither she nor Addy had actually been in them. They had planned to get some fake ID this year and start exploring. With Addy deserting her for New York, that plan was on hold.

"There are a few places in town. Ben always goes to a place called Revolution." Then she remembered this was a gay bar and probably not somewhere Gray might want to go, though you never knew. He seemed straight though.

"You haven't been there? Where do you go?"

Marcy tried to cover. "This past year I've been so busy with study that I haven't got out much. And I had a part time evening job in a restaurant." This was true, but now she had probably made herself sound really boring.

He smiled, figuring out what she was trying to conceal. "I'm guessing if you're still studying you couldn't legally go last year anyway?"

Not last year. Nor this year. Nor the next two either, but she wasn't going to tell him that. Was he fishing for her age?

"Not quite."

He was grinning at her now, seeing that she was discomfited. "It's okay, I'm not asking for your ID."

"I won't ask for yours then." But she really wanted to. How old was he? Maybe Ben could guess. She thought he looked at least twenty-one. Eighteen and twenty-one wasn't too much of a gap anyway.

Gray drained his beer. "I wonder if you can get arrested for drink rowing?"

Marcy had only sipped one beer as she wasn't used to alcohol, but he'd had a couple. She wished they could have stayed longer on the lake but they had only hired the boat out for a couple of hours and their time was nearly up.

"We could go back and hire some more time," he said, reading her mind.

He must be enjoying spending time with her. She smiled. "I'd like that."

Unfortunately when they reached the jetty, there were already people lined up waiting for their rowboat. No wonder, on such a great day. Reluctantly Gray handed over the oars, and climbed out first. He reached out a hand to help Marcy out.

When their fingers touched she felt a jolt. After spending two hours so close to him, only talking, the physical contact was kind of a shock.

She caught his eye and thought she saw the same reaction there.

They went for a walk through the trees along the shore, and he slipped his arm around her. Until he did so Marcy hadn't realised how tall Gray was. She herself was about average height for a girl, but he must be well over six foot.

She kind of liked being so much shorter than him, over a head below him, it made her feel sort of feminine and petite. Plus he was older than Josh or any other of the boys she had dated. He seemed stronger, more protective.

Not that she was expecting any wild bears to leap out at them, but it was good to know he could probably wrestle one with his bare hands if he tried.

Thinking about this she laughed and Gray asked her what was up.

"I was just imagining if a rogue bear came charging out of the woods."

"There are bears here?" He looked mildly alarmed.

"None, I'm not sure why I thought of it." She wasn't going to confess her fantasies this soon.

They passed other walkers and a couple of people jogging, taking advantage of the shade in the hot day. Marcy always loved the pale golden-green light underneath the trees here. It was like being a leafy castle.

After a little while Gray stopped and turned her to face him. "Tell me if this is too soon," he said.

"If what is?"

"This." He tilted her head up to his and brought his lips down on hers. They were simultaneously soft and firm, and warm. Her stomach gave a flip.

Her lips parted in response and he deepened the kiss, tasting her. It felt so right, so perfect, like quenching a thirst.

I really like him, Marcy thought. Even though it probably was too soon she had no doubt about her feelings. She was just surprised it could happen this quickly.

Again reading her mind, he broke off. "I wasn't expecting this."

"This?"

"You. Meeting someone practically the first day I arrive in town."

The way he said "meeting someone" gave Marcy a shiver. It made it sound significant, somehow.

"I had to make it up to you for the crash somehow. To give you a better welcome," she joked.

He raised his eyebrows. "Is that the only reason you kissed me?"

He was joking as well, but she played along. "Of course. Just being hospitable."

Gray narrowed his eyes. Without a word he took her in his arms again, more forceful this time, his lips plundering hers. She melted against him as his hands gripped her sides, his thumbs brushing near her breasts.

She was out of breath when he finally let her go. Shell-shocked, while he was grinning. "How would you like to extend me some more of that hospitality tomorrow night?"

Marcy was momentarily startled but he broke in again. "I mean have dinner with me. Nothing more," he told her.

Nothing more? She found herself half-wishing he did mean something more. But still the kisses… both of them… this wasn't "just friends".

"I'd love that."

Maybe this year wasn't going to be such a disaster after all. Maybe it was for the best that Josh had dumped her.

Thinking about how Gray's lips felt on hers, she was sure it must be.

4. Girls' night

Marcy felt sad as she walked over to Addy's house as it was going to be one of their last girls' nights together. She couldn't believe Addy was deserting her for New York. A virtual girls' night over Skype or FaceTime just wouldn't be the same.

Just when she needed her friend more than ever... Addy's mother had to go and get that amazing job. Life was so unfair.

They had decided to meet at Addy's as she and her mother were in the midst of packing for their move, and Marcy thought it would be fun to help out. Addy's mother was pretty cool, even if she overheard their conversation she wouldn't judge or get mad. They could talk about most things within her earshot.

Addy hugged Marcy at the door. "This might be the last time I get to welcome you to my home here! Though it's not much of a home right now."

This was an understatement. Boxes of stuff were piled everywhere, leaving just a narrow corridor through the hallway.

"You have been busy," Marcy said.

Addy rolled her eyes. "It's been a nightmare. We're getting professional removal men but Mom was worried they'd break stuff. So she ended up making us pack half the stuff that the removal company would be doing."

She ushered Marcy into the kitchen, where thankfully the seats still remained along the breakfast bar. "Most of the crockery's packed, we've just kept a few things. So much is going to end up in storage though. New York apartments are so tiny by comparison."

Addy's mother owned the house but planned to rent it out. Leaving half their things would have been awkward, and the rental agent said it would be easier to get tenants for a fully unfurnished property.

"It's like you're packing up your life," Marcy said. "It's all happening so quickly."

"I know. It's not easy. I kind of power through it all by keeping busy, there's so much to do which helps. I also have a whole box of stuff for you. Some of it's for safekeeping, so we can look at it when we're old ladies and weep bitter tears."

Marcy felt a bit better at the thought of them still being in touch and hopefully close friends in old age. "I'll hold you to that."

"No Josh stuff though. Or maybe we'll have a folder of the awful ones, to laugh over."

"Was he really that awful?"

"Truthfully? I think he was a vain idiot. And not that great looking either. You could do so much better. Which reminds me, what happened with that guy whose car you wrecked?"

Marcy had been burning to tell Addy but felt strangely reticent as well. The thing with Gray was so *big*, somehow, that she wanted to get her own thoughts about it a bit clearer.

"We went out earlier today. He was nice."

"Nice!" Addy looked like she was going to shake Marcy. "That's what you say to your parents. Tell me the truth! What did you do, did anything happen? Are you seeing him again."

A big yes to that one, Marcy was already nervous about it. "He was great. We kissed. We're going out tomorrow night."

"Wow! So was it a good kiss? Do you like him, I mean really like him?

"I think so." Marcy looked troubled as she said this, which Addy instantly picked up on.

"So what's the problem?"

"He thinks I'm at college. I mean from what he said, he thinks I'm about twenty-one."

Addy shrugged. "So? You'll be at college in a year. It's no big deal. You're above the age of consent. It's not like it's a crime or something."

"I know. I just feel awkward about it."

"So how old is he?"

"I don't know. I think maybe around twenty-one," Marcy said.

"That's fine then. I mean if he was forty-one, now then I would be putting you in a straitjacket and wheeling you off to a convent."

Marcy laughed. "No, he's definitely not that old. I wish you could meet him before you go. It's just so early though."

"Text me where you are tomorrow night and maybe I'll drop past and spy on you. Now, I need food."

They used the contents of Addy's kitchen being in disarray as an excuse to make some comfort food. In this case, microwave mug brownies. Addy tipped a packet of Walnut Fudge Brownie mix into a bowl, stirred in some eggs and oil, and poured it into mugs. She got chocolate everywhere, which was usual for Addy.

The TV wasn't packed up yet so they sat on the couch and watched Saved! They both loved it because the mean girl reminded them of a girl at school, Brittany Paige, and in the movie the mean girl got her comeuppance.

They were officially supposed to be friends with Brittany, all being part of the top social clique, but in truth they couldn't stand her. Brittany was rich and blonde and supposedly beautiful. She regarded herself as the Queen of the school, so everyone else had to bow down to her if they wanted to remain popular.

Marcy saw that Addy was looking uncomfortable when a section of Saved! came on that they usually laughed at. "What's wrong?"

"It just reminded me of something. I wasn't sure if I should tell you, but I guess you'll find out anyway," Addy said.

"You can't leave me in the dark now. Come on, nothing could be worse than all the other bad news recently."

"It's kind of related to that. It's about Josh."

Marcy felt slightly sick. Even though she was more than over him, his name was a reminder of her humiliation at being dumped, and the fact she'd have to face him at school in a week's time. "Unless you're secretly dating him, it can't be that bad. What is it?"

Addy half laughed at the idea of dating Josh. "Not even wearing gloves and surgical scrubs. So not my type. Seriously though, I found out about that girl he's dating. It's Brittany's cousin."

Everything felt darker for a moment. "Brittany knew about us though. She always seemed fine with it."

"Yeah, well I don't think she's truly fine with anything she can't directly control. This way she's got him back in her claws, kind of," Addy said.

"But she doesn't even like him!" Marcy said.

"I know. But he's one of her minions, or whatever you call them. My grandmother would would say suitors. If he's dating her cousin, with her blessing, then she still kind of owns him."

They were both silent for a moment, thinking about this horrible turn of events. And how Brittany might gloat and lord it over them even more.

"She lives out of state though, so that's something," Addy told Marcy. "At least you won't have to face her. Anyway, in a week's time hopefully you'll be so loved up by Mr New Guy that you won't notice or care about Bitchany Paige."

5. Getting closer

Gray was picking her up at seven o'clock. Marcy's parents had gone out a little earlier so they wouldn't get to meet him this time. But they were cool, they trusted her judgement. After all she was practically an adult.

Marcy had also mentioned that she might stay over at Addy's later on. If the date went badly, she would head there for ice cream and sympathy. She and Addy always had a backup plan like this for a first date, as nothing was worse than going home and crying alone.

Feeling a little nervous and dressed in her cutest outfit, she waited for him to arrive. Finally the doorbell rang and she opened it to see Gray there looking absolutely amazing. His shirt brought out the deep green of his eyes.

Just as she stepped outside she tripped and fell over a flying fur ball hurtling into the house. Gray managed to catch her, preventing her from hitting the ground.

"I think you have an invader," he said.

"It's only Pegasus. He's a bit fast." Marcy was dying with embarrassment at how clumsy she must have looked. Just when she was trying to appear her most sophisticated and elegant.

Gray opened the car door for her and closed it afterwards, which felt really chivalrous. Josh had never done that kind of stuff.

He had music playing in the car but it was nothing she recognised. It wasn't even in English.

"Is that French?" she asked.

"Yes. We can put something else on. I listen to it occasionally, it helps stop me getting rusty," Gray told her.

"No, it's nice. Please leave it." Maybe it would help her French as well, it was one of her better subjects but she still needed to improve. She couldn't understand any of the lyrics though.

Gray drove them into town. "You obviously know this place better than me, but I found an Italian restaurant which looked good. If it's got a terrible reputation we can go elsewhere."

Perfect choice, she loved Italian food. "If it's Luigi's then it's great." It was also quite expensive, she wasn't sure if she should mention this.

"That's the one."

Inside they were shown to one of the best tables, in the window. Marcy never got to sit there when she went with her family as they only had two-person tables there.

Gray ordered a bottle of wine and they looked through the menus. It turned out that they both liked pepperoni on pizza so they got one to share.

He told her about France, as she asked him how often he'd been there. It turned out that he'd actually spent a year at the Sorbonne, a university in Paris.

"What was it like, Paris?" Marcy imagined endlessly sitting at stylish cafés drinking black coffee and discussing French philosophers.

"It was pretty cool. The food was great. It's a long way from home though," he told her.

The wine was getting to Marcy, relaxing her and making her head swim. It also made her more flirty with him than she would have been otherwise.

They skipped dessert and headed to a bar. She was terrified that they would ask for ID and she would have to reveal her age, but accompanied by Gray there were no questions asked.

Inside they drank some more and flirted some more. Eventually they were kind of leaning against one another, the sexual attraction stronger than anything Marcy had ever felt. She could feel his hardness through his jeans. If she had had only slightly more to drink she would have made out with him then and there.

"You want to come back to my place?"

Marcy hesitated. She did want to, but she had a feeling where it might lead. Except she pretty much wanted it to lead there, or close.

He saw the conflict in her eyes. "If you have to get back it's okay."

"It's fine, I'd love to come."

Since he couldn't drive he left the car in town and they walked to his apartment, which wasn't far. It was in a really smart, quite new block that Addy's mother had once considered purchasing in.

They took the elevator, Marcy feeling a little nervous but thrilled to still be with Gray.

Inside he turned to face her. "We should get coffee or something." And then his arms were around her and his lips were on hers and they were both embracing like they were parched with thirst for one another.

Marcy could feel the hard planes of his body underneath his shirt. His smell of soap of cologne and warm skin. She was intoxicated.

Gray led her into the bedroom and onto the bed. She loved the feeling of his weight on top of her as they continued to make out. His hand went under her top, brushing over her bra.

"I don't usually want someone this much, this fast," he said. "But there's something about you."

Marcy figured this was not the time to reveal her lack of experience. He might freak out and reject her. She and Josh had never gone all the way because somehow it hadn't felt right, though Josh had started to pressure her a bit. They had had a kind of understanding that it would happen in senior year.

And now here she was, in the bedroom of some guy she'd met three days ago. She should have been shocked at her own behaviour, but instead she realised for the first time why she had never wanted to do this with Josh. Because he had never, ever made her feel like this.

Gray had pushed her top above her head, taking it off her. Marcy had already run her hands under his shirt, marvelling at the sculpted feel of him. It shouldn't come as a surprise, given all the physical pursuits he had mentioned doing.

Then she felt his hands reach underneath her, his fingers moving and suddenly her bra was unclasped and he had removed that too.

Gray's green eyes met Marcy's for a moment, hazy with lust, then he bent his head and put his mouth on her breast. She bucked as electricity ran through her body. How did anyone ever stop themselves half way through?

When he tugged her pants down and slipped his fingers inside her underwear she was momentarily embarrassed because she could feel she was soaking wet. He didn't seem to care though. The feeling of his fingers on her sensitive folds was amazing, he knew exactly what he was doing.

"You feel incredible," he said.

He was teasing her, tugging at her skin gently. Then his thumb slid directly over her nub and she actually gasped.

He rose up and rapidly threw off his own shirt, so he could lie skin-against-skin with her. Somehow he got rid of the rest of his clothes and they were both entirely naked, she felt his hardness pressed against her thigh. He felt huge.

Gray kissed her some more, running his hands over her body, over her breasts. Marcy's entire body was on fire.

Then he leant over to reach for something, and she heard the tearing of a little packet. Deftly he slipped it on.

This was the point of no return.

He moved back over her, kissing her again, his tongue entwining with hers. She found that her body naturally shifted to give him access.

She felt him at her entrance, she was so swollen and wet that she longed for him to enter her and the desire overcame any fear.

In one smooth movement Gray was inside her, but she winced at the sudden sharp pain and then tried to hide it.

He paused and broke off from the embrace. Raised his head and looked down at her. She saw the confusion and alarm in his eyes.

"Marcy, were you...?"

"Yes." She could feel herself going red despite the throbbing throughout her body and hoped he couldn't tell in the low light. "I know it's crazy late to have waited this long."

"It's not at all, but Jesus. I wish you had told me, we could have taken things far more slowly. Do you want me to stop?"

"No." She really didn't. She wanted him so badly.

"Sure?"

"Totally."

He started moving into her again, taking it much more gently this time. It gave her a chance to get used to him. It wasn't exactly hurting now, she loved the feeling of closeness and fullness.

Eventually she was making soft moans at his rhythm, closing her eyes to focus on the new and wonderful sensations in her body.

Gray slipped his hand between them, pulling up her folds slightly which drove her nearly wild as his fingers aimed for her most sensitive place.

Once he hit it there was no going back.

It was a sharp, sweet release. Marcy could feel herself squeeze and spasm around him, this rock hardness inside her body. Waves of it ran through her body and her head felt all dizzy and out of control.

Then Gray was thrusting inside her much more vigorously, straining as he came as well, until they collapsed together, hot and wet with perspiration.

6. No regrets

Thank goodness she had told her parents she might be staying at Addy's.

That was the first thing Marcy thought when she woke, to find herself cradled by Gray's arm. He was still fast asleep. She had never woken up in a guy's bed before and her second thought was how warm and comfortable it was.

She had barely had a chance to notice his apartment the previous night. They had been all over one another and off to bed the moment they had got through the door.

Now she enjoyed a peek, wondering if his place would reveal more about him. Unfortunately there wasn't much to see, he clearly hadn't moved all his stuff in yet. There wasn't anything on the walls or any kind of decoration. It wasn't as stark as a hotel room but it didn't feel fully lived in yet.

He had his own bedclothes at least. They were dark blue and smelt of laundry powder combined with his scent. They must have been fresh and clean last night.

Now of course they were all rumpled from the night-time action. Marcy felt herself blush just thinking about it.

She really needed the bathroom but had no idea where it was and didn't want to wake Gray. She lay there for a few increasingly uncomfortable minutes, before deciding that she really couldn't hold it in any longer.

Very carefully and gently she raised herself off the bed, slipping out of his embrace. He stirred slightly but didn't awaken.

Once out of the warmth of the blanket Marcy shivered and felt awkward for being naked. There was a towel hanging over a rail so she grabbed it and wrapped it around herself before finding the bathroom.

In there she finally went and then had a peek at Gray's bathroom toiletries when she washed her hands. He didn't have a lot of stuff, just a razor, some toothpaste and a toothbrush in a yellow plastic cup, and a can of shaving gel next to them. She kind of liked the fact that he wasn't overly fussy and vain with twenty kinds of hair gel and cologne.

The metrosexual thing didn't really do it for her, it was Addy who preferred her guys super groomed. Marcy just liked them clean and natural.

She splashed her face with water. Her make up was all smudged but it didn't look too bad, just sort of smoky. She longed to have a shower. She wasn't quite sure if she should hang around or get busy and leave, but all her clothes were strewn about the bedroom so she had to return there.

Slipping back to the bedroom still wrapped in the towel, she saw him open his eyes as she entered. "I thought you'd run out on me."

"No, I just visited the bathroom."

"Want to revisit it and shower with me?" he asked.

Marcy tried not to go red. She had never ever showered with a guy before. This was all happening so quick.

He saw her embarrassment. "It's okay, no pressure. There's plenty of hot water. You can go first if you like."

Except she wanted to try showering with him. She smiled shyly. "But then we wouldn't be saving the earth."

"Saving the earth?" He looked confused.

"Wasting water unnecessarily."

Gray realised what she was saying and grinned. "That's the only reason to shower with me, is it? To use less water? Okay, let's go and save the planet."

He hopped out of bed and crossed the room wearing nothing, confident and unashamed. Marcy wished she could get over her inhibitions. But then it was different for guys.

Under the water and hot steam his mouth was on hers almost immediately. Making hers open for him, probing and exploring her, while the water ran down them and into her mouth. Hot and wet and slidey.

They soaped one another's bodies, she loved the feel of his hands over her. "You're so smooth and slippery," he said.

"I think that's the shower gel."

He laughed then reached between her legs. She flinched slightly, she hadn't realised she was a bit sore there.

Gray immediately picked up on it. "I'm sorry, I should have realised. You probably need a bit of recovery time. I wish you had told me it was your first time. I nearly didn't guess though, you were amazing."

"Likewise. It makes me wonder why I waited so long."

There was a strange intensity in his eyes. "I'm kind of glad you did."

It was weird, Marcy barely knew him - he'd been a total stranger just two days ago - but now she felt so intimate with him. Things felt right, and she hoped it wasn't just in her head. That he was feeling it too.

She was certainly glad to have given up her v-card to him. Whatever happened, it had been a wonderful experience. Half of her couldn't wait to tell Addy, and half of her wanted to hug the secret to herself for a bit longer.

They were kissing again, and he had started to lead her out of the shower back towards the bedroom when his mobile rang. "Damn. I really want to ignore that but I was waiting on a call. Stay right where you are."

He picked up the phone, and held a brief conversation, frowning as he did so. "It's my old landlord," he told her. "The new tenants want to move in early. I hoped to have another week to move the rest of my stuff out but I'm going to have to head up there today, or he'll lose the deal."

"That's difficult," Marcy said.

"I know. He appreciates it though, he's a good guy. He's going to refund me my last cheque as I was paid up until the end of the month."

Marcy wanted to ask how long Gray would be gone for but didn't want to sound clingy.

32

"Anyway," he continued, "let's grab some breakfast, then I'll drive you home."

He cooked them eggs and toast with black coffee. Marcy was surprised at how hungry she was.

"I hope it's okay, I haven't had the chance to do much grocery shopping yet," he said. "I ran out of fruit."

"It's great. If your new job doesn't work out Ben would hire you for these eggs alone," Marcy told him.

She was glad he was driving her back, though she felt kind of icky putting on her clothes from the night before. She had heard other girls joke about the "walk of shame" when you returned home in your going-out clothes from the night before, after spending the night with a man. By giving her a lift, Gray had spared her that awkwardness.

"I didn't want to do a huge 'About last night' but you are okay, aren't you?" he asked her. "No regrets?"

"None at all." Truly, Marcy had no regrets. He hadn't said he wanted to see her again but even if he didn't, although she'd feel pretty miserable and disappointed for a few days, she could cope.

She was still glad her first time was with such an amazingly kind and hot guy. Anything else was a bonus.

The journey back to hers wasn't long. It was early, so the downstairs drapes were still closed. This was a good thing: no peeping eyes.

At her house Gray got out and opened the door for her. "I hate rushing off like this, but I'll only be gone a week. There's a few other things to tie up. Then I'm back for good, and I'd really like to see you again."

Her heart flipped with excitement and relief. He did want to see her again! "I'd like that." She tried to sound friendly but casual. Inside she was spinning around and doing a little dance of joy.

They already had one another's numbers so there was nothing more do to than kiss goodbye - Marcy fervently hoping her parents wouldn't see who she had arrived back with - and part for now.

She was going to see him again.

She just didn't know yet how shocking the circumstances would be.

7. Some bad news

As soon as they had parted Marcy decided that a week would seem like forever. But it also took her thoughts away from school, which if she was going to admit it, was a big shadow of dread hanging over her.

She was staying over at Addy's that night, for real this time. Her parents weren't too surprised as they knew it was their last week before Addy moved to New York.

"I expect Addy's house must be nearly packed up, are you sure they can host you?" Marcy's mother asked her.

"I'm taking a sleeping bag and a pillow." It was going to be like camping. They even planned to toast marshmallows over a candle.

Marcy's mother put an arm around her. "I know you'll miss her, dear, I am very sorry she's moving so far away."

"Me too." She tried not to look as miserable as she felt about it.

"Your father and I were talking about taking a trip around the end of the year. How about Christmas shopping in New York and catching a show on Broadway?" Marcy's mother knew her passion for theatre.

Marcy was overwhelmed. "That would be amazing. I can't wait to tell Addy." Having something to look forward to would keep her going throughout the long semester ahead. Even it was months and months away.

Her mother looked searchingly at her. "I trust it the date went well last night."

Marcy glowed. "It was perfect. He's lovely, you would like him."

"Better than Josh?"

"Infinitely," Marcy said.

"I figured, given how quickly you got over that heartbreak." Her mother smiled and offered her a plate of cookies and Marcy took two and went upstairs.

She went to stuff her night things in a bag and take a rolled up sleeping bag from the closet where they were kept. She also grabbed a bag of marshmallows from the kitchen. So weird to think that she wouldn't be able to just pop over to Addy's like this anymore. They had been best friends for so many years. Addy featured in more of the photos on Marcy's corkboard than any of the rest of her friends.

From the photos you could see just how much everyone had changed since high school started. I wonder what we'll look like now, to our future selves, Marcy thought. They'd find out at a high school reunion one day when people got the yearbooks out, she supposed.

At Addy's house she prepared herself for a grilling about Gray. They always shared the gory details - up to a point - though Marcy wasn't sure if her friend would be shocked at her behaviour. Not that she was the judgmental type, but what Marcy had done was kind of out of character for her.

When Gray had driven her back home Marcy had momentarily worried that a big "V" with a red line through it must be hovering above her head, but her mother didn't seem to have noticed anything. She might feel a sophisticated and scarlet woman inside, but outside she was just regular old Marcy.

"So?" If speech came with punctuation marks, Addy's question would have had about six question marks and eight exclamation works.

"So it's a lovely evening, isn't it?" Marcy replied, deliberately teasing her friend.

"You know that's not what I meant. Spill. Every last detail. Where did you go for dinner? How did he seem? Did he kiss you again? Has he asked you out again? When are you seeing him again?"

"Too many questions!" Marcy said, pushing past her friend towards the kitchen. Addy's mother was out that night at a business event so they had the place to themselves.

Addy chased after her. "No juice: no microwave brownies." Marcy could tell that Addy had been baking again from the warm aroma of chocolate in the air. And the chocolate smeared all over Addy herself. "And no marshmallows."

Marcy waved her own bag. "I came prepared."

Addy sat down on one of the stools. "Seriously. There's obviously something or you wouldn't be drawing it out like this. And it's obviously good, or you wouldn't be grinning all over your face. And blushing. And... oh my God, Marcy, you didn't, did you?"

"Didn't what?"

"You know what I mean! I thought you always wanted to wait for some reason. Not that it's not totally cool that you didn't. Assuming you didn't screw up and I have to start babysitting for you in nine months," Addy said, getting ahead of herself.

"Woah woah woah! I haven't confirmed or denied anything. And you know I'm not an idiot," Marcy said.

Addy grinned. "I can read you like a book. You've joined the club, haven't you? The Pink Ladies."

"Is that what it's called? If you must know, yes, I went a little further than I expected to. But Addy he's so wonderful! It just felt right. And he says he wants to see me again." Then her face fell.

"What's wrong?" Addy asked.

"He's away for the next week. So I can't see him for another seven days, until after school starts."

At the mention of school a flicker of concern went over Addy's face, but she tamped it down. "So was it good?"

"More than good. It was amazing! Why didn't you let me in on the secret? Though I'm glad I didn't give it up for Josh, thinking about it." Yes, that would have been terrible, Marcy thought. Given how she now felt as though she was falling for Gray, particularly after being so intimate with him, to have done that with Josh and then suffered his betrayal would have been unbearable.

At least she had gone into things with Gray with no expectations. With an official boyfriend, you felt entitled to some proper commitment afterwards.

Just then her phone buzzed.

Hope you're well. See you in a week, don't crash any more cars

Marcy liked the fact that he texted with proper language. It looked sophisticated and elegant. She'd have to reply the same way, none of the usual abbreviations and codes she used with Addy and others.

"Well, I'm now totally jealous. Even though I still don't know what he looks like," Addy said.

Marcy promised to send her a photo as soon as tactfully possible. "I don't want him to think I'm one of those girls that snaps photos of all her beaus like big game hunting trophies."

Addy burst out laughing. "Who on earth does that?"

"Brittanny Bitchy Paige, for starters."

The mention of Brittanny brought the cloud back to Addy's face. This time Marcy saw it.

"What's wrong?" Marcy asked.

"I found out something. If you thought the thing about Josh dating Brittanny's cousin was bad, then this is worse. Very much worse." Addy looked grave.

"What could be worse? They're getting married and I have to be maid of honour?"

"No, it's even worse than that. Apparently she - the cousin - has transferred. Her family moved over here or something. She's going to be starting at Springdale in the fall."

Suddenly the world went darker. It was going to take all of Marcy's courage to face the first day.

8. A huge shock

Nothing, absolutely nothing, could have prepared Marcy for the horrors of that first day of school.

She was expecting things to be bad enough with the whole Josh, Gretchen and Brittany thing.

What she wasn't expecting was complete social ostracism.

The day started with science, and Marcy ended up being five minutes late because she had to pick up a form from the principal's office. By the time she arrived back in class there was only one seat left, by a geeky guy she didn't know that well, so she didn't really notice any cold-shouldering from her usual crowd. Geek guy was a great lab partner so that kind of went okay.

As it turned out she didn't have many classes with Brittany and Josh. Or the dreaded cousin Gretchen. So it wasn't until lunchtime that she got the biggest shock. Or what she thought would be the biggest shock in store for her that day.

Taking her tray over to join her regular table, she noticed a girl with dark blonde hair sitting between Josh and Brittanny. She looked a bit like Brittany, a bit proud. Supercilious was the word. Marcy guessed she must be Gretchen.

She truly wasn't that pretty, Marcy thought. Even putting aside her obvious bias, Gretchen wasn't the ravishing glamour queen that Marcy had feared. She was more Brittany-lite, a bit less blonde, quite a bit less attractive. Addy had been right about why Brittanny would have been comfortable with one of her male friends dating her cousin. Push come to shove, she was no real competition.

Brittanny pursed her lips as Marcy went to sit down, opposite and a few seats along. The other people around her seemed oddly on edge and not welcoming.

"Actually Marcy, it's probably best if you don't sit with us any more. It's really awkward for Josh. I'm sure you understand."

And just like that, Marcy was out in the cold. Addy would have had her back, but she was thousands of miles away.

She got about one semi-sympathetic look from one girl which quickly froze when Brittanny glared at her. Gretchen was looking smug and Josh had the grace to look slightly embarrassed.

Marcy felt as though she had been thrown into a cold wind. She picked her tray back up, turned and walked away. There was nothing to be said.

There was also nowhere to sit. The only table left with seniors on it was taken up by some awkward nerds and the school weird girl, a drop out with the bizarre name of Revel. Marcy never knew whether she was supposed to look Goth or emo or whatever, but no one really spoke to her. She had piercings and at least one tattoo, and kept herself to herself.

Revel looked up as Marcy passed by, hoping to find a space somewhere.

"You can sit here."

The offer was all wrong and weird. Revel giving her permission to sit at the outcasts' table. Marcy was supposed to be one of the in crowd, she should have been the one deigning to let Revel join her.

But the world had changed that day, and she felt so isolated right now that she no longer cared that she was committing social suicide by sitting there.

"One year," Revel said. "One year and you'll never have to see any of them ever again."

Marcy both resented Revel for commenting on her life, while also feeling a flash of gratitude. It left her conflicted, so she said nothing. She also realised that people had clearly been talking and bitching about her behind her back and Revel must have picked up on it. Probably everyone had.

What had she done to deserve this? All she had done was date someone, and Brittanny had never given her the slightest indication that she minded.

Thinking this also made Marcy feel angry. What right did Brittanny have to mind? Or to interfere, and set Josh up with her hateful cousin. She couldn't bring herself to look over at Brittanny's table as she felt sure they would all be sneering at her.

She ate her food, feeling numb.

The rest of the day was pretty miserable. She was ignored by all the usual crowd and she ended up sitting by people she didn't know that well. It felt like starting a new school except this was her school, dammit. She was supposed to be having the best year of her life, her last year, and it looked like months of social ostracism stretched out before her.

If only Addy's mom would decide she hated New York, or was too homesick for Springdale to stay there. Marcy felt like everything would be okay again if only Addy was back. School was such a hostile, horrible place when you had no allies. And until now, she'd never realised how precarious popularity could be.

The last class of the day was French. She got there early, because it was better having some nerd choose to sit by her than being blocked from every seat except nerd-seats herself.

Miserably she stared down at her textbooks while everyone else filed in around her. She didn't want to catch any more sneering eyes. Why were people so mean? Brittanny had got what she wanted, hadn't she? Her cousin welcomed into the cosy fold and provided with a Brittanny-approved girlfriend.

Finally everyone was settled and their new French teacher came in through the door. Marcy knew it was someone new, because Mrs Vansittart, or "Madame Vansittart" as she liked to be called, had left at the end of the previous year to have a baby.

"Good afternoon, class. My name is Mr Grayson."

What?

Marcy, who had only been half paying attention, flicked her eyes up fully on hearing his voice.

It couldn't be.

"I'll be taking over from Mrs Vansittart this year - "

It was him. Gray. There was no mistaking it. Not even if he had an identical twin.

" - since she's left to have a baby."

What the hell was he doing here?

What should she do?

She actually wanted to be sick. Any second now he was going to see her.

His eyes were travelling around the room as he spoke... and finally he saw her.

Gray started, momentarily. Probably no one else would notice but Marcy did.

He immediately looked away and continued, but seconds later caught her eye again briefly, as in disbelief.

She could read shock there, fury. Fear.

Marcy couldn't move. She was stricken.

All she knew was that she had to get out of there.

Feeling like a robot she managed to get to her feet, mumble something about needing the restroom, and stumble out.

In the cool of the girls' bathroom Marcy went and locked herself into a cubicle. Finally it was all too much. The day had turned from a nightmare into some kind of hell farce.

She covered her face with her hands and wept. Not caring if she smudged her make up, or got into trouble for running out of class. She just wanted to be away from it all. She honestly couldn't face any of them ever again.

She couldn't stop thinking about Gray's face. The horror on it. She replayed it over and over again in her mind. The guy she was crazy about was her teacher? This kind of thing just didn't happen. She had lost her virginity to her teacher. It was impossible to process.

Marcy didn't know how long she had sat there for when she heard a voice above her. "Want to get out of here?"

She looked up. Revel was leaning over the top of her cubicle.

Normally Marcy's reaction to cubicle invasion would have been to freak out and tell the person to get lost. But then she wasn't actually using the facilities at present.

Getting out of school seemed like the sweetest thing in the world.

"Don't you have class?" Marcy asked.

"I cut early. I have a shoot to get to. You should hurry, they'll all be out in a few minutes," Revel said.

Marcy wasted no time. She got her things as they went past her locker and she fled, of all people, with Revel Holmes. Any port in a storm. All she wanted was to be shot of Springdale High and never have to return.

9. The shoot

As they walked out of the school gates, Marcy wondered what Revel had meant by a shoot? Did she do target practice?

She knew Revel didn't drive. Or didn't drive to school, anyway. She had no idea where she lived. Ordinarily Marcy would have offered her a lift out of politeness, but her car was still being fixed.

"I don't have my car here," she said as they crossed the parking lot.

"Yeah, I heard."

Was there any woe or misery from Marcy's life which hadn't made the school grapevine? She said nothing.

Revel looked at her. "You can come if you want," she said.

"Come where?"

"The shoot."

The weird thing was that it was as though Revel was extending Marcy a privilege. This term was so switched around. Normally someone like Revel was expected to be bent over with gratitude if someone like Brittanny or her set even acknowledged her.

But come to think of it, Marcy considered, Revel never had played Brittanny's game. She'd always remained kind of aloof. Which made her particularly weird, at high school. You had to have a group. Even if they were geeks or nerds or Christians.

Images of Gray were still going round and round her head. If nothing else, it eclipsed Brittanny and her petty spite. This was huge.

She walked alongside Revel for several blocks before they got to a part of town with some smaller shops and businesses. It was a beautiful September afternoon but Marcy barely noticed.

Revel stopped at an art shop that Marcy had only ever seen the outside of, and entered, with Marcy following. Behind the counter was a guy with untidy hair and a close cropped beard.

"Hey." He clearly knew who Revel was, didn't make any remark when she went through the back and up some stairs signposted Staff Only.

Upstairs was crammed with art supplies, from rolls of paper to old easels. New ones as well, flat packed. One corner of the room held a photography studio. There was a weird, chemical odour that was unfamiliar to Marcy.

"Hi Nick." Revel greeted a man who was adjusting some lights, evidently the photographer.

A photographic shoot. Marcy still didn't have much of a clue what was going on, but this was more interesting than a rifle range.

"Nearly ready, babe."

"Okay, I just need five." Revel put her backpack down and went around the back of some easels. Marcy stood there, awkwardly. The Nick guy didn't say anything to her, he was now busy fiddling with his camera gear. Adjusting a tripod or something.

Revel called out from her hiding place. "That's Marcy by the way. She's at Springdale too."

"Hey Marcy." The guy didn't look up from his work.

"Hey." She felt more and more awkward. Yet these people didn't seem to mind her presence.

Revel eventually emerged with her hair down and a flimsy robe around her. Oh God, was she naked under there? Fortunately Marcy realised Rebel clearly had pants on, and shoes. Tight black leggings.

When Nick finally stood back and switched the lights on, Revel slipped off the robe to reveal a kind of bra top. It wasn't overly revealing, just cropped. Like a short corset, perhaps.

Marcy watched, fascinated, as Revel posed for Nick. The school weirdo was completely transformed in her eyes. Revel was clearly used to modelling, and she actually looked like a real model. Not like the skinny types you saw on the catwalks, though she was thin, but the kind you saw in art shows. This was obviously some kind of art shoot, nothing creepy or sleazy.

Marcy just found it hard to reconcile her notion of the weird, antisocial Revel with this cool model girl.

Revel turned this way and that, occasionally cracking a joke while Nick photographed her from different angles. When they'd finally finished he turned to Marcy. "You want some pictures taken?"

Revel gave a laugh. "Yeah, why don't you? Nick's amazing."

Marcy hesitated. Both because she really wasn't the photogenic type, and because she wasn't sure if she might have to pay him, and if so how expensive that might be. She was trying to save up her money for various things at the moment.

"It's very kind - " she hesitated.

"It's just for fun. You're doing Nick a favour," Revel told her. "New face for a change."

Embarrassed, Marcy slid onto the stool that was currently positioned in front of the photographic screen. Was she supposed to smile? Pout?

"Just look at me here," Nick said. Marcy did so, and he took several snaps before she'd had the time to decide what to do with her face. "Now look over there. Turn towards the door." He took a couple more and they were done.

They would look awful, Marcy thought. She would look like a scared rabbit.

Revel farewelled Nick and the guy downstairs in the shop as they exited. "I need a drink." Instead of going to one of the cafés where everyone else went, Revel went into a bar. It was one that Marcy hadn't been in before, but fortunately they didn't seem to check ID at this time of day.

The way things were going Marcy wouldn't have been surprised if Revel ordered hard liquor and drank it from the bottle, so she was more surprised when Revel just ordered a coke. They could have got that in the café. Marcy got one too, and then was surprised that she didn't have to pay.

"It's okay, I work here," Revel told her. Then seeing Marcy's confusion she explained. "Not behind the bar obviously. I sing here sometimes. You don't need to be of age for that."

Revel modelled and sang? It was so much to take in that Marcy's mind was almost distracted from her stress over Gray.

46

Then as soon as she realised this, she started thinking about him all over again.

Revel saw her shoulders slump. "Shitty day, hey?"

"Yeah." You don't know the half of it, Marcy thought.

"One more year, we'll be through with it."

Marcy was starting to realise that Revel actually didn't care what people thought about her, or the way they disregarded her. She had always assumed Revel minded being cold shouldered all the time. She and Addy would have been mortified not to have any friends - well, Marcy was mortified now.

But Revel was just biding her time apparently. Making no effort to fit in.

"So what you do you sing?" Marcy asked.

"Jazz mainly. Here anyway. Some musical theatre."

"I didn't know you sang." She didn't know anything about Revel, truth be told.

"Since I was a kid. It's in the blood," Revel told her.

Given she was actually holding her first ever conversation with Revel in two years, or however long it was since Revel moved here, Marcy decided to ask her about something she had burned with curiosity over.

"How did you get your name?"

Revel was unruffled by the question. "It's my middle name. My mother was enamoured of some book character called Virginia Revel, partly as it was her own name. But I'm not really a Virginia."

She wasn't, Marcy had to admit. "What do your parents do?"

"Not much. They're dead."

Marcy was mortified. She started to apologise.

"It's okay. It was years ago. I was pretty small. A plane crash. I live with my grandmother. That's why I'm here, not in New York."

Marcy got the sense that Revel had given this summary a few times, to avoid further questions. But something was ticking in her mind. Music being in the family. Virginia. A plane crash. New York. She studied Revel's face more closely, trying to see if she could recognise a likeness.

"Your mother wasn't Virginia Lake was she?" And then felt completely stupid for asking. Virginia Lake had been a huge Broadway star, killed in a light aircraft crash at the peak of her career. Marcy's parents had some of her records and Marcy had seen old clips of her on TV. Everyone would have known if she was Revel's mother, surely.

But Revel's eyebrows shot up. "You've heard of her?"

"Of course. She was incredible. I'm so sorry for what happened," Marcy said.

"Most people haven't heard of her these days."

Marcy suspected the issue was more that Revel had never mentioned her famous parentage for anyone to comment on. "Theatre is kind of a thing for me, it's what I want to do one day. Write plays that is, not perform," she said hurriedly.

"Great. I look forward to starring in your first production," Revel said.

Marcy couldn't tell if she was mocking her or not. Revel actually seemed sincere. "You plan to follow in your mom's footsteps?"

"That's the plan. If I can get into Juilliard."

Just one year. One more year of this high school hell, and then all their dreams could come true.

Except Marcy had a dream she wanted now, and it had just been snatched from her grasp.

10. Confrontation

Marcy didn't expect Gray - Mr Grayson, she reminded herself - to text her that evening. It would be way too compromising given what had already occurred. He had doubtless deleted her number from his phone by now anyway. She thought he might decide to treat her with cold formality, at a distance, but really she was just guessing.

She had no idea what to expect in such a circumstance. Who did?

As for her, she couldn't bear to erase his number and messages. She wanted to keep them a while longer. She changed his name from "Gray" to "G" just to disguise it a bit in case anyone else found it.

Then she rang Addy.

So much had happened that day that she was feeling numbed to it all. Numb enough to talk about it with Addy without breaking down. She hoped, anyway.

Addy's New York school hadn't started back yet, so she didn't have a lot of news to share there. Her first question, of course, was about Gray.

"So is he back yet? Did he call?"

"He's back. He didn't call. He won't be calling," Marcy said.

"What? Why?" Addy's confusion was clear down the other end of the line.

"I found out what his job was."

"And it's something you don't approve of? He works in a abattoir? He's a male stripper?" Addy threw out wild guesses while Marcy took a couple of deep breaths.

How to broach this? "You know how Miss Vansittart left last summer to have a baby? Well, we have a new French teacher. Mr Grayson."

"So? What's Mr Grayson go to do with anything. Tell me what happened with Gray - " the penny started to drop "- wait, Mr Grayson - Gray - no way. No way, Marcy. No way no way no way!" She was yelling at Marcy down the phone, Marcy's silence telling her all she needed to know.

"Yes way."

"Oh my god. Marcy I'm so sorry. How did this happen. Didn't he tell you what his job was? Surely he recognised the school you went to?" Addy asked.

"He didn't think I was at school, remember. Not high school I mean. He thinks - he thought - I was at college." Marcy had never explicitly told him this, but she had deliberately failed to correct him.

"Oh. My. God." It was still sinking in. "So what will you do?"

Marcy had no idea. "Change schools. Ask my mom to home-school me." They both knew this wasn't a realistic option. Marcy's parents would never let her drop out, not in her final year. And her parents could never, ever know why she wanted to leave.

"Did he definitely recognise you?" Addy asked.

"Addy, I slept with him. I spent the night with him. He saw me with makeup, without. His face when he realised..." she tailed off. She could hardly bring herself to remember it.

"Was he sad?"

Sad? "No, Addy, he looked shocked and furious and then he hid it, and I ran out to the bathroom and never went back."

Addy swore. "I just can't believe this!"

Thinking about it, Marcy had made the whole thing even harder. Now she had to face him again tomorrow, on top of the issue of running out of his classroom. That would normally warrant a detention, but she doubted he would want to hold her back after class.

The thing was she had really liked him. Really, really liked him. She had been so excited when he had said he wanted to see her again, and when he had texted her. And despite being paralysed with horror when he introduced himself as "Mr Grayson", she had noticed how incredibly hot he looked in a shirt and tie, his hair newly cut. He made such a contrast to the pathetic high school boys like Josh that it was almost sad.

"You still there, Marcy?" Addy was worried about her.

"Yes. I'm just wondering if military academy is an option."

"For him or you?"

Marcy grimaced, though Addy couldn't see. She wanted to change the subject. She had imagined pouring out tales of hearts and flowers to Addy, while Addy reciprocated with stories of hot New York guys. Instead all she had to offer was "I slept with my teacher." It sounded like an episode of some slutty chat show.

* * *

Next day was slutty chat show time. Marcy had to face Gray - Mr Grayson - and sit through his class somehow. She couldn't fail French and there was no other class she could transfer to.

Deep breaths. You can do this, Marcy, she thought.

French was in the morning that day, the last period before lunch. The rest of the morning passed in a kind of blur, with Marcy oblivious to any nasty looks or spiteful comments from Brittanny's set. She had far bigger things on her mind.

She knew it almost certainly wouldn't matter how she looked, but she checked her hair and make up in the restroom anyway. At least there was nothing to laugh at: no smudged mascara or anything like that.

Bracing herself, she joined a crowd of people entering the French classroom and found her way to a desk. All without managing to look at the teacher. She felt his eyes burning into her back, but that could have just been her imagination.

Keeping her head lowered, Marcy arranged the things she needed in front of her. It was time to face the worst.

Holding her face steady, wanting to bite her lip but not daring to show any emotion, she raised it to look at the front of the classroom.

Only to see Gray's eyes directly meeting hers. He looked away again almost immediately, but he had clearly been watching her. Marcy hoped no one else had noticed.

What was the expression in them? She still thought she saw anger there, but there was something else she couldn't quite figure out.

Mr Grayson studiously avoided looking directly at her during class or addressing any questions to her. Marcy wanted to roll her eyes when she saw how some of the other girls simpered at the merest word from him. They were practically all over him, playing with their hair and trying to seem cute and dumb. Well they were dumb, most of them.

If Addy had been there she would have been rolling her eyes and making secret vomiting gestures to Marcy. Marcy missed her so much.

At least Mr Grayson didn't seem to be responding to them. He treated everyone in the same friendly but businesslike way.

Looking at him, she couldn't really blame others for drooling all over him. He was TV star hot. In fact given that he'd mentioned he liked acting she found herself wondering why he hadn't gone that career route. It had to be better paid than teaching.

"Anyone? Marcy... Winters, isn't it?" he said, looking down at his register and feigning that he didn't know. "What would your interpretation be?"

Oh God. Her face flushed bright red. One moment's daydreaming and she had lost track of what he had been saying.

Keep calm, she thought. "Could you please repeat the question?"

There was a snicker behind her from one of the guys near Brittanny.

Mr Grayson raised his eyebrows. "What is Monsieur Martin asking the hotel concierge for?"

She hadn't even read it. Fortunately Marcy found French relatively easy. She glanced down at the book. "Whether he has a non-smoking room."

He was silent for a brief moment. "Good." Then he looked away and addressed another question to someone else.

The lesson continued, an endless ordeal for Marcy. She had one eye on the clock, willing the hands to go round faster.

Finally they ticked over to noon. The lunch bell sounded. Marcy practically slumped with relief. Grabbing her things together quickly, she got up to make a rush for the door.

Only to be stopped by a command.

"Marcy Winters, would you stay behind please?"

11. Facing Gray

Having anticipated the worst, his first question took her by surprise.

"How come you're not doing Advanced Placement?"

Everyone else had left the class now and it was just the two of them, facing one another in the empty classroom.

"I don't know." Marcy did know, it was because she and Addy hadn't wanted any extra pressure in their final year. French didn't seem vital for her planned career and she was already doing AP English and Theatre Studies.

Gray was looking at her as though he was her teacher, nothing more. Which he was of course. Mr Grayson, she reminded herself.

"I saw your records. You easily have the ability."

Marcy said nothing. She had no idea what to say. There was an awkward pause.

"I'd also like to know why you lied to me?" Gray said. His eyes were a hard, dark green.

She wanted to sink through the floor. "I didn't exactly lie."

"You led me to believe you were at college. An adult. God, Marcy, do you realise the position you've put me in?"

Marcy wished she could cover her face and make it all go away. But her arms were hugging her bag.

"I didn't think it mattered. It wasn't like it was illegal or anything. I had no idea you were going to be teaching at Springdale."

They hadn't ever really discussed his job, which was odd when you thought about it. Or maybe not. Marcy had shifted out of the subject of college and careers as much as possible, to avoid revealing her own situation.

"Going into a bar was illegal. Buying alcohol for you was illegal. Taking you back to my place…"

"…was not illegal." She finished for him.

"That hardly matters now, does it? I could lose my job at the very least."

"I'm sorry." She really was. "I just liked being with you so much." I liked you, she thought. I still do.

Something softened in Gray's eyes when she said this.

His voice was husky. "I liked being with you too." Then he became stern again. "But that's it, Marcy, I'm your teacher now. Nothing more can happen. And no one can ever find out what did."

Good thing Addy was in New York then. "I understand." She did, though she didn't want to. Every fibre of her being was pleading with him to just take her in his arms and kiss her. She looked at his lips and wished he would kiss her just one more time. A final, goodbye kiss that she could remember for always.

"I do want you in Advanced Placement though. You're wasting your ability otherwise. Here's a form, please get it signed and you can join the class later this week."

Marcy took the form. Her fingers momentarily brushed his hand and she wondered if he felt the same jolt she did. She looked up at him. She saw in his eyes that he was as unhappy as she was about the situation. He might still be shocked and angry, but behind the "Mr Grayson" that she had to get to accept as his new identity to her, she could still see Gray.

Her Gray. Or so she had thought.

"Don't forget the form, Marcy. Or today's assignment."

He didn't say "have a good day" or anything trite like that because they both knew he wouldn't. And nor would she.

Marcy thanked him and left, her thoughts whirling.

The burning question was whether he would have still been interested even if he wasn't her teacher? If she had been upfront with him from the start about her age, would he still have ruled it out? Or if she had told him on their next date, and he was working in some job that wasn't teaching, would he still have wanted to see her?

Marcy walked into lunch in a kind of daze. She wished she had brought a packed meal so she could go and hide somewhere by herself. Instead she collected a tray of pretty awful looking food and then faced the gauntlet of walking past the popular tables to find her place among the outcasts.

"He's sooo hot!" she heard Brittanny drawling to her friends. "I just know that he wants me back, I can tell from the way he looked at me when he handed the assignments out."

"Don't let Jayden hear you." Jayden was the captain of the Springdale football team and supposedly Brittanny's boyfriend that semester. She was such a walking cliché, Marcy thought.

Brittanny made some dismissive response that Marcy didn't fully catch because she had walked past.

Mr Grayson wasn't going to be short of attention that year, that was certain. Still, at least if he had ruled Marcy out based on the student-teacher situation then Brittanny stood no chance. Not that this gave Marcy a lot of satisfaction.

"Homeless again?"

It was Revel. Gratefully Marcy slid in the place opposite her. She appreciated how Revel didn't probe, didn't ask her how she was. She obviously noticed what had gone on, Brittanny was so prominent that her campaigns of bitchiness were hard to miss, but Revel didn't make Marcy relive the ordeal.

"When do you get to see the photos from your shoot?" Marcy asked.

"Whenever. Nick has an exhibition soon, so…"

She didn't specify what she meant by "so" and Marcy didn't like to ask. Perhaps it was supposed to be obvious.

"You mentioned you sang jazz?" she said to Revel.

Revel was picking out raisins from some trail mix she'd brought with her. "Among other things."

"Do you take lessons?" Marcy asked. She was curious to know more about Revel.

"I used to." She didn't mention why or when she had stopped. "If you want you can come down on Saturday night, I'm singing at the bar."

Marcy frowned. "I don't have any ID…"

"You won't need it. I'll put your name on the door," Revel told her.

Marcy thanked her. It would be a change of scene at least. She'd have to fib to her parents about what she was doing, as they wouldn't approve of her hanging out in an adult venue. Still, really it was no different than going to a concert. After all she probably wouldn't drink there, she was only going to watch Revel perform.

Throughout classes that afternoon Marcy was dying to just go home, lie on her bed and close her eyes. To not think about Gray. Or truthfully, to phone Addy and talk about Gray for an hour. She couldn't help remembering the expression in his eyes when he had admitted he had liked being with her.

Walking home later that day she wondered what Gray got up to in the evenings. He had said he did a lot of exercise and sports. Or maybe he would have to mark their assignments. And now she had all that extra French ahead of her if she enrolled in the Advanced Placement.

Doing so would of course result in her seeing him even more often. Had he realised this?

She tried to suppress it, but deep down a small hope flickered that maybe he wanted her in his other class for another reason.

12. Advanced French

There was a parcel for her when she arrived home. Marcy instantly recognised the handwriting: it was from Addy. She had sent Marcy an assortment of deliberately tacky New York souvenirs and a postcard.

"Just getting you excited to visit me! I miss you up here, it's too far. A."

There was a pen in the shape of the Empire State Building, an "I heart NY" key ring, several fridge magnets, and a cool pendant with a piece of vintage New York map set into it, under a glass dome. Marcy put it around her neck. Best of all, given her current mood, there was a foil-wrapped chocolate Statue of Liberty.

Unwrapping it and biting off its head, Marcy headed to her room to phone Addy. Before she could do so her mother called out to her.

Marcy went to the kitchen where her mother was cutting up some carrots.

"Mrs Helberg has been on my back again about her theatre group. They're desperate for some new young people. Why don't you join, Marcy? It's only a couple of nights a week."

"I've told her before, acting's not my thing," Marcy said.

"You wouldn't have to go on stage. They need people to help with other things. I told her you might be able to help design the programs." She saw Marcy's face fall. "She's a good-hearted person, I know she can be a bit..."

"...overbearing?" Marcy said. "Pushy? And a total busybody?"

"She has her faults, but she's always been a good neighbour. She's been very kind looking after Pegasus when we go away."

Pegasus, as fat and grey as ever, was curled up smugly on a cushion. Marcy ran a hand over his plush fur.

"I might not have time. They want me to enrol in Advanced Placement for French," she said. She avoided saying who "they" were. She couldn't yet bring herself to say the words: "our new French teacher".

Her mother was delighted. "That's wonderful!"

"It means extra classes so I'm not sure I can help Mrs Helberg out this time. What with my job and all," Marcy said.

"See how you go. If it's all too much you can drop something."

Upstairs, Marcy was about to call Addy when her phone rang. "You must be psychic."

"So? What happened? I've been literally burning to know since we spoke yesterday. And I do mean literally burning, I was messing around with a candle and I singed my hair. All your fault, because I was distracted."

Typical Addy. "I managed to face him."

"Gray? Or Mr Grayson? What was he like? Are you going to have a secret affair?" Addy asked.

"Hardly. We'd both get kicked out of school. He was kind of angry at first, but he did admit he liked seeing me. But that no one could ever know and it was all over."

Addy made a sympathetic sound. "I'm sorry. But you never know, maybe when the year's over?"

"I don't think so," Marcy said. "He's bound to be dating someone else by then, he really is that good looking. I'm kind of amazed he was single. Oh, and he's making me do AP French."

"What?!" Addy was practically bouncing around at this, at least as far as Marcy could guess thousands of miles over the phone.

"I have to enrol in Advanced Placement for French. As if I didn't have enough on my plate," Marcy said.

"There's only one reason he wants you in AP and that's because he wants to see more of you."

Marcy managed to laugh. "I don't think so. You know that Mrs Vansittart also mentioned it, she probably put it in my notes."

Addy was not convinced. "If he really meant to keep you at arm's length then he wouldn't try to spend any more time with you."

Secretly Marcy hoped there was some truth in this, but in reality Mr Grayson was probably just being professional and helping her to get the best education. "Your parcel arrived, thank you so much! I already ate Liberty."

"I figured you might need some chocolate, facing Brittanny and everyone. I didn't know about Mr Grayson then or I would have sent a crate."

* * *

There weren't many other students in Advanced Placement French that year. They were just six, all up. Marcy didn't know any of them very well. One girl, Emilie, had moved with her family from Quebec a couple of years ago, so obviously spoke great French.

Mr Grayson came in and Marcy tried to focus on him just being her French teacher. She had to admit that he was a really good teacher. He'd managed to ignore all the girls swooning over him in class, he kept good order and so far people seemed to like him.

In his shirt and tie, instructing them from the front of the classroom, he also seemed older. It gave Marcy the horrible feeling that she must look much younger.

She loved the way one strand of hair randomly fell over his forehead, and he had to push it back. He had such a great body, you could tell through his clothes, even though she obviously had more intimate knowledge.

Marcy pinched herself. She had to stop daydreaming. They were supposed to be going over a French magazine article and she found the vocabulary pretty challenging. She really didn't want to put her hand up and have to ask what a word meant.

They were reading around the room, a line each: first in French, and then translating. Marcy's line was just awful, full of long words for which she had no clue of the meaning. The only thing that gave her courage was that the students who had already read seemed like they were struggling even more.

She made her way through the line. The pressure was worse because she knew Mr Grayson had French parentage, so it must have sounded even more terrible to his ears.

Then it was time to translate. She knew the article was something to do with the environment, but beyond that she was stumped.

"What's *sécheresses*?" she asked.

Mr Grayson's eyes met hers. His expression seemed neutral. Cool, but not cold.

"Can you guess? Can you remember what *séche* is, or *sec*?"

She knew that one. "*Vin sec*" was dry wine. "Dry".

"So from the context, what do you think it means?" he asked.

"Drynesses - " suddenly the light bulb went on " - droughts!"

"Very good." He smiled at Marcy, the first time since the school semester had started, and she felt her stomach flip over. "Now this is an example of many words you can figure out through context, without needing a dictionary. It will making reading French much smoother if you don't keep stopping to check," he said, addressing the whole class.

When it was finally time to go Marcy rushed to get her things together so she could get away first. She didn't want Mr Grayson to think she was lingering to talk to him or something.

But as she was about to go, he called her back to his desk.

"Yes?" she asked. The other students made it past her and out of the room.

He looked directly at her. "You did well today. I'm glad you signed up for this class."

Once again her stomach was fluttering. She returned his gaze, looking into his green eyes, and felt certain he wanted to say something more.

But he couldn't. They both knew how it had to be.

"Me too." She hoped she could somehow convey everything in her expression. How she was sorry, how she really liked him, how she missed him already even though she had only known him for a short time. That she had no regrets, and that she understood.

Even if she wished things could be different. She thought - she hoped - that he felt the same way.

13. Surprise encounter

It was the first time Marcy had been to a bar by herself, at night. She was super nervous. Revel wasn't singing until ten o'clock so Marcy had decided to get there just a few minutes early.

As promised, the doorman checked her name on a list and let her straight through without asking for ID. Marcy didn't plan to drink anyway, just in case.

She couldn't see Revel there, she was probably getting ready out the back or something. The bar was very crowded. It was popular with college students in the town, particularly with groups of guys. Addy had described it as a "pick up joint" and had always wanted to go there.

Marcy was wearing skinny jeans and a top that wasn't too low cut, but was just suggestive enough to be sexy enough for going out. She could feel a lot of eyes on her as she tried to make her way to the bar, and was paranoid that they were people thinking she was underage for drinking.

She ordered a Coke. While she waited there were a couple of really lame chat up lines from really lame looking guys, but she politely declined. "I'm with someone."

It wasn't exactly a lie, she was kind of with Revel. She was Revel's guest, anyway.

Pushing her way through the crowds she tried to find a position near enough to get a reasonable view of where Revel would be singing. As luck would have it there was a table with a spare barstool. A girl initially had her purse on it but saw Marcy standing and moved it for her.

"Thanks."

"No problem. I was keeping it for a friend, but she just bailed." The girl indicated her phone. "You here for the band?"

Marcy wasn't sure. Was Revel singing with a band? "My friend's singing in a few moments."

"Ah yeah, the singer. She's good. I'm not really into jazz but my roommate's boyfriend plays sax so we get dragged down here. I'm Didi," the girl told her. She had black hair, cut straight across at the front.

"Marcy. Thanks again for the seat." She really hoped she didn't look like a high school student. Didi herself looked almost too old for college.

"That's him, the guy with the hat." For some reason the saxophonist was wearing an odd looking hat.

Marcy sipped her Coke and then saw Revel step up to the microphone. She was wearing tight black pants - Marcy couldn't remember ever seeing her in a skirt, even in summer - with a long top made of some shiny silvery fabric that fell off one shoulder. She looked amazing, Marcy thought. She couldn't believe she never noticed how stunning Revel was, in a kind of dramatic way.

The band struck up and Revel started singing. Marcy had expected "jazz" to be old songs by Ella Fitzgerald or whatever. She was surprised to find that it was all much more upbeat, like a mix of jazz and hip hop. Revel had a beautiful voice, very smoky, but powerful too. She also rapped. Marcy could easily imagine her performing musical theatre.

Occasionally there was something she recognised, but mixed up with newer songs. She wondered who wrote them. Currently Revel was singing "Fly me to the moon" much faster than the song was usually performed, rapping in between.

Marcy didn't know what instinct made her look around, back towards the bar, but when she did her stomach nearly fell through the floor. Gray - Mr Grayson - was there, looking directly at her. She froze. Maybe he would ignore her.

But no, he made his way over to her.

"You shouldn't be here." He did not look pleased.

She could smell alcohol on him and his hair was ruffled at the front. It was sexy, it reminded her of the other night with him.

"I'm only watching my friend sing. It's Coke, look," she said, holding out her glass towards him after his eyes went to it accusingly.

"You need to be twenty-one to get in here."

"I'm on the guest list," Marcy told him.

He was still glaring at her. "It's still illegal."

"Well, I was invited so it's not an issue." She didn't actually know whether it would be an issue or not if there was a police bust, but it was hardly a rowdy bar.

"That's your friend?" Gray asked, looking at Revel. "How old is she?"

"She's a senior at Springdale as well."

Gray swore. "I can't even drown my sorrows in peace without being surrounded by students."

Marcy realised he had had quite a bit to drink. "Drown your sorrows?"

He obviously hadn't meant to say it. "Forget it."

They were in front of one another, closer than he probably intended because of the crush of people. She was nearer his eye level due to being on the stool.

She could smell his cologne, his skin. Practically feel the warmth from his body, he was so near her.

She looked at his lips, firmly set in anger yet still soft. She knew how they would feel on hers.

He swayed even closer towards her. For a moment she thought he was going to kiss her, and every fibre in her body longed for him to do so.

But then he straightened up and got a hold of himself. "When the band is over, you need to go home, Marcy."

Her disappointment was almost like a lead weight, dragging her down, as he walked away. He moved out of sight and she thought he had probably decided to leave altogether.

Wound up about it all, Marcy tried to concentrate on the rest of Revel's singing. She eventually finished her set with a modernised version of "When I fall in love" which Marcy found almost physically painful to hear. Music occasionally got to her, but never this strongly. It was as though every lyric somehow spoke about how she had been starting to feel for Gray, or would have done if the whole teacher-student thing hadn't strangled it.

Afterwards Revel came over to their table, and Marcy wasn't able to leave as Revel had asked someone to get them more drinks. Someone else had left, so Revel slid up onto the seat next to Marcy.

Marcy knew by now that Revel wasn't the kind of person to directly ask what someone else thought about her, or care. But Marcy had enjoyed her singing, so she said so.

Revel smiled. "It's fun. I'll do it until I get bust."

"They don't know you're eighteen?"

"Hell no." She swigged her drink. "Well, probably they do, but not officially."

"How did you meet the band?" Marcy asked.

"They were auditioning singers, I tried out."

There were guys flocking round Revel: no wonder given how she looked. A couple of them started chatting to her and Marcy, the usual kind of thing, how they liked the music, did Revel sing there often, did they work or were they at college.

The one talking more to Marcy was quite nice looking but way too old for her, he looked about twenty-eight. He would probably be even more horrified than Gray to find out she was a decade younger than him.

They talked for a while, Marcy losing track of the time. She was on her third coke when she felt someone grab her arm. She was pulled off her stool and against someone.

Before she could react, there were lips on her, fierce, crushing hers. She registered almost instantly it was Gray. He forced her mouth to open for him and was kissing her in a really possessive way.

Marcy was turned on beyond belief. She felt her insides melting just at being touched by him. Her thoughts were whirling. What was he doing? He was the one that had vowed it was all over, professional student-teacher relations only. Now he was practically devouring her.

God, how she wanted him. She just wanted to roll the clock back to last weekend, sleep with him again, then transfer to a different high school by Monday so he would have never found out.

His tongue was probing her, tasting her. His hands gripped her hips hard. She yielded to him, feeling his pelvis pressed against hers, his heat warm against her.

Abruptly he broke off. He had clearly had even more alcohol since he had spoken to her earlier. "I can't stand seeing you with those guys."

Then he turned and left. She wanted to go after him but some instinct stopped her. Over the throng she saw him swing the door open and leave alone, into the night.

Back at the table Revel was laughing. "Who the hell was that?"

She didn't recognise him? Marcy remembered that Revel didn't do French. "Just someone I had a thing with." She hoped it didn't make her sound really slutty.

"More than a thing, I'd guess," one of the guys said.

"Yeah, it didn't end well," Marcy told them. Fortunately they sensed her discomfort and changed the subject, but Marcy could see a glint in Revel's eyes. She was amused. Whatever she had expected of Marcy, it probably wasn't this. She probably thought that Marcy was miserable due to lovesickness over Josh since their dating and breakup was public knowledge.

She must not find out, Marcy thought. Even though she thought that Revel was someone who could probably be trusted, it was far too dangerous for anyone else to know. She would have to keep her own secret, with Addy her only outlet to spill her woe.

14. Texting

Revel didn't stay much longer so they walked out of the bar together. Marcy was so confused over what had happened that she was keen to get out of the crowds and noise. She needed a long time along to think about things. And to freak out.

Revel was chuckling again.

"What is it?" Marcy asked.

"You. You're such a dark horse. Here I was, figuring you were heartbroken over that dweeb and you're involved with much hotter stuff. Way older, too. Don't worry, I'm not going to snoop on your secrets. It's just funny, is all."

Marcy was grateful that Revel didn't plan to probe. She honestly didn't know what she could have told her anyway. She was curious about Revel's own love life: before she would have assumed that Revel went home alone and did nothing. Now, she found herself wondering more about her.

But she had to extend Revel the same courtesy of not probing her love life, so she made a more general comment.

"I hope your life is less of a train wreck, at least."

"I'd take a train wreck like that any day. Angry and gorgeous. Just how I like a guy," Revel said.

They were nearly at Marcy's car which was finally back from repairs. She had been amazed at how well they had patched up the damage. Marcy offered Revel a lift.

"It's no problem, it's all fixed up now," she told her.

"Sure, thanks."

It turned out that Revel lived not far from Marcy, it was just a slightly different direction if you were going there from Springdale, which is why Marcy had never seen her walking back home from school before.

Revel's house - her grandmother's house - was a big, old property that looked dark and leafy at this time of night.

"Come round some time. It's like a time warp," Revel told her.

Marcy thanked her for the invitation and drove off. She didn't know exactly when or how she was supposed to take it up, just show up there sometime? Maybe Revel would more formally invite her another time. She was interested to see what Revel's home was like, wondering if there were photos of her famous mother. Then she remembered Revel lived with her paternal grandmother, so probably not.

What Marcy wanted to do was call Addy. Desperately. Except the time zones were all wrong and even though Addy, surprisingly, was often an early riser, no way would she appreciate being woken up before dawn.

Although it was pretty big news...

Marcy decided she was best off sleeping on it. She needed some time to gather her thoughts anyway

* * *

First thing that morning she messaged Addy.

Too much to text. Call me. Emergency.

She got a reply back within thirty seconds.

You're pregnant?

Marcy was about to reply "No!" when her phone buzzed again.

Sorry about last night. It won't happen again.

She was confused.

What won't happen?

Then suddenly she realised she had just sent the message to "G" not "A".

Oh God. He had texted her. Gray. He must still have her number. Now he probably thought she was being facetious or moody or something. She was struggling with how to explain her confusion when he messaged her a second time.

Good. See you in class.

68

So abrupt. He must have thought she was pretending to play along that it had never happened. Which of course was probably the wisest strategy.

Her phone rang. For a second she thought - hoped - it was him.

"So?"

"Oh, it's you." Marcy said.

"You just asked me to call you!" Addy was bewildered.

"Sorry, yeah, I just got other texts in between."

"Who from?" When Marcy paused Addy instantly guessed. "Oh! No way!"

"Yes. That's why I was calling, or getting you to call me. Something kind of happened again last night," Marcy told her.

"You didn't sleep with him again!"

"No, no. But I was in a bar with Revel and he grabbed me and kissed me."

Addy was now totally confused. "Hold on. Scroll back. Revel as in Revel Holmes? Weird Revel?"

"Yes," Marcy said. "Only she's not that weird, so it turns out. But I'll get to that later. The thing is that Gray was there, he'd been drinking, and he saw me and told me to go home. Then a bit later he kissed me, really angrily, then he suddenly left."

"How did you get into there in the first place? Did you manage to get fake ID?" Addy asked.

"Revel sings there. So she put my name on the door and I didn't need it," Marcy explained.

"Revel sings? Like, what, with a band or something?"

Marcy didn't want to waste time talking about Revel. "Yes, a band. But I'll get to that later. Tell me what I'm supposed to do about Gray?"

"I really need to see a photo of this guy, it's hard to judge otherwise. I mean is he nice-hot, take it or leave it, or is he drop-dead risk-everything-for hot?" Addy asked.

"Risk everything. Except he doesn't want to," Marcy told her.

"Except he did last night. And now he's texting you."

"Only to tell me that it's over. Again." She related his exact text messages to Addy.

Addy groaned. "I can't believe the most wild things ever are finally happening at Springdale and I'm thousands of miles away. I want to come back!"

Marcy wished she would and told her. "But how's your new school?"

"It's not bad. Pretty intense. Half the kids there are super over achievers and the rest are really intimidatingly cool, you know? Like they're from New York and they know everything and everyone's parents work on Wall St or whatever." Addy described what her new life was like and Marcy listened, kind of glad for the distraction. "Anyway, so that's enough about me. The question is what are you going to do on Monday?"

Marcy had no idea. "Pretend it never happened, I guess."

"But you want him, right?"

She did. "If it wasn't so illegal."

Addy was unfazed by this. "You're of age, the only issue is his job. It sounds like he's pretty crazy about you. You should just flirt with him and try and end up at that bar again, for a repeat performance."

15. Suppressing feelings

If Mr Grayson was crazy about Marcy you could hardly tell from the way he acted toward her in French that week. Half to her relief, half to her disappointment he was flawlessly professional, there were no looks or special attention, and he didn't call her back after class. Her Advanced Placement transfer hadn't been finalised yet due to starting late, so she was still having to attend both classes.

One more week and hopefully she would no longer have to face Brittanny flinging herself at Mr Grayson. What Brittanny lacked in attractions she compensated for with her father's wealth. If she couldn't win someone, she bought them.

Maybe that's why she hates me so much, Marcy thought. Because she never really won me or Addy. They had never fawned over her like others in the group. It was also possible that someone had heard Addy refer to her as Bitchany Paige and told her.

So long as Marcy had dated Josh, she and her best friend were kind of untouchable. Now she was out in the cold and fair game for tormenting.

The only good thing about Brittanny's crush on Mr Grayson was that her malice towards Marcy subsided a bit, at least in French. In the first week, before the fateful night in the bar, Brittanny had tried making some sneering remark about Marcy to another girl. A searing look of disgust from Mr Grayson cut her dead.

He wasn't just defending Marcy though, much as she would have liked to have imagine she got his special attention. On another occasion Brittanny was deliberately rolling her eyes and smirking when a slower student was struggling over a translation.

"Do you think that kind of response is conducive to a supportive learning environment, Brittanny?" Mr Grayson had asked her.

Brittanny probably didn't understand what conducive meant, but she picked up his general tone. He didn't find bitching and gloating appealing. She had gone bright red, and a few others who were routinely victimised by her had in turn tried not to smirk at the takedown.

After that she was a lot nicer - or less nasty, more accurately - in French.

Mr Grayson didn't ignore Marcy completely. He still called on her in class, but no more than anyone else.

AP French lessons were a bit less tense even though there was a smaller group. Somehow Mr Grayson seemed more laid back with fewer students. The Canadian girl Emilie turned out to be a livewire and often held the floor, joking and even answering back.

Marcy might have felt jealous except the rumour was Emilie preferred girls. Brittanny mocked Emilie about it behind her back, and no one dared call her out for being a homophobe.

* * *

Marcy now sat with Revel as a regular thing at lunch. She liked her a lot, though Revel was very different to Addy. Addy spilled her guts, Revel was more reserved. It wasn't that she held stuff back deliberately, or was really private, just that she didn't feel the need to share everything.

"Nick has your photos if you want to come over after school," Revel told her. It was Friday, finally the end of another long week. "I'm not singing tonight but we could go for a drink at the bar later if you want, get some food somewhere."

Marcy looked glum. "I wish I could, but my mom forced me into this theatre thing," she told Revel. She was embarrassed even to mention it to Revel, given Revel's background.

"Theatre?"

"Just a local group. Our neighbour is really into it. Everyone else in it is over seventy." This was an exaggeration, but it was fair to say that the Springdale Players had fairly mature age members. Which was why Mrs Helberg, well into her fifties, still cast herself in ingénue roles.

"That sounds like fun," Revel said.

"Honestly?" Was Revel joking?

"Yeah. All that off-stage drama. Haven't you ever done amateur theatre before?"

"They take themselves quite seriously," Marcy said.

"Exactly. That's why it's funny. And kind of touching. You want me to sign up with you?"

This sidelined Marcy. She simply couldn't imagine Revel lowering herself to join Mrs Helberg's troupe. After all Revel was the daughter of a Broadway star, hugely talented herself, and already practically a professional performer.

"Won't it interfere with your band?"

Revel shrugged. "I can juggle it. What hours do they rehearse?"

Marcy told her that it was Tuesday and Friday nights, from six to nine o'clock.

"Then that's fine," Revel said. "Plenty of time to do both."

Suddenly the miserable prospect of dragging herself to the Springdale Players twice a week seemed a lot brighter. Marcy's mother had also sweetened the pill by increasing Marcy's allowance, as she would have to give up her Tuesday shift at the café.

With Revel there, it might even be bearable. She couldn't imagine Revel being pushed around by Mrs Helberg. Marcy also wondered how Mrs Helberg would react to Revel's talent. She probably wouldn't like a challenge to her role as star.

* * *

There was plenty of time to view the photos before they had to get to the rehearsal. Several of Revel's were pinned up around the studio-come-storeroom, along with some of other girls.

"Nick shoots film and develops himself. The darkroom's back there," Revel said, indicating the place she'd gone to change her clothes the other week.

Marcy, who had never been in a traditional photographer's studio before, now guessed that the unusual odour must be developing chemicals. She wandered over to look at some of the pictures of Revel and others pinned to a piece of string tied across the room, like a temporary clothes line. The photos were pinned on with actual clothes pegs.

Revel looked absolutely amazing in them, just like a professional model. They were really arty shots, in black and white, and a couple of them reminded Marcy of the old-style publicity photos used for Hollywood stars of the Golden Age. Even with her piercings in, Revel just had the right look. Dramatic, alluring.

As she moved along the line Marcy was mortified to realised that one of the images was of herself. It took her a moment to recognise herself because of the angle and the black-and-white style. She looked strangely solemn and wistful.

Revel came up over her shoulder. "That is just beautiful. You have to get a copy of that one."

Marcy blushed. She felt the photo didn't really look like her, it was too sophisticated. The shadows made it look as though she was wearing more eye make up or something. It was hard to describe. And her skin looked way more flawless than it did in the mirror. Though that was the same in all the photos of all the subjects. They had a kind of pearly white marble tone to the skin.

Nick appeared from the dark room area, drying his hands on a towel. "Like them?" he asked.

"As ever," Revel said. "Which ones are you using?"

"The first six on the line, then those in that corner," he told her.

The first six on the line. That meant Marcy's photo. She had no idea that he had planned to use it in his exhibition, and wasn't really sure how she felt about it. She looked so timid or something, compared to Revel's pictures. At least they weren't full body shots.

"Great. Do you have copies?" Revel asked.

"Over here." He opened a folder and drew out some prints. As well as the washing line one of Marcy there was one in which she was smiling in an embarrassed and awkward way. In Marcy's opinion, anyway. It reminded her of how awkward she had felt in front of the lens.

Revel handed Marcy's to her, and Marcy put them carefully in her backpack, inside a book so they wouldn't get bent or crumpled. "Thanks," she said to Nick. She wondered if she should be more effusive, but followed Revel's lead. She tried to look pleased, though it made her feel vain to do so.

It had been a weird day. And it was about to get a lot more weird.

* * *

Marcy and Revel stopped to get food before going to the Springdale Players. They only just arrived in time, Marcy knew that Mrs Helberg would complain to her mom if she was late.

As it turned out not everyone had arrived yet anyway. Mrs Helberg was flitting around, introducing Marcy to the other members. A couple of whom she vaguely recognised from previous productions she had gone to see with her parents.

Mrs Helberg was initially thrilled that Marcy had brought another "young person" to the group. But when she got close enough to see Revel's piercings, Marcy saw her expression twitch with disapproval.

She got everyone to sit around on chairs, forming a circle. "As president of the players, I'd like to welcome two new young members to our company. It's always nice to have new faces." Marcy noticed her again give a rather sidelong glance to Revel. "Now I should hand over to Len, our director-producer, to update us on casting."

Len was a thin man who looked around sixty, he had glasses and wore the kind of sweater that people gave you for Christmas.

"I'm not sure we're all here yet - " he began, whereupon Mrs Helberg dived in again.

"That's right, we still have another couple of members not arrived. Phyllis isn't here, is she? Nor Thaddeus. And of course our new male lead. Now as you know, we've nearly finished casting for the production, but there's always room in the chorus." She smiled encouragingly at Marcy. "But of course I should be handing the floor back to our director."

Once again Len took the floor. Just as he started to relate what roles were still available, Mrs Helberg once again interrupted him with an explanation.

"And here's Phyllis now! Phyllis dear, hurry and join us. And Thaddeus, do bring a seat over here. Do bring a seat over here, we're just getting started."

Phyllis was a sweet and mild looking old lady with snow white hair, and Thaddeus also had a thick thatch of white hair. Marcy couldn't work out if they were a married couple or not, as Mrs Helberg hadn't mentioned their surnames.

In the confusion, which involved Marcy and Revel having to shuffle their chairs around as the circle was expanded, they didn't notice the final arrival.

The ringing tones of Mrs Helberg broke through once again.

"And here's our new young man, who will be taking the part of Sky. As you may know, dear," she said, addressing Marcy, "we've chosen Guys and Dolls this year."

Marcy looked up at the newcomer.

It was Gray.

16. Dramatic meeting

Gray. In the Springdale Players. Marcy would have liked to fantasise that Fate was pushing them together, but in reality it wasn't much of a coincidence. He'd mentioned he was looking to join an amateur drama group, and she had mentioned the Springdale Players to him.

She had also implied she would rather drop dead than join up herself, so he had probably assumed he'd be safe not bumping into her there.

She could see the immediate shock in his eyes when he saw her. He covered it pretty quickly.

"Welcome, welcome," Mrs Helberg said. "Pull up a seat and join our circle of players."

Gray did so. He briefly caught Marcy's eye. She couldn't read his expression.

She also had no idea what Revel would think. Would she recognise him as the guy in the bar? Would she recognise him as Mr Grayson from school? Even if she wasn't in his classes she must have seen him walking around by now. Marcy glanced at Revel. Her expression was neutral, inscrutable, just like Gray's.

"Len was just taking us through the latest updates. Len, if I can pass back to you?"

Len opened his mouth to speak, but Mrs Helberg was too quick for him once again.

"Just one more thing! I nearly forgot, the most exciting thing as well. The scripts have arrived. They'll be ten dollars each. Yes, Betty, they did come in very slightly under that, thanks to my negotiations with the script company, but any surplus goes straight to the Players as our Treasurer will confirm."

Mrs Helberg smiled brightly at Thaddeus, who was apparently the treasurer. "Now I'll check off against everyone's names on my list when you've got your copy and when you've paid. Don't worry," she said, turning to Marcy and Revel. "I did have the foresight to order a few spares."

Finally, by some miracle, Len managed to do his update. All the major leads had tentatively been cast, though there was possibly room for some adjustments. As predicted, Mrs Helberg had cast herself as the lead female role, Sarah, opposite Sky.

The prospect of the two of them on stage playing a romantic couple was so absurd that Marcy couldn't bring herself to look at Revel. She could sense Revel was trying to suppress her laughter. Marcy also couldn't bring herself to look at Gray, so she just looked across at someone else's feet, attempting to maintain her composure.

Mrs Helberg suggested that they start by "trying the new talent out". Phyllis, who turned out to be the accompanist, sat down at the piano.

Marcy did her best to get out of it. "I don't sing, I'm afraid. Or act. I hoped there might be some way I could help out?"

She addressed this to Len but it was Mrs Helberg who answered. "I'm sure we can find something for you to do. Now what about you - " she had forgotten, or had pretended to forget, Revel's name.

"Revel. Revel Holmes. I sing."

Mrs Helberg looked arguably less impressed by this than by Marcy's refusal to sing. She would clearly have preferred to stick Revel and her piercings in the prompter's box, well out of sight.

"Any preference, dear?" Phyllis asked her.

Diplomatically, Marcy thought, Revel chose Adelaide's Lament rather than one of the lead songs by Sarah.

Revel's performance blew everyone away.

It was flawless. Revel's voice was strong, she was funny, the accent was perfect. The Springdale Players had never witnessed anything like it.

There were various murmurs, and Gray also looked impressed. Everyone gave her a round of applause afterwards.

The obvious thing would have been to recast Revel in the lead role, but Marcy could only imagine the apocalypse that this would bring down.

Mrs Helberg quickly stepped in to protect her territory. Revel's choice of song had made this slightly easier for her.

"Wonderful... Revel. Now I know that we had already cast the role of Adelaide, but I do feel, Betty, don't you - " she addressed poor Betty, who was clearly about to be demoted to the chorus " - that this might be a very suitable change? Everyone agreed?" she asked, before anyone had a chance to respond. And just like that, Revel was suddenly one of the stars of the Springdale Players.

They were starting with a read through, but a couple of people had gone to visit to the bathroom so there was finally a moment to talk.

"Mr Grayson," Revel said.

"The singer," he replied, instead of using her name.

Revel raised her eyebrows. "My lips are sealed." She turned and walked back to her chair, leaving Marcy and Gray together.

"I never guessed...."

"I had no idea..."

They both started speaking simultaneously, and then there was an awkward pause when neither of them knew who was supposed to talk. Marcy found herself wanting to gaze at him, so tall, attractive, somehow even hotter outside of school.

She looked at his lips, and the firm lines of his jaw. The breadth of his shoulders.

She wondered if she should suggest withdrawing from the group, though how she would explain that to her mom she had no idea. As she hesitated over what to say, Gray spoke.

"Thank you for... after the other night. I drank too much and I am hugely sorry."

Marcy wasn't sorry at all. She fantasised about it all the time, being crushed in his arms. I can't believe I've actually slept with you, she thought. And now they were supposed to act like polite near-strangers. Well, if that was the case, she would have to put on a brave face and try to act natural and friendly around him.

"Congratulations on getting the lead role," she said.

She saw a slight flicker of surprise in his eyes. He obviously wasn't expecting her to be so calm. In reality she was boiling up with nervous tension and giving an Oscar-worthy performance of hiding it. Or a Tony-worthy performance, given this was theatre.

"Thanks."

Before they could speak further, everyone was called back by Mrs Helberg and the read-around began. Marcy was glad she could just sit there and listen, and not have to read any parts.

Mrs Helberg, in fairness, wasn't as bad as she could have been. If she had been cast in a more mature role, or perhaps with a co-star nearer her own age, it might not have been so absurd.

No one was singing currently, it was just the spoken lines, but Marcy knew that Mrs Helberg had a rich contralto voice. Her singing on stage would be good even if she looked about as much like a slim young girl as Thaddeus did.

Revel was amazing, but that went without saying. Gray was also surprisingly talented, he got the accent just right. Marcy once again wondered why he hadn't gone into acting. Martin, the man playing Nathan opposite Revel's Miss Adelaide, was also very good. He was probably in his late twenties or early thirties, and clearly an experienced actor.

There was a coffee break half way through, at which time Mrs Helberg accosted Marcy. "Now Marcy dear, I was wondering how we might best make use of you. How about the prompt?"

This was absolutely the last thing Marcy wanted, to be stuck in the prompter's box from start to finish, having to concentrate more on the script than anyone else. "I'm not sure I'd be very good at it. Perhaps I could help backstage, with props or something?"

"We do have Alan usually acting as our stage manager, he's not here tonight of course, but you may be able to help him."

What Marcy would have really loved was an Assistant Director role, under Len, but she rightly suspected this position was unofficially held by Mrs Helberg.

Revel had been talking to Thaddeus and Phyllis, but broke off as Marcy came over. "Did she fix you up with something?"

"Kind of. Stage hand, depending what the stage manager says," Marcy told her

"Alan would be delighted for any help," Thaddeus said. He had a kindly face, Marcy thought.

"Such a beautiful voice your friend has," Phyllis said. "I was just telling her what a delight it is to accompany someone so talented."

Revel smiled. "Be careful, or my head will swell and Miss Adelaide will need a larger wig ordered."

They returned to their seats, and continued the reading. Marcy was really enjoying herself, listening to them all. The rhythm of it and the interplay of voices were giving her ideas for her own play.

Before everyone left, Gray spoke to Marcy one more time. "It's a shame you don't act."

She was surprised. "Why?"

"As dedicated as Cora is," he told her, referring to Mrs Helberg, "you'd be a better fit as leading lady." For a moment she saw heat flicker in his eyes as his gaze met hers.

Marcy blushed and her stomach dissolved. I'm not imagining this attraction, she thought. I can't be.

But then he was gone, and the night suddenly felt emptier.

17. Tension builds

Revel had said nothing to Marcy about the Mr Grayson situation after they left the theatre.

She guessed, perhaps, that it was complicated and that Marcy needed to gather her own thoughts. Best of all, Marcy didn't feel that Revel judged her. Addy had been wildly amused and excited for her, but that was Addy.

Many people would have been shocked and judgemental. Some would have been jealous and nasty; others morally outraged by a liaison between a student and a teacher, or the age gap, or the fact they'd slept together so quickly.

Marcy spent Saturday working in the morning then catching up on homework - there was such a huge amount this year, all the AP classes didn't help - then on Sunday she had to visit her Great Aunt Esme.

In truth while it had originally seemed like a chore, as she got older herself she increasingly enjoyed the elderly lady's company. Esme had never married but had worked as a seamstress for much of her life. She was very talented at handicrafts, and they often sat around her table drinking tea and eating homemade cake, while Marcy helped her with a project.

Great Aunt Esme had been away the past month, staying with old friends interstate, so it was the first time Marcy had seen her since school started.

"How's that young man of yours?" Esme asked.

Marcy started for a moment, her thoughts instantly turning to Gray. Who wasn't her young man at all, of course. Nothing could be further from reality. Then she realised that Esme must have meant Josh.

"That didn't really work out," Marcy said.

"All for the better, I expect. You didn't sound terribly smitten when we last spoke."

Hadn't she been smitten? Marcy had thought at the time that she was. That she was feeling the most anyone could feel. Of course now she knew very differently.

"He's seeing someone else now."

Esme shook her head. "Fickle is as fickle does."

Marcy rather winced at this, since her affections had switched just as quickly - within the same day, in fact. Though that was better than cheating. Josh had effectively cheated on her. She highly doubted he had kept Gretchen at arm's length until his phone call to Marcy that day.

Esme was putting together some patchwork to make a baby's quilt for a neighbour's grandchild. She had an endless store of old pieces of fabric in beautiful shades and patterns. The parents of the baby didn't yet know the gender so Esme had chosen circus colours of red, orange, purple and yellow, suitable for a boy or a girl.

Marcy finished tacking another hexagon in a shiny violet and handed it to Esme. "It's going to be such a beautiful quilt. Such a lucky baby."

"I hope to still be around to make one for your little ones."

Marcy laughed. "You may have to live past a hundred then." She couldn't imagine it happening to her for decades. All celebrities had babies after forty these days, didn't they? You needed the time to establish yourself in a career first.

Great Aunt Esme frowned. "In my day, a girl your age would already have been married and having a family. Not that I'm suggesting a return to the olden days for you modern young women. We didn't have the educational opportunities you do."

"You went to college, didn't you?" Marcy asked.

"Only after a monumental battle with my father. I only won because my brother, your Great Uncle Ernest, chose to go into farming rather than Yale."

So Esme had been the bluestocking of the family. But despite her brains, there hadn't been the career opportunities for her that Marcy and her generation would enjoy when they graduated.

"So don't you settle down too early," Esme continued. "And don't leave it too late either."

Faced with this conflicting advice, Marcy stayed silent and continued sewing. She wondered what her great aunt would have thought of Gray.

* * *

At school on Monday Marcy felt less stressed about French class. Mr Grayson was at least being civil now: he hadn't got angry about them both ending up in the theatre group.

She saw Revel first at recess. They sat out on a wall, getting some late September sun.

"I truly didn't recognise who he was in the bar," Revel said. "Someone pointed him out last week at school and he looked familiar, but I couldn't place him. The penny didn't drop until I saw him again at the rehearsal."

It was unusual for Revel to volunteer this much information. In typical Revel style, she didn't say anything more, or prompt Marcy to say something. Revel's silence was always very relaxed, she wasn't sitting there waiting for Marcy to offer an explanation, or confess, or whatever else.

It was because of this that Marcy felt able to confide in her.

"I met him in the last week of vacation. We had a couple of dates, I had no idea who he was," she told Revel.

"I'm guessing he didn't know who you were, either."

Marcy felt a nudge of guilt. "No. He assumed I was in college, and I didn't - " she struggled to find the right phrase " - correct him as such."

"Anyone would have done the same."

Marcy was surprised and reassured by this. She had expected to be judged for not being upfront about her age.

"I mean look at him," Revel continued. Mr Grayson had suddenly appeared at the other end of the lawn and was walking into another building. "He looks like a matinée idol."

Trust Revel to use a term like that. But she was right, Gray really was that good looking. Once again, Revel wasn't directly probing Marcy for her story. So once again, Marcy offered up the information.

"Anyway, then we both got the shock of our lives the first day back. Certainly the shock of mine, anyway. He spoke to me after class and was really furious. Then nothing until that night at the bar."

Revel had a curious expression on her face. "I wonder how long he'll hold out?"

"Hold out?" Marcy felt weird butterflies at this.

"You know what I mean," Revel said. She swung down from the wall and they made their way back to their next classes.

* * *

When Marcy entered her next AP French class, Mr Grayson actually caught her eye and smiled, which left her totally confused and more than a little distracted the entire lesson.

They were studying some French poem and Marcy was struggling to understand a line which read "*Que l'astre irise*". She had looked up the words, and it seemed to be something about an iris and a star, but it made no sense.

Called on by Mr Grayson to translate, Marcy had to confess her failure.

"Verlaine is using *irise* as a verb here. So the object is *astre*, star, and the object is on the former line, *firmament*, which is an English word too, but you could translate it as sky, or heavens."

Marcy was still lost. "What's 'to *irise*'?" she asked.

"To make something the colour of an iris," Mr Grayson told her. "In this case purple."

The star was making the sky purple. It didn't make much sense, but it was beautiful nonetheless. It reminded Marcy of something but she couldn't remember what.

Mr Grayson read the entire poem out to them once more. His accent was so flawless, he sounded incredibly sexy speaking French. She might have thought a guy reading poetry would sound soft or geeky, but he sounded really masculine.

On the last words - *"l'heure exquise"*, "the exquisite hour" - his eyes briefly flicked to Marcy.

She felt her cheeks flood red because all she could think of was their first night together, and she was sure he was too.

When class finished he called her back. She went and hovered by his desk while the others left. No one looked suspicious, why would they be? she thought. It wasn't as though anything was going on and no one would have known about what happened in vacation.

"Don't look alarmed, you're doing really well in class," he told her, once they were alone.

Marcy wasn't actually feeling nervous about that. It was being so near to him that set her on edge, in a scary, good way.

"I just wanted to check you were okay. I mean with everything," he said. She could see genuine concern in his eyes,

She was and she wasn't. What could she say?

They stood there, looking at one another. He was directly in front of her, after taking a step closer. She could smell him, feel the warmth of his body.

He swayed towards her and for a desperate, intense moment she thought he was going to kiss her. He was so close to her. The world stood still for a moment and she nearly closed her eyes.

But then he moved back. Took a breath. "I'll see you tomorrow night, Marcy." His voice was low.

Tomorrow night? She was confused.

"Rehearsals," he reminded her.

Feeling dazed, she left the classroom and into the hallway. If they had come close to kissing at school, what was going to happen at the theatre?

18. Rehearsing

Marcy had been looking forward to Tuesday night with a mixture of excitement and nervous anticipation. She was dying to see Gray again outside school. She felt like a stupid girl with a crush but just getting to see him again and spend more time with him, even if it was in a group, was something.

She trusted Revel not to say anything. It was funny, Marcy hadn't known Revel that long and still didn't really know her that well, but she felt she could trust her with her life.

Her thoughts were so focused on after school that the usual things happening kind of washed over her, not bothering her. Brittanny had made some mean remark in English and Gretchen and a couple of other girls had sniggered. Josh had actually looked uneasy, Marcy thought. After all, meanness isn't a very attractive trait. Particularly in someone like Brittanny who wasn't smart enough to be clever with her spite.

Marcy was now following Revel's policy of not reacting and not engaging. It was getting easier, because Marcy truly no longer cared what Brittanny and her friends thought of her. Compared to the other things in her life, and the fact that someone as mature and intelligent as Gray had liked her, the bitchy gang seemed kind of petty and worthless.

Not that they saw themselves that way. "I think Mr Grayson wants to ask me on a date," Brittanny said.

"No way! He'd get fired!" Gretchen said.

"I couldn't go, of course. You know, because of Jay. If he does ask me I'll just have to break his heart, I guess."

"Whose, Jay's or Mr Grayson's?" another girl asked.

Brittanny snapped at her. "Mr Grayson's, of course. After all, Jay is my boyfriend and we're totally committed to one another."

"What makes you think Mr Grayson likes you? Has he said anything?" the girl asked.

This was not a wise thing to ask Brittanny, who glared at her. "Of course not. Not yet, anyway. But he's given me a look, you know? If you had a boyfriend you would know about these things," she said, and flounced off with Gretchen.

That girl will be out in the cold for a while, Marcy thought. Challenging Brittanny was very dangerous.

English went well. It was pretty much her favourite subject. Except for French, but that probably shouldn't count because if Mrs Vansittart had returned it would have gone right back down the list.

They were studying Shakespeare's The Tempest, which Marcy loved. She liked the fairy-tale plays far more than Shakespeare's historic drama. Though Macbeth was always fun, with the ghosts and witches.

She was still busy writing her own play though she hadn't had the courage to show it to anyone yet. It wasn't the first play she had started writing, but it was the only one she had continued with.

* * *

Marcy and Revel managed to be early at rehearsal that evening. Len was going to be blocking out the scenes - telling the actors where they should stand and move in each scene. Marcy saw that his script was covered with pencilled notes and highlights.

Another woman in the chorus would be arranging the choreography, but not just yet. Tonight would just be regular movements on stage.

Gray arrived along with several other cast members. Mrs Helberg exclaimed with delight when she saw them appear. It was clearly her own little kingdom. Marcy feared for Len's chances of getting his own stage directions across.

Gray greeted Marcy and Revel with a "hi" and a nod, but nothing more. Marcy felt a bit deflated but after all, what was she expecting? He looked so hot as well. He had changed out of his teacher's clothes into jeans and a shirt and his hair looked damp. She thought he must have been for a run and a shower.

The memory of being in his shower with him made her shiver. She could remember only too well the water running off his hard muscles. And the way he had held her…

Snap out of it, Marcy, she told herself firmly. She had to start being more professional and viewing him as her teacher at school, and her platonic colleague at theatre. Though it was pretty hard.

She wondered if other members of the company knew that Gray was her and Revel's teacher. After all, he'd presumably told them his job when he first joined up, and Mrs Helberg knew that Marcy went to Springdale High.

To Marcy's surprise, Len turned out to have something of an iron will as a director. She had thought him a rather timid man, easily bowled over by Mrs Helberg. Instead he took full command, and any attempts by Mrs Helberg to suggest something else were met with a calm, unyielding refusal.

"We'll try it this way for now, thanks Cora," Len said.

Marcy was also impressed by the way Len organised the scenes. He could clearly see in his mind what he wanted. Alan, the stage manager, was also in charge of the sets, and he made notes while Len blocked it all out. Alan had a short, pointed beard and a round face.

Since there was nothing to do backstage at this time, Marcy was free to hang out at the front near Len and Alan. For now she absorbed everything. A couple of times she thought of something that might work in an interesting way, but she buttoned her lip for now. She didn't want to be another Mrs Helberg.

Her chance came in a scene between Revel and the actor playing Nathan. Len's idea worked pretty well, but it meant Miss Adelaide would be obscured at one point. Timidly, Marcy suggested her change. Len looked a little surprised but gave it a go, and it worked beautifully. Revel shot Marcy a grin of thanks.

At the half way break she was standing by Gray at the coffee machine.

"You have a real eye for this, don't you?" he said.

Marcy tried not to blush at the praise.

"It was just something I thought of."

"Show me?" He took her wrist and pulled her script from her hand. Inside were some of Marcy's own thoughts about the production. Gray chuckled at one of them. "Don't show that one to Cora!"

It was an idea Marcy had had to try and downplay the shape of Mrs Helberg next to Gray. His height and fitness made her look even more stout than she was. Len had positioned them in profile, facing one another, for a particular scene. Marcy had adjusted this to have Mrs Helberg three-quarters on.

"I guess if it was opera, these things don't really matter," she said. Opera seemed to be full of terribly fat female singers playing young maidens. Far heavier and older than Mrs Helberg.

"If it was opera," Gray said. And then he fell silent and they were looking into one another's eyes again.

Marcy missed him so badly. In the short time they had spent together she had felt that they were a team. He was on her side. As her teacher, he was kind of in opposition to her.

Before either of them could say anything, there was a loud summons from Mrs Helberg and everyone had to finish their drinks and get back to rehearsing.

As Gray went back onto the stage he turned back to look at Marcy one more time. She wished she could read his thoughts. She was very glad he couldn't read hers.

19. Stolen kiss

In the second half Marcy was sent backstage to fetch a script that someone had already managed to lose. She handed it to the actor whose script it was and then decided to watch from the wings for a while. You got a very different perspective on the scenes this way.

It was dark and curtained and had that smell of the theatre that always awoke something in Marcy. It was as though all the emotion and adrenalin from past productions somehow seeped its way into the building. Plus the faint smell of greasepaint and that dusty, slightly mildewy backstage aroma that theatres always seemed to have.

Marcy was watching the scene where the heroine Sarah's grandfather sings her a song about love - except there wasn't any singing tonight - and then Sarah and Sky have an argument, with Sarah storming off. The fact that Thaddeus, who played the grandfather, was barely old enough to be Mrs Helberg's father didn't seem to matter so much once they were reading the lines. Thaddeus had a really beautiful, resonant voice when he read his lines.

He finally exited stage right, the opposite side to where Marcy was standing, then slipped back out to the front to watch.

Next Gray and Mrs Helberg had their duologue, and then Mrs Helberg also exited stage right.

The scene ended, with Gray exiting Marcy's side.

He seemed surprised to see her there. "Hey."

She felt embarrassed for a moment, as though she had been spying on him. "Len sent me backstage. I thought I'd watch from another angle."

They were both silent again. Marcy had stepped backwards as Gray exited, and was standing against a piece of set from some former production. Of course it wasn't anchored down, so when she leant back on it for a moment it moved backward. She nearly lost her balance and Gray managed to catch her and pull her to standing.

In doing so he had pulled her right up against him. He let go of her wrist, but instead of dropping his arm to his side his hand went on her waist.

They stood there, looking at one another.

Then his lips were on hers, gently but firmly, his tongue deepening the embrace.

His hand gripped her body, drawing her even more closely to him.

Marcy felt like she would melt against him. Yet at the same time a little voice in her head was crying out that this was her teacher, what was she thinking?

Knowing that he was her teacher, and supposedly in a position of authority over her, just heightened the intensity. Knowing how wrong this was. Knowing how much he had been fighting it, but still wanted her.

He broke off for a moment and his other hand brushed her hair back from the side of her face. "I've missed this." His voice was barely a murmur. "We shouldn't be doing this, I know. I have to get back out there."

* * *

Her mind whirling and her body longing for him, Marcy watched Gray through the next scene. It was with Martin as Nathan. She marvelled how Gray could just get up there and act like normal.

She slipped offstage after the scene to join Len and Alan again. This time Len actually asked her for an opinion on one part of the blocking, which was flattering. Marcy was still desperately hoping she might get a job assisting him rather than doing props or something. She wouldn't mind doing props during the performance, as it would be all hands on deck, but she wanted something a bit more demanding for now.

Revel slid into the seat next to Marcy after finishing another scene with Martin. The current scene featured nearly all the male characters on stage, save for Thaddeus.

"I think it's going to be okay," she said.

Revel could say so little and mean so much. In that phrase lay all the doubts that she and Marcy had privately had about whether the entire thing would turn into a farce or not. Even though they hadn't related their fears to one another. It also held all the reassurance that Marcy needed. Revel seemed to know about this stuff. If she thought a production could work, then it likely would.

After the final scene was blocked everyone got ready to leave. Martin suggested that he, Gray, Marcy and Revel went for some food. Marcy felt weird being included in this invitation, as Martin was so much older, but Revel didn't seem fazed and accepted. After all, compared to all the others there, they were the youngest four by a mile.

Gray hesitated. "Normally that'd be great, but..." He looked uncomfortable. Marcy could guess the issue.

"You have to be somewhere?" Martin asked.

"It's these two. I wasn't sure if you knew, but I'm actually their teacher."

Martin's look of surprise told them he hadn't known. "I should have guessed. Cora mentioned you were a teacher, but I didn't put two and two together."

It was something of a dilemma. On one hand there was nothing wrong with Marcy and Revel going for a burger with Gray and Martin. On the other hand, if someone from school saw them socialising with a teacher and an even older guy, it could look pretty bad all round.

"I can see how that might be awkward," Martin said. The look in his eyes suggested he found it pretty amusing. "A shame, though."

"It's okay, I have to get back right away anyway," Marcy said. It wasn't true, but she wanted to let him off the hook. That way Martin and Gray could still go without having to disinvite her and Revel.

"I've actually got to be somewhere too," Revel said. "Another time maybe."

Marcy didn't know if Revel did have somewhere to go, or whether she was just being tactful as well.

Gray shot Marcy a glance, and she could see regret in his expression. "I'll see you both at school."

Marcy offered Revel a lift and they walked off to the parking lot together, while the two men headed towards the town.

* * *

"Can I hook up my phone?" Revel asked Marcy, as they drove back.

"Sure."

Revel fiddled with the Bluetooth settings on the car stereo, and managed to connect it with her iPhone. The music that blared out was Guys and Dolls. Revel flicked forward to "More I Cannot Wish You", the song sung by Sarah's grandfather.

"I love this one," she told Marcy. "It was cut from the 1955 film. Have you seen it?"

Marcy hadn't.

"I have it on DVD. Come round and watch it sometime. Thursday if you like," Revel offered.

Neither of them was working Thursday night so it was settled.

"This teacher thing is a bore," Revel said. "Any other situation and we could just hang out. I'd suggest the bar as no one would see us in there, but your Mr Grayson would probably decline that one as well."

"He's not my Mr Grayson," Marcy said.

"From the way he was looking at you, he is," Revel told her.

Marcy wanted to ask what Revel meant but didn't want to sound like she cared. Though she did, desperately. She just wasn't quite ready yet to admit to Revel that she still liked him.

"I think if it wasn't for you, he'd probably hang out with us," Revel said.

"How do you mean?" Marcy asked.

"He's wrestling with his conscience. It's written all over his face. Anyway, let's give it time. If word gets round school that we're all rehearsing the same production, maybe it won't be such an issue."

94

Marcy thought this was a great idea, and said so. She wasn't exactly sure how to spread the word though. Without Addy, who spread any news needed like a public service announcement, they'd have to find another way to announce this one.

She was replaying the kiss in her mind, as well as the way Gray had ended it. *"We shouldn't be doing this, I know."* It had kind of sounded like he wanted to keep doing it.

He'd vowed nothing would happen again, twice now, and there he was kissing her, while sober.

Would it happen again? Marcy burned for him. She desperately hoped so.

20. An attack

Back in school Marcy was trying to get a pile of things out of her locker while also putting other things back in. She failed, and a heap of stuff fell on the floor.

As bad luck would have it, Brittanny and her group were passing at the same time, and started mocking her. But Josh, surprisingly, didn't join in.

Instead he bent down and helped her pick everything up.

"What are these?" He was holding the photos of Marcy that Nick had taken, she had forgotten that she had put them inside a book, and now they had slipped out.

Marcy wanted to sink through the floor with embarrassment.

"Just some photos."

"They're really great." He looked from the photos to Marcy. "When did you get them taken?"

Before Marcy could answer him, Brittanny stepped in. "Let me see." She snatched one of them out of Josh's grasp. "They're not great, they're really ugly and pretentious. Poor Marcy. You just don't have what it takes, do you? Trying to become a model. It would be funny if it wasn't so sad." She tried to do an exaggerated imitation of Marcy's pose in the photos, then smirked at Gretchen.

"I think they're nice," Josh said. He took the photos from Brittanny handed them back to Marcy and walked off, leaving Brittanny, Gretchen and a couple of others just standing there.

"What the fuck?" Brittanny's mouth was practically hanging open. Then she turned on Marcy. "What the hell is your problem, Marcy? Are you so sad and desperate that you just can't accept Josh doesn't want to be with you any more? Was this some lame, failed attempt to get him back?"

"Josh is with me now," Gretchen told her. "Just remember that."

Marcy was torn between a desire to laugh and to slap Brittanny hard. Instead she tried to channel Revel, and ignored them. This annoyed Brittany even more.

She pushed Marcy against the lockers, quite hard. Pinning her up there she started ranting about what a sad, desperate wannabe Marcy was, and how if she didn't stay away from Josh she would regret it.

Marcy was so stunned she didn't react for a moment. Before she could, she heard a voice.

"Exactly what is going on here?"

It was Mr Grayson.

Brittanny turned and instantly sprang back when she saw him. "She tried to attack me, Sir. I was only defending myself. She's jealous because her boyfriend dumped her for my cousin."

If Marcy had wanted to die a thousand deaths, it was never more than before.

Mr Grayson raised his eyebrows and looked from Brittanny to Marcy. To Marcy's relief she read cool amusement in his eyes, not anger. Either he didn't believe Brittanny, or he didn't care. Marcy hoped it was the former.

"Brittanny, what I saw was you attacking another student. No - " he stopped her trying to interrupt him " - I don't want excuses. I'll see you both in detention after school."

Before he left them, he noticed the photos that Marcy was holding. He angled them so he could see. "Those are beautiful, Marcy."

Then he left, leaving a shocked and seething Brittanny and Marcy in complete turmoil. But Brittanny wasn't stupid enough to resume the fight.

Instead she muttered something to Gretchen about "must feel sorry for her" and they walked off to their next class.

* * *

Marcy would have been upset about getting detention unfairly except for the fact that it was with Mr Grayson. After all, she had done nothing wrong and was completely the victim.

But an extra hour in Mr Grayson's presence would be more of a pleasure than a pain. Besides, she had so much homework this final year that it made no difference whether she sat in a classroom and did it or studied at home later.

She was a few minutes early arriving at detention because her last class had been nearby, and she hadn't needed to fetch anything else. Mr Grayson was at his desk, marking work.

He looked up as she entered. "Hi Marcy. I wanted a quick word with you."

Surprised, she went over to his desk. He had made a point of not singling her out at school, despite the kiss in the theatre. She had no idea what was going through his mind.

"I know you probably had nothing to do with that fight. But I've noticed Brittanny giving you a hard time, and I didn't want to draw out the situation today and potentially add to that. This detention won't be on your record."

Marcy smiled in relief. "Thank you."

"I also figured an hour in my presence wouldn't be too painful for you. Hopefully." He caught her eye, and she could see a glint in his, but before she could respond some more students arrived.

She found a desk by the window, about half way back and got out her English homework. She was in the mood for The Tempest. It was such a strange and exotic story that she could escape into it, letting the words and her imagination create an entirely new world for her. Except Ferdinand now looked strangely like Mr Grayson.

Brittanny marched in looking furious, a scowl making her look even meaner than usual. "I really shouldn't be here," she told Mr Grayson. "I'm the victim in all this."

He paid no heed. "Please sit down, Brittanny."

Brittanny shot a venomous glare to Marcy as she took a place in one of the back rows. "You'll pay for this," she said, under her breath.

Mr Grayson couldn't hear but he could see. "Something you'd like to share, Brittanny?"

But Brittanny just glowered and took her seat. How she could possibly delude herself that Mr Grayson liked her was anyone's guess, Marcy thought. But she fully expected Brittanny to spin this all to her advantage. Likely she would tell everyone that he had only given her a detention so he could spend more time with her.

Marcy looked up at one point from her Shakespeare to see Mr Grayson's eyes on her. They held her gaze for a few seconds, then he looked down at his marking again. She hoped Brittanny had been too self-absorbed to notice.

Marcy had no idea where she stood with him. He hadn't actively rejected her after their last encounter, but nor had he crossed the line again. Maybe she would just have to wait until Friday night.

Amazing to think that until last week, Marcy had been doing everything she possibly could to avoid being dragged into Mrs Helberg's theatre group.

Now she could barely wait for the next rehearsal.

21. Plans and dreams

Marcy was entranced by the 1955 movie of Guys and Dolls. The cast was stellar: Frank Sinatra, Marlon Brando, Jean Simmons - it was the most golden of the Golden Era of Hollywood.

"Something to live up to, isn't it?" Revel said.

Marcy thought that out of all the cast, Revel was the only one anywhere nearly talented enough to do so. Gray and Martin were great, and she was sure Mrs Helberg's singing would be beautiful, but Revel was in a league of her own.

What inspired Marcy was the thought of having famous actors read something she had written. She wondered how the screenwriters of Guys and Dolls felt. And also what it must be like if you weren't happy with the casting, or thought your lines were being performed wrongly.

Revel's grandmother's house was lovely inside. It was a large house, much lighter inside compared to how it seemed from outside, with the high hedges and all the foliage. The rooms were airy and the decor old fashioned, but in a timeless and elegant way.

Revel's room had an antique iron bedstead and a white counterpane. It was the kind of bed that people went to antique shops for, but Marcy suspected this bed had always been there. If there had been an old-fashioned wash stand there, with a bowl and jug of water, it wouldn't have looked out of place. Even though Revel had plenty of modern touches in her room.

There was a stunning black and white portrait photograph of Revel's mother on one wall. Now Marcy had seen Nick's photographs of Revel, she could see the resemblance even more strongly.

Revel's grandmother had been out when they arrived, but she came back while they were taking a break to get a drink and more snacks from the kitchen.

"Virginia. I hope school went well? And this must be Marcy. How do you do?" She was a tall, woman with steely grey hair, very upright and elegant, and the house fitted her like a glove.

Marcy returned the greeting, feeling a little overawed. Hearing Revel called "Virginia" was a bit of a surprise.

"We're just watching Guys and Dolls, Grandma. The one we're doing for the theatre production." Revel had poured an extra tea for her grandmother while she was getting her and Marcy's drinks.

"Thank you Virginia. Are you able to stay with us for dinner, Marcy?"

Marcy hadn't given it any thought, beyond hanging out with Revel for a couple of hours and eating snacks in front of the television. She wasn't sure how to respond.

"You can stay, can't you?" Revel asked.

"Sure, I guess. Thank you," Marcy said.

"That's wonderful. Now I'll manage everything, so you girls can go and resume your theatrical study."

Back in front of Guys and Dolls Marcy texted her mother to let her know she wouldn't be home until later. "It was kind of your grandmother to invite me," she said to Revel.

"I meant you to stay anyway. The movie's two and a half hours," Revel told her.

"Your grandmother seems very nice."

Revel laughed. "She's completely vintage. She is wonderful."

Try as she might, Marcy could not help thinking of Gray every time Marlon Brando had a scene. While the movie script and theatre script had many differences, there were still entire phrases that she had heard Gray speak.

"So you're writing a play yourself?" Revel asked. "Is it under wraps or can you talk about it?"

Marcy felt a little embarrassed. Her idea would probably sound really lame to anyone else. "I don't have a title for it yet, but it has a fairy-tale setting," she said. "I know that probably sounds really dumb. But it's actually aimed at adults."

"Not dumb at all. No one complains about A Midsummer Night's Dream, do they? Or The Tempest, or whatever else. Besides, even with Disney there are tonnes of adults that watch it," Revel said.

Marcy was relieved Revel hadn't immediately cringed or laughed in her face.

"It's kind of based on Rapunzel, but it's about people not being able to afford healthcare. Because in that story the couple have to give their baby to the witch as they couldn't afford the herbs. So I'm using that to comment on how it works today."

"I think it sounds fascinating. I'd love to read it once you're done."

"Thanks." Marcy was grateful that Revel took her seriously. She had not dared to let anyone at school know about it, even Josh when they were dating. People tended to mock that kind of stuff, like if you wrote poetry or whatever.

"I'm singing at the bar tomorrow night, as it's Friday," Revel said. "I was thinking that you should come, and I'll ask Martin. He can then ask Gray if he wants, and I bet Gray will come."

"You don't want to ask him directly?" Marcy asked.

Revel shook her head. "He won't come if I do that, he'll feel obligated to decline because of the whole teacher/school thing. This gets him off the hook. He's going at Martin's invitation, not ours."

Marcy understood. She still wasn't sure Gray would accept though.

"Who knows? You may even get a repeat performance," Revel said, joking.

Was Revel trying to push them together? "I doubt it. He'd had a lot to drink that night." Marcy didn't mention the subsequent, fully sober kiss during the Tuesday rehearsal.

"The intent's still there though. He just needs to loosen up. He's so obviously crazy about you, it's written all over his face. I mean I can see it," Revel said to clarify, as Marcy looked alarmed, "though I'm sure the others have no idea."

Marcy was getting a warm and nervous feeling hearing this. She marvelled how little Revel seemed to care about the student-teacher thing, or the age gap. She spoke of Gray and Martin as though they were colleagues, her equals. But then most of Revel's friends - at least the people she seemed to know outside school - were older.

If anything happened in the bar, and Martin saw, and it got back to Mrs Helberg and then her parents... Marcy shuddered, the warmth gone. It would be a living hell. She'd probably be grounded until she was forty. Not that her parents were super strict or anything, but even they would draw the line at their daughter dating her teacher.

What if Gray was just a guy who worked in the café? Or a graduate student? Marcy wondered if they would mind as much, even though he was older than her. She thought they would probably get used to it. After all, she was eighteen and officially an adult. And her parents were seven years apart, which was more than her and Gray.

Revel's grandmother eventually called them in to dinner. She also invited Marcy to call her Rowena. Marcy struggled to do this, as she instinctively felt that Revel's grandmother was the kind of person you should call ma'am.

It was wonderful, old-fashioned home made food. A chicken and bacon pie with proper hand made pastry, woven in strips on the top. Followed by a spiced apricot and brown sugar tart. Marcy said how delicious she thought it was.

"You can praise Virginia, she made the tart," Rowena said.

Marcy turned to Revel. "Really?"

"It's Grandma's recipe."

"It was your Great Aunt June's recipe," Rowena told her. "Though I think your changes to it are an improvement. Cardamom, if I'm not mistaken?"

Marcy was happy to have a second helping. Rowena led the conversation, telling Marcy about the house and some of its history, and the gardens. She also asked Marcy about her own ambitions. "Virginia wishes to act, of course, always a risky profession. But I believe she has some of her mother's talent. Time will tell."

Marcy hoped Rowena would be suitably blown away when she saw Revel as Miss Adelaide. Revel didn't really need any more time to prove herself, she already had it. She told Rowena about her own dreams of moving to New York and studying theatre writing.

"How very appropriate. Perhaps one day you'll room together if Virginia attends Juilliard," Rowena said.

It seemed like a very far off dream right now, but a good one.

22. Friday night

Friday night was the first singing rehearsal. Marcy was happy to discover that Gray had a great voice, and matched Mrs Helberg very well in their duet.

Revel of course was the stand out. As Miss Adelaide, she was backed up by several "Hot Box girls". These comprised of Betty and several other women, and they all sounded pretty good. Marcy figured that even with some of them being a little vintage in years, they would look fun as showgirls. Kind of like the Golden Girls.

As it turned out, Betty hadn't minded too much about losing her role of Miss Adelaide to Revel. Dance was her forte rather than vocals, and she was quite the tap dancer: very agile despite her years.

They were arranging the choreography so she and Revel could do a short tap dance number together during the nightclub scene, for the song A Bushel and a Peck. Revel had brought along some tap shoes - she said she hadn't had lessons since she was a kid and was very rusty - but they had some fun experimenting on stage.

"You've got the advantage of youth," Betty told Revel. "Some practice and you'll do fine. Be thankful you haven't got these old bones." She tapped her thigh, which was still very firm and shapely. Marcy guessed Betty was in her sixties. Dancers seemed to keep their figures like that.

There was no real time that Marcy could have spoken with Gray, since everyone was out front. But she got the sense he was keeping his distance. Maybe she was being paranoid, but that's how it felt.

She didn't mind though. Because if he was deliberately avoiding her, that meant his feelings towards her weren't entirely casual.

Marcy herself was increasingly helping out Len, making herself as useful as possible and carving out a role as his assistant. She'd be happy to help Alan backstage during the week the performances were on, but her true love was watching and helping the production take shape from the front.

Sometimes she itched to rewrite a line, or add something. But Len seemed to be sticking to the exact script so she didn't say anything. She would save her creative energies for her own play instead.

"So I have a gig singing tonight in town," Revel was telling Martin. "Would you like to come? It's at the bar off Main Street. Ten o'clock."

"Aren't you too young to be let into a bar?" Martin asked.

"Not as a performer. I'm there to work, not drink. Marcy's coming too, she helps out with equipment."

This was the first time Marcy had heard of this.

Martin looked intrigued. "A female roadie, hey? This I must see."

"Don't worry, the guys can always use some help moving crates," Revel told Marcy under her breath as they got ready to leave the theatre. "Now let's go on ahead, then hopefully Martin can bring Gray for you."

She also called him Gray outside school.

"I don't need him to be there," Marcy said.

Revel grinned. "You're crazy about him, and he can't take his eyes off you. It amuses me to play Cupid. Or chaperone or something."

Marcy thought how incredibly kind Revel was. "Thank you!"

* * *

The band Revel played with were only too happy to have another pair of hands, once Revel had assured them that Marcy knew what she was doing.

Marcy didn't actually know what she was doing, but she was good at taking directions. They were nearly set up anyway by the time Marcy and Revel arrived there from rehearsal.

Keeping busy helping them, while Revel changed her clothes and fixed her makeup in the bathroom, meant that Marcy hadn't had a chance to see if Martin and Gray had come or not.

"All ready." Revel stepped out, transformed once again. Tonight she was wearing a clinging black top with a line of sequins from the neck over one shoulder. It was cut off at her midriff, and she had a sparkly stone wedged in her navel.

"You should have worn that to rehearsal," Marcy said. "It's very Miss Adelaide twenty-first century."

There was just time to grab a Coke so Revel could moisten her vocal chords, then it was time for them to play. Marcy found a stool in the corner that was tucked away, where she could watch from without drawing attention to herself.

She was sipping her drink, listening to the music, when she was interrupted by a voice.

"She's talented, your friend."

It was Martin. And there, just behind him was Gray.

Gray didn't look surprised to see Marcy though she thought she detected a slight wariness. He didn't try anything, but then he couldn't with Martin there.

They watched the band together for a while, the volume making it hard to hold much of a conversation. Finally Martin went off to get them more drinks.

Gray stood next to Marcy. "I should have guessed you would be here."

Marcy felt bold. "You did guess, that's why you came."

He smiled. "Something like that." He looked at her for a long moment. "I really want to be alone with you."

"Me too." She didn't know what else to say.

"We need to talk. Properly. It's been ages."

They clearly couldn't do that here, their current conversation was only possible because Revel was singing a softer number.

"Can you come back to my place?"

Marcy had been dreaming of something like this. She tried to play it cool so Gray couldn't see quite how relieved and happy she was. "I could probably manage that." She was sure Revel would cover for her.

"We'll need to be discreet. Once the band finishes and Revel's done, I'll drive you both home."

This shouldn't look too suspicious to Martin. A teacher driving two students home to make sure they arrived back safely after a musical performance. Besides, it wasn't like Martin had anything to do with their school.

When Martin came back with the drinks he was standing to the side, with Gray directly behind Marcy's stool.

Gray was so close to her it felt intoxicating. She started as she felt his hand lightly rest on her hip, his finger tracing up and down. No one else could see that he was touching her which made it all the more thrilling. The two of them had this small connection that nobody else was aware of.

Gray clearly didn't intend to keep her at arm's length, whatever he had in mind. Revel had been right about him breaking his resolve. Marcy had thought it would take ages for him to make another move, if ever, and she had assumed he would need to be drunk again to lose his inhibitions.

They stayed there, watching Revel and the musicians. Marcy was alternating between joy that Gray was with her, that they shared this secret connection, and giddiness that Mr Grayson, her French teacher, was currently fondling her waist. His fingers sending a tingling up through her body.

No one in the bar knew he was her teacher of course, except for Martin and Revel. To everyone else they would just look like a regular couple.

23. Midnight misbehaving

Gray's place was more furnished than the previous occasion, now he had moved all his stuff down there. Marcy suddenly felt super nervous being there again. He had just been a hot guy the first time. Now they were student and teacher. It was forbidden.

They had driven Revel home keeping up the pretence that Gray would drive Marcy back to her house next. But Revel knew, and Marcy knew Revel knew, and probably Gray did too, just what was going on. But it was a kind of game they had to play, to cover their backs.

Marcy stood in the middle of the floor feeling briefly awkward.

But not for long. Gray came up to her, cupped her face in his hands, and brought his lips down on hers.

Finally.

Her own lips parted for him and he explored and drank her in, deep and sensuous. Once again she could smell his skin, so wonderfully familiar and intimate, and the trace of alcohol from the bar and the soap he used in the shower.

They had a desperate need for one another. Gray's hands had moved to encircle her waist, he was pulling her hard against him.

His lips left hers and he kissed her down past her jawline, down her neck to the tender hollows beneath it. He buried his head there for a moment, his arms wrapped tightly around her, breathing her in.

"I've wanted you so badly." His breath was ragged.

She hoped he was going to take her straight to the bedroom but he stopped, let her go and stood back.

"We really can't do this. Not like before. Not until you leave school, anyway."

Marcy was bewildered. "What's the problem, it's perfectly legal?"

"Except you're now my student and I'm your teacher."

He wasn't looking at her like a teacher, though. More as though he wanted to rip her clothes off. And Marcy wanted him to so badly.

"It's not like we have to tell anyone," Marcy said.

"This is bad enough. Wrong enough. I know I should be waiting until you graduate but I see you in class and it drives me nearly wild. As for theatre..." he broke off, he didn't need to continue. She knew exactly how it felt because she felt it too.

"I am really sorry, you know," Marcy told him. "For misleading you about my age."

He stroked a hand down her face, his thumb brushing her lower lip. "I'm sorry for being so angry and overreacting. It wasn't entirely your fault. I never actually asked your age, and you never actually told me."

"So is it too young?"

"It should be." Then he kissed her again, showing her that it wasn't, to him anyway.

He was so incredibly handsome. He could have had any girl he wanted. Marcy was still amazed he liked her so much.

"Can I stay with you tonight?" Her voice was husky partly from shyness, partly from desire. She just wanted to be with him.

"I shouldn't let you."

"But you will." This time she kissed him, putting her lips on his and taking the lead in the embrace. She head him groan as she pressed her body against his, loving his tall, hard form that she could crush herself against.

"You can stay. God help me, I have no willpower around you. I'm supposed to be the responsible adult. We're going to hold off though, until school ends."

* * *

Gray handed her a clean t-shirt to wear in bed. It was huge, practically like a nightshirt on her, and smelt wonderfully of his laundry powder.

Marcy had one aim and that was to get Gray to strip the t-shirt off her again.

He also gave her a new toothbrush, still in its wrapping. "I actually got this one for you, after the last time you stayed, until…"

"…until the worst French class in the history of the universe," Marcy finished for him.

"Something like that." He grinned. "It wasn't the easiest start to my teaching career."

Marcy still felt cold when she remembered the shock. "I nearly quit school, let alone French."

"I wouldn't have let you. I would have come and found you," Gray said.

"For the sake of my education?"

"That's what I would have told myself." He turned to face her. "The truth is, Marcy, I was totally falling for you. That's why this has been so hard. At first I wondered if it was all some high school game to you."

"It wasn't."

"I know that now," he said. "Then I saw in your notes how well you were doing, and that your previous teacher recommended you for AP French. You were clearly a dedicated student, not just some irresponsible teen. Which made it even harder because I couldn't just dismiss what I was feeling."

Marcy looked into his eyes. "You seemed so angry the next day."

"I was. But mainly with myself, not with you. Given what I did to you," Gray told her.

"What we did," she reminded him. "It's not like you forced me. Though I suppose that now you're my teacher, that puts you into a position of authority…"

"Marcy." Gray's eyes held a flicker of desire and warning. "We're not going to go there again. Not yet. Now let's get some sleep."

Gray was very determined that they should not get up to anything in his bed. Marcy lay there burning with frustration. She was sure he must feel even worse.

She tried the most obvious tactic. "I'm cold."

"Want me to get you another blanket?" Gray asked.

"It might not be enough. Feel how cold I am." She took his hand and slipped it up under the t-shirt, over her breast. She knew full well how warm her skin was.

"Marcy." There was a groan in his voice.

"Just one kiss?"

She knew, and Gray knew, that one kiss would be like lighting the fuse. But in the semi darkness he bent over her and briefly kissed her lips. "Good night."

"I meant more like this." Marcy pulled his head back down to hers, and kissed him. He gave way as she deepened the kiss, almost instantly he was kissing her back, devouring her.

She moved his hand back to where it had been, so he could feel how her nipples hardened at his touch. She heard him swear, and then his mouth moved down her neck and to her collarbone.

Marcy squirmed against him. She could feel his hardness through his boxer shorts. She tried reaching for it.

"Stop that. This is supposed to be just a kiss." He took both of her hands and held them above her head, pinning her down. It had the effect of driving Marcy completely wild with frustration. She loved and hated that he was in control.

No matter what, she was going to get him to break his resolve.

She tried to wriggle out of his grasp but failed. "You know I'm completely in your power like this?" Marcy said.

"If it's the only way I can keep your hands above the waist, so be it." His lips came down on hers again, kissing her sensuously, tenderly, but his body arched so it wasn't pressed against hers.

Marcy wanted to feel his weight on her. "Isn't this role reversal?" she asked. "Isn't it me who's supposed to be the one holding out?"

"We should both be holding out," Gray said.

"We could just not-hold-out one more time." She was going to explode if he kept up this above-the-belt thing.

"Marcy..." There was a warning note in his voice.

Marcy wanted him too badly to care. "Can't you just lie on top of me for a moment?" They both knew where it would lead.

But Gray's determination was being eroded. Having Marcy lying there, practically begging for him, was a superhuman effort to resist.

Wordlessly he lowered himself on her, pressing the full weight of his body along the length of hers.

She sighed. He felt so right. He was kissing her again now, slowly, and she could feel his hardness pressed against her thigh.

"Be naked with me for just one moment." She spoke nearly in a whisper, but she knew even before he acquiesced that she had won. He shrugged off his t-shirt and boxer shorts, and she slipped the t-shirt off her head quickly.

Now they were lying flesh against flesh, no barriers between them. A part of Gray was still trying to hold out. But it was as though Nature had made their bodies to slide together and fit. Just by moving against him slightly he was soon between her thighs,

Marcy was so wet for him that there would be no resistance. She was moving her hips against him in a small, circular motion. Grey, despite himself, was grinding back. She felt his knees push her thighs apart and there he was, just on the brink.

She felt him at her entrance, still delaying. He pushed forward just a couple of millimetres and she thought she would go crazy. Was he still trying to hold out or was he just trying to go slow? To draw this out and torture her?

Then both his hands gripped her wrists again, holding them above her head, and she nearly cried out with frustration. But just as she thought he had finally decided to hold back again, he pushed straight into her, making her gasp. A long, steady entry.

He held there for several seconds, just the two of them joined. Fused. Body to body. Marcy totally in his power, even though she was the one who had overpowered him.

Then he started moving in and out of her. He shifted his grasp so he had both her wrists in one hand, and ran his other hand over her breast and the sensitive curve of her waist.

Gray was kissing her as well, but at one point he broke off and looked down at her. "I'm really falling for you, Marcy."

"I feel the same."

"That's what makes this so hard. I thought I could resist you but I can't. But it's so wrong, I'm your teacher." His lips were on hers again and finally he let her hands go so she could run them over his body, through his hair, down his back. Feeling the hard defined muscles on his shoulders and upper arms.

They were both increasing the pace now, beyond stopping. If he keep this rhythm up much longer it was going to bring Marcy over the edge.

Just as the sweet bright sensation began to build in her lower belly, drawing all her sensitive zones together towards a peak, Gray suddenly swore and pulled out. He cried her name and a moment later she felt a hot, wetness over her stomach.

"I nearly forgot, I got so carried away. I didn't even use anything," he told her as he recovered.

"Will it be okay?"

"It should be fine, I got out in time." He grabbed a towel to wipe her stomach. "It was too early for you though wasn't it?"

It was. She still throbbed with unsated pleasure, but she felt bad confirming it.

Not that she needed to say anything. Lying on his side alongside her, Gray kissed her again. His hand slipped between her legs and his finger found the focus of her desire.

The firmness and the pressure were so intense that he only had to swirl his finger around for a few seconds before Marcy was quivering helplessly in his hands.

She almost felt a little embarrassed that he had finished and was still doing this for her. But she loved that he cared about her own pleasure as well. She'd heard enough horror stories of guys that couldn't care less.

"Do you think you're warm enough to get some sleep now?" he asked her.

She was warm and exhausted. "I think so."

She saw Gray smile in the dim light, then he kissed her once more and cradled her to him, as they fell asleep together.

***

Marcy awoke feeling truly happy. She was snuggled up against Gray, against his warm, firm, masculine body.

She only hoped he wasn't going to regret breaking his resolve. After all, there was nothing illegal going on and in less than a year's time no one would even thing to remark on it. What was the issue?

When they were together like this she couldn't think of him as Mr Grayson, her French teacher. He was simply Gray.

But she looked at his profile and was reminded of the times she had gazed at him in class, wondering if she would ever get to be with him like this again.

Now she was in his bed, in his arms. She looked at him and he opened his eyes. "Good morning."

"Good morning."

"After your performance last night, you really deserve a detention. Several," he told her. He was only half joking, part of him was frustrated that she had made him overcome his better intentions. And so easily.

"Maybe I should get a spanking instead?" Marcy said. She was only half joking as well.

Gray managed to look shocked and turned on at the same time. "I need a cold shower. Want to come and shower with me again?"

Marcy did. "But not if it's cold."

"You don't think I could warm you up?" He was playing along now.

"You can try."

They showered in hot water, steamy and slippery, their hands all over one another. "Next French lesson will you look at me and remember this?" Marcy asked, teasing him.

"Now I will. You'd better not wear anything too cute or distracting."

Marcy silently vowed to wear the sexiest outfit she could get away with at school, just to see his reaction.

Afterwards he made breakfast again, Marcy tried to help but Gray wanted to show off his pancake making skills. Admittedly they were very good. Marcy also found she had a huge appetite: probably all that activity last night.

"This is where it gets hard," Gray said.

Marcy looked up from her pancake, which was strewn with blueberries and maple syrup. "What does?"

"Us."

Marcy was thrilled that there was an "us". "How do you mean?"

"Normally I'd like to spend the day with you, go back to the lake, whatever. Go out with friends. But we can't take that kind of risk."

"So you do want to see me again?" Marcy was fairly certain of the answer but she wanted to hear Gray say it.

"What do you think?"

"Even though it's risky?" she asked.

Gray ran a hand through his hair, pushing it back from his brow. "Against all my better judgment, I don't seem to be able to stay away from you. The theatre group hardly helps." He poured more coffee. "But we're going to have to be extremely discreet, and patient. More patient than last night."

Did he mean that they were back to above-the-belt until the end of school? Marcy desperately hoped not. She liked sleeping with him not just for the physical excitement, because also because of the intimacy. She felt close to him.

"So we'll have to be incredibly careful," he said. "Otherwise…"

He didn't finish the sentence. They both knew what "otherwise" was. It was the end of Gray's career and probably Marcy getting kicked out of school and grounded until she was eighty.

But looking at him, at that strand of dark hair falling tantalisingly over his forehead again and his eyes dark green as he looked at her, she knew it was worth the risk.

24. Learning lines

Marcy was walking on air all the rest of the weekend, even after Gray dropped her home mid morning. He had a lot of work to do and he wanted to try and take things slowly, however hard that was. It wasn't like they could just go and hang out openly in Springdale.

She kept herself busy the rest of the day, getting homework done, emailing Addy and putting some work into her own play. It had been a bit neglected recently, but the way she was feeling about Gray inspired her.

Her phone beeped.

Last night was great. I'll see you Monday.

It made Marcy's heart leap.

You too. Good luck learning those lines.

The actors were supposed to be learning their lines by next Tuesdays rehearsal, though Marcy imagined scripts would be relied on by some of them for longer. Just so long as she didn't end up as prompt. It was her primary aim: not to be stuck in the prompter's box on opening night.

Revel rang later that afternoon. "Are you home?"

Marcy was.

"I wasn't sure if you'd be out," Revel said. She meant still out with Gray, Marcy guessed.

"No, I've been stuck doing assignments the last few hours."

"Want to come over later and run lines with me?" Revel asked. "Grandma is out, but she left cake."

It sounded like fun. "Count me in. What time?"

"Whenever suits."

Marcy felt slightly guilty going over to Revel's for a girl's night. She had a twinge about the fact that she was going there rather than Addy's, though of course she could hardly go to Addy's any more. An Asian family were now renting her house in Springdale. They seemed like nice tenants according to Addy, although she hadn't actually met them, but it was strange to think of Addy's house there, empty of Addy and her mom after all these years.

The other twinge was that Marcy wasn't sure if going to Revel's would be as fun as going to Addy's. Revel was still kind of remote. She didn't let her hair down in the way that Addy did. In fairness Addy didn't need to let her hair down, it was always down, figuratively and literally. Marcy felt a pang just thinking about the distance. She still hoped to see Addy around Christmas.

Revel's grandmother's house had that strange, foreboding look as Marcy walked up the drive. It was all the shadowy leaves and trees. Dark ivy cascaded over the garden walls while Virginia creeper covered most of the front of the house.

Inside it was bright and airy, and Revel was there wearing jeans and a t-shirt. "Welcome."

They went through to the kitchen where Revel got them sodas and big slices of Rowena's home-made cake. It was a Hummingbird cake, several layers high. Marcy thought she'd never manage such a huge piece, but after one bite knew she would do so pretty easily.

"Thanks for doing this," Revel said. "It's easier than memorising them by myself. Song lyrics are no problem, but spoken lines seem that much harder."

At least there were no super long monologues. Most of Revel's scenes were with Nathan, so Marcy was reading Martin's lines. Then there was a scene near the end between Miss Adelaide and Sarah where Marcy took Mrs Helberg's part.

"You read well," Revel told her afterwards. "Even if you don't like singing you should give a speaking role a go."

It really wasn't Marcy's thing. "It's not that I haven't done it before, but it just doesn't do it for me. I'm more stressed than enjoying it. And I itch to be at the front of the stage, in the audience, watching it instead."

Revel laughed. "I guess Cora Helberg needn't worry about glass in her ballet shoes then."

After they had gone through the lines a second time, with Revel now getting close to word perfect for most of it, they took a break.

"There's something you should know," Revel said. "it's Martin. I have a feeling he may have guessed about you and Gray. Maybe not that there's anything happening, but that Gray is into you."

Marcy's blood ran cold. "Are you sure? How?"

"It's not definite. It was just something he said, like a throwaway remark. I didn't get the sense he disapproved or would say anything to anyone."

But if Martin had guessed or even suspected, others might as well. They really were playing with fire.

"Things are okay, though?" Revel asked.

Just thinking about last night and the answer to this question made Marcy's body sing.

Revel looked amused. "I can tell from your expression it's all good. Lucky you. And him, of course."

Addy would have wanted every last detail but Revel didn't ask. So Marcy volunteered.

"It's sort of on, but it's under wraps. We have to be really careful," she said.

"I can imagine. If you ever need cover, you can say you're staying here."

Marcy wondered if Revel had ever been in the same situation. What excuses did she give to her grandmother?"

"Are you… dating anyone?" She hoped Revel didn't mind her asking.

"Nothing serious. Nick and I hook up occasionally, but it's only casual."

"Nick?!" Marcy was a little shocked. The photographer was sexy in a kind of dishevelled way, but he looked as though he must be past thirty.

"He's a little younger than he looks," Revel said, reading Marcy's surprise. "He's twenty-eight. I know it's a gap, but like I said, it's just casual. We get on, but we're on different paths. I'm splitting for New York as soon as I'm done with Springdale High, and he's a small town boy." She drained her Coke.

"Besides, he's still hung up on his ex, I think. They married out of college but it didn't work out."

Marcy was trying to take it all in. No wonder Revel had never cared for high school guys if she dated men like Nick. No wonder, also, that she hadn't been judgemental about Gray and her.

"I guess you'll be busy with Juilliard next year," she said.

"Hopefully. What about you? Are you going to study playwriting?" Revel asked.

"I hope so. Or maybe English as an undergraduate degree, then do a Masters in playwriting." Marcy hadn't completely decided. "I was looking at NYU."

"So then, you're in the same boat as me. Can't get serious about a guy if you're going to love him and leave him for the Big Apple," Revel said.

It was such early days with Gray that Marcy had never considered this. Springdale seemed like forever, she had been there so long. Yet her time there would likely draw to a close in less than a year.

What would happen if she and Gray were still together next summer, as miraculous as that seemed right now? Was it maybe unwise to take such a huge risk if they'd have to split up anyway?

Marcy couldn't imagine ever not wanting to be with Gray. He was the most amazing thing that had ever happened to her. Suddenly the distance between New York and Springdale cast a dark shadow over her happiness.

25. A suitor returns

Another amazing thing happened on Monday. Except it was more awkward than amazing.

Josh was hanging by Marcy's locker when she arrived there morning.

"Hi, how are you?"

Marcy was surprised and also suspicious that this was some set up by Brittanny and her cronies. She retrieved the things she needed and closed the door. "I'm fine, thanks."

She turned to walk away, but Josh caught her arm.

"I just thought... it's been a while since we hung out."

Marcy turned to him, bewildered. And not a little outraged. "And why do you think that is?"

"I know I've made mistakes. I didn't handle things very well." He looked contrite.

Marcy wanted to laugh. But more than that, she wanted to be rid of Josh. The last thing she needed was any more grief from Brittanny and Gretchen. "It's fine. I've moved on. No hard feelings." She tried to make herself sound as genuine as possible so Josh couldn't think it was an act.

Because it wasn't. She truly didn't care for Josh any more, and everything that had happened with Gray had eclipsed the Josh-and-Gretchen thing to such an extent that she couldn't care less about it any more.

"Marcy, I know you're still upset with me. Deep down," Josh said.

"Deep down, really, I'm not."

"You don't have to put on an act."

"It's not an act," Marcy told him. "Sure, I was upset at the time, but it's been some time and I've moved on."

Josh looked hurt. "We went out for months, Marcy. How can you be over it so quickly?"

Marcy stopped and turned to him. She fixed him with a cool gaze. "I asked myself that same question of you, when you chose to ditch me for someone else over the summer. And now I understand why, because the whole thing was pretty meaningless and pretty forgettable."

She continued on her way to class leaving him there, stunned. Josh had obviously expected she would be hanging out to get him back. Marcy would almost have felt sorry for his hurt pride, were he not such a jerk who deserved every morsel of it.

* * *

Marcy had a shift at the café after school on Monday. She couldn't conceal how much happier she was feeling and Ben picked up on it almost instantly.

"Who is he? Romance back on track with Josh-the-Jock?" Ben had always made fun of Josh, whom he claimed was a shallow stereotype of high school life.

Marcy's grimace at Josh's name told Ben all he needed to know.

"So who is it then?"

Ben was a terrible gossip but he could be discreet when it counted. Also he had no connection to Springdale High, so Marcy figured it was safe to tell him.

"You remember that guy I met here for coffee some weeks ago? At the end of the vacation?"

'Who could forget him? Mr Super Hot. You can't have been keeping him under wraps all this time?"

Marcy wasn't sure how to phrase it. "Not exactly…"

"Don't tell me he got a new car and you totalled that one too?"

Marcy wanted to protest that she hadn't totalled his car in the first place, she was as much a victim as Gray had been. But they were getting off on a tangent.

"Nothing like that. We had a couple of dates, it was really great..."

"Just really great, or stay the night and get your rocks off great?"

Marcy laughed and pretended to hit Ben with a damp cloth. "The latter, not that it's any of your business. But anyway, that wasn't the issue. The issue was - " she braced herself, took a mental deep breath " - that when I arrived in my French class the following week, he turned up there as well."

Ben was confused. "So he's a student at Springdale."

"Not a student."

Ben was still confused, then the light dawned. "You're hot for teacher? This is just exquisite. We need to celebrate."

"No!" Marcy was adamant. "You can't tell anyone. Except Jason." She knew asking Ben to not even tell his partner would be futile.

"Jase will love this. You have to bring Mr Hotness down here. We'll be subtle."

Marcy knew all too well what they would be like. Ben and Jason were like mischievous school kids when they got in the mood.

Ben had once served Josh a coffee with an obscene foam drawing on it. She wasn't going to let Gray suffer that.

* * *

It never rains but it pours. That night when Marcy got home from her shift at the café there were flowers waiting for her. A large bunch of white roses interspersed with dark foliage. From an expensive florist too, judging by the card and wrappings.

Her heart leapt for a moment thinking they might be from Gray.

Then it sank when she opened the envelope. *"I miss you and I'm truly sorry. J."*

"Those are beautiful," Marcy's mother said, coming past her in the hallway. "Who are they from?"

"Josh," Marcy told her. His name sounded leaden as she spoke it. She would rather have had the flowers from anyone else but him. It just made an awkward situation even more complicated. God forbid Gretchen ever found out.

"You don't sound very happy. Just a few weeks ago you were head over heels about him."

Marcy went to get a vase for the flowers. "That was then."

Her father also commented on them. "Young men make lavish gestures these days. In my day - "

" - in your day I was lucky to get a wilted flower picked off the sidewalk," her mom interrupted.

"I was being careful, saving for our first house deposit." Marcy's dad adjusted his spectacles.

Marcy adored her parents. Even when they bickered they were madly in love.

What was she doing to do about the damn flowers? She felt bad keeping them given she still had no desire nor intention to see Josh, even just as friends.

"We're supposed to have moved on. He's seeing someone else," Marcy said.

"Then you just concentrate on your school work," her dad said. "Getting into a good college will serve you far better than boys."

This was doubtless true, except Marcy's choice wasn't exactly between college and high school boys. It was something quite different.

* * *

To her delight, Gray texted her that night.

Are you free tomorrow night? I'll cook.

Marcy was free, but there was no way she'd get away with staying out all night mid-week. Not without an exceptional reason, and "sexy times with my teacher" was hardly that.

She hated having to imply she had a curfew. She didn't really have a formal one anyway, just an understanding that she'd be back at a reasonable hour. Until now she'd never really had cause to push the limits.

Love to. But I can't stay late.

He didn't seem concerned.

We'll eat early. Save our strength for the weekend.

For the weekend? Marcy felt a flicker inside her at what he might have planned. The thought of any time alone with him was amazing, as was pushing the limits with something already so forbidden.

26. Dinner with Gray

Marcy felt nervous getting ready to go to Gray's that evening. He had offered to pick her up but she felt safer going in her car, in case her parents - or God forbid, Mrs Helberg - saw him outside her house. Mrs Helberg was a bit of a problem, all things considered.

She had already mentioned to Marcy's mother how they had had "several young people" join the Springdale Players, and that one of them was a teacher at Marcy's school.

"It's wonderful to get so much community involvement," she had said, in a pointed remark to Marcy's mom to try and get her to reconsider joining. Marcy's mom remained resolute. She had sacrificed her daughter to Mrs Helberg's theatrical passions, one family member was enough.

For her part Marcy was hugely relieved. While if Revel wasn't there she would have loved to have done theatre with her mom, as they got on well, the thought of her parents managing to observe her and Gray together was danger beyond compare. If Martin, who didn't even know Gray or her very well, had guessed, just imagine what her mom might notice.

Marcy also felt a little strange about going to Gray's because she had just had him teaching her French the past couple of days. Switching from "Mr Grayson" to just "Gray" was a bit of a head trip. In some ways it was kind of a thrill, knowing she was dating her teacher. In another way it was as though she had to snap between worlds which was a bit stressful.

Increasingly she thought of him simply as Gray though, even at school. She just had to be careful she never let it slip in class.

She drove over to his place and parked in a street nearby. She had told her parents she had a date with "a cute guy who came into the café", which wasn't exactly a lie.

"Is he at high school?" Her mother was starting to ask this, aware that Marcy was getting to an age when college guys might be showing interest.

"He's also at Springdale," Marcy said. This was actually literally true. Her mother hadn't asked if he was a student at Springdale, had she? Though that was clearly what she meant, Marcy had to admit to herself. It was a lie in vibe, if not in words.

"I hope Ben doesn't mind you fraternising with customers."

"He's cool." Ben had met his boyfriend Jason at a previous café he'd worked at, so he could hardly complain.

Checking her hair and make up looked okay, Marcy rang the bell and Gray ushered her in. There was a truly delicious aroma coming from the kitchen.

"Have a seat. And a drink, it's nearly ready." He offered Marcy wine but she chose water. After all, she was driving and just being here was risk enough.

Marcy noticed Gray's script of Guys & Dolls on the kitchen counter. "How are your lines going?"

"Not great," Gray said. "I was going to ask if you wanted to run through them with me later."

"Sure. I spent the other night doing them with Revel, she said it was easier with another person."

"It is. And more fun, for certain scenes." Gray didn't specify what but Marcy could guess. Not that actual stage kissing was supposed to be sexy, at least she hoped it wouldn't be for him and Mrs Helberg. Sarah and Sky only had one kiss in the music anyway.

Marcy flicked through Gray's script. It was full of notes. She found herself imagining her own play one day, covered with actors' and directors' notes and highlighting.

"So does Revel have her lines down yet?" Gray asked.

"Nearly. It's a lot to memorise, in such a short time."

"She's a natural though, that girl," Gray said. "I assume she plans to do something like this for a living?"

"Yes, she's applying to Juilliard. You know her mother was an actress?" Marcy said.

"It doesn't surprise me. Was she successful?" Gray asked.

"She was Virginia Lake."

Gray was stunned. "The Virginia Lake? As in Broadway star, deceased at the height of her fame?"

'The very same."

"Jesus. That explains a lot. Poor kid, growing up without her parents," Gray said. "She's certainly inherited her mother's talent."

He brought the food to the table. "It's Adobo chicken. My sister-in-law's recipe, she's from the Philippines."

"It smells amazing," Marcy said.

"And tastes even better. It took months of begging to get this exact recipe from her. It's a family secret apparently. Eventually I convinced her that if she and Rob were going to make me an uncle, I would be family."

"They have children?" Marcy asked. She didn't know anyone who was becoming an aunt or uncle yet. Except for a girl in her history class whose father had been married before. She had nephews and nieces only a few years younger than her.

"Just the one, still on the way. My first nephew or niece. He or she is due around Christmas."

Gray's sister-in-law's recipe turned out to be awesome. Marcy had never had the dish before and she really liked it.

Afterwards they sat on the couch, Marcy reading various parts so Gray could test his memory. She had already read Nathan and Sarah before with Revel. Reading the lines in romantic scenes was kind of a trip, though.

Marcy had been reading out the stage directions as well. "Sky exits stage left." "Sarah dances on the bar top." Finally she came to "Sarah and Sky kiss" only to find that Gray wasn't moving on to the next line.

"I need some practice with that direction," he told her.

Marcy looked at him. His gaze held flirtation but also desire.

"So how do we do this?" Marcy asked, deliberately trying to wind him up. "Clever head angles, like in old movies?"

"It's the theatre. There are people watching from all angles. I'm afraid it has to be real."

128

"How real? Like this?" Marcy leant over and gave him a brief peck on the lips.

Gray had a glint in his eyes. "More convincing than that."

She leant over again and kissed him open mouthed but nothing more, just pressing her lips to his. "Like that?" she asked, breaking off again to try and frustrate him further.

"Like this." He leant over and took her in his arms. His mouth came down on hers, gently forcing her lips apart. His tongue probed her mouth, wet, entwining with hers. His hands gripped her shoulders to show her he meant business. Then he ran them down her body as he pulled her close to him.

After what seemed long enough for the audience to have booed from boredom, left the theatre and got taxis home, Gray finally broke off. "More like that."

Marcy was still giddy and tingling from his embrace. "I'll be interested to see how Mrs Helberg responds to that."

Gray laughed. "She may have to be satisfied with the first version."

"Maybe we should go for some more practice in your bedroom," Mary said.

Gray looked tempted and seemed to be wavering for a moment. "I know where that will lead. And as you've pointed out, it's a school night. If I was going to take you to bed now it would be for hours."

Marcy was turned on just hearing this. She tried to plead one more time but Gray was resolute. "Friday night. If you can say you're staying with Revel again."

Right now Friday night seemed forever away. Marcy tried not to feel disappointed. But she loved the fact that Gray wanted to be with her even if they weren't getting down to it right now. It meant he liked spending time with her, and that meant so much more than a booty call.

27. School stress

Marcy was not expecting to be confronted by a furious Brittanny Paige by her locker when arriving at school that morning.

"I thought I told you to stay away from Josh."

"Excuse me?" Marcy really didn't have time for Brittanny and her pathetic demands that morning. She also didn't need her mood broken: she was still buoyant from the previous evening with Gray.

Though it was weird having to come back to school and switch back into student-teacher mode.

"You know what I mean. You two are over. Josh dumped you. He doesn't want to be with you. So stop trying to mess up his life," Brittanny said.

Marcy was irritated and bewildered. "I have no clue what you're on about. I have nothing to do with Josh any more. But it's none of your damn business what I do or who with."

Brittanny rolled her eyes and looked contemptuous. Ugly soul, ugly face, Marcy thought.

"You're screwing up him and Gretchen. He's had to cool it with her because of you."

"Because of me?"

"Because you keep crying and calling him and asking him to hang out all the time," Brittanny said.

"Did Josh say that?" Marcy asked.

"For God's sake, Marcy, don't try to deny it. Just leave him - and us - alone. It didn't work out with you two and it never will." Brittanny was getting more and more irate.

Marcy smiled, knowing nothing would infuriate Brittanny more. "He's all yours. Or should I say all Gretchen's. I have no interest in him whatever."

"Yeah, like I believe that."

"Believe what you want to." Marcy turned and walked away. Brittanny wasn't in her next class at least, which was a relief. She felt pretty furious with Josh though. Trying to two-time Gretchen and blame it on Marcy.

* * *

Unfortunately the Bitchy Gang were in Marcy's history class later that morning. Fortunately they were ignoring her, because they were having an involved discussion about something else.

"He could just be saying that though," Gretchen was saying. "Like to keep people off his back. It's not like he has a ring or anything."

Marcy first thought they were talking about Josh again.

"And he's new in town. He could hardly have met someone already," another of Brittanny's cronies were saying.

"I'm sure he does really like you," Gretchen said. "He probably just doesn't want to make a move because of the risk."

"Also he may have seen you around school with Jay," the other girl said to Brittanny. "Like he might not want to mess that up."

"Maybe if there's a field trip or something, outside Springdale," Gretchen suggested. "To a French museum. Maybe he'll say something then."

Marcy realised to her amusement and horror that they were talking about Mr Grayson, and Brittanny's romantic prospects with him. She wanted to laugh, except the fact that they were scrutinising his love life was kind of horrifying.

She wouldn't have put it past them to try and do their own investigations outside school: follow his car home or something, if they hadn't already done so. If they ever saw hers in the vicinity… it didn't bear thinking about. Marcy and Gray would have to be a lot more careful.

Damn Brittanny. As if Gray would ever be interested in someone as shallow and immature as her.

Marcy was feeling rattled enough without the thing that happened next. Josh.

He came and slid into the empty seat next to hers. "OK if I sit here?"

"Shouldn't you be sitting with Gretchen?" Marcy said, already feeling cold icy dagger stares on her back.

"We broke up," Josh said.

This was all she needed. "Did you tell them I'd been calling you?" she asked, under her breath.

Josh looked sheepish. "Kind of. I thought it would be easier that way. She wouldn't be so hurt."

He was such a coward, Marcy was disgusted with him. "You've made things a thousand times worse. Like I said before, I'm not interested in getting back with you. And now Brittanny is on my case because she thinks I split you and her cousin up."

"I know you're still mad, Marcy, I can be patient."

He was so exasperating! Maybe if she told him there was someone else he would get off her case. Or maybe that would make it even worse? She didn't need him snooping her business as well.

"Please Josh, just give it up. I am genuinely so busy right now, what with AP classes and everything. I know I was sad when we broke up -" in fact it seemed so long ago now and so trivial that she could hardly remember either way "- but it's all turned out for the best. Just focusing on my studies as much as possible is helpful right now."

But Josh wasn't going to give up. "What about Friday? Just come over to my place and we'll watch a movie. Friends only."

"Truthfully I can't. I'm doing this theatre thing, and we have rehearsals," Marcy told him.

"I thought you said you only had time to study right now."

Marcy wanted to shake him. "It's part of that. You know that I want to get onto a theatre degree. I need this for extra-curricular points." This was more or less true. It was great experience, either way. She almost felt grateful to Mrs Helberg for pressuring her into it. Even if Gray hadn't joined it would have been worthwhile.

132

Josh looked suspicious and sulky. "You've changed. Something's up with you."

Before Marcy could reply their history teacher arrived, and conversation had to stop.

* * *

Revel found it hilarious when Marcy related some of the conversations at lunch. "If only there was a French museum trip so you could watch Brittanny in action. I'd pay to see that seduction attempt."

She agreed that Brittanny's crush on Mr Grayson made things more dangerous for Marcy. If Brittanny even got a hint that Marcy and her French teacher were on friendlier than average terms, there would be hell to pay.

"It's a good thing you're in AP French at least. Otherwise he might give himself away."

Marcy refuted this. Gray was totally professional at school.

"That's what you think," Revel said. "I've seen him at rehearsals even when he wasn't supposed to be with you. He's hopeless at concealing it."

Just then Mr Grayson came past them and stopped briefly. "Hi Revel, Marcy. Word perfect for Friday?" he asked Revel.

"Pretty much."

"See you tomorrow then. Have a good afternoon."

He caught Marcy's eye as he left, and the expression in it made her heart leap. It was a knowing look, it made her feel like blushing. She desperately hoped she wasn't going red, because that would really give things away.

Just as he had gone she glanced across and saw Brittanny and her friends looking over at their table in fury, and muttering amongst themselves.

"Don't sweat it," Revel said. "You can always say it was about an AP assignment. Or even the theatre thing, they're all going to find out some time."

Josh already knew, of course. Though not that Mr Grayson was also a cast member.

"What do you think she'd do if she found out?" Marcy asked. "I mean that Mr Grayson is part of the same theatre group that we are?"

Revel dipped a carrot stick in mayonnaise. Marcy had noticed that she never ate ketchup. "Try to join, I suspect. And then try to poison Cora Helberg or something."

Brittanny as Sarah opposite Gray as Sky was an atrocious thought. The horror showed on Marcy's face.

"We can't let her know. I'll warn Gray," Macy said.

"It's wisest. At least wait until it's so far along they couldn't let anyone else join, at least for this production." Revel had finished her lunch and stood up. "Let's go. And if you want to 'stay at mine' so to speak on Friday night, it's cool."

28. Boy trouble

Marcy should have guessed that Josh wouldn't give up so easily. After breaking up with Gretchen he had nothing to lose.

She was in the hallway just before recess when he showed up yet again.

"Hey babe."

Marcy resented the style of greeting. It sounded kind of presumptuous, like she was still his "babe". When she was so far from that it wasn't true. But she didn't want to pick a fight or sound petty.

"Hi Josh. Can't talk right now, I've gotta run." She certainly wasn't going to hang around for more of his pleading.

Unfortunately, he had decided to try a different tactic.

But before Marcy could get away Josh had taken a step towards her. Suddenly his hands were pinning her against the lockers and his mouth was on hers.

It was a shock. It was awful.

And then things got worse.

Just as Marcy tried to push him away - which was immediately - the unwanted kiss was broken up for her.

"Exactly what is going on here?"

At any other time that voice would have sent thrills of happiness through her. Right now it sent chills of fear and frustration.

Mr Grayson. Looking white with fury. Even angrier than Marcy felt towards Josh, if that were possible.

Before she had a chance to explain, Mr Grayson was reprimanding them both.

"This is completely inappropriate behaviour in school hours. You can both take detention. Report to Mr Hailsham's room after class."

Marcy tried to catch his eye before he left, to send him some kind of look to explain it was totally unwanted on her part, but he looked at Josh rather than her. Then he left, and she could hardly chase after him.

Damn. Damn. Damn. She was in absolute turmoil, freaking out over what he must think. Absolutely furious with Josh, she wiped her mouth with the back of her hand, wanting to rid herself of his saliva. She'd forgotten what a sloppy kisser Josh was.

"What the hell did you do that for?"

Josh at least had the grace to look sheepish. "I'm sorry, I didn't mean for us to get caught."

"Us? There was no us about it. You assaulted me."

"C'mon Marcy, you were into it too. If that French asshole hadn't gotten all uptight."

Marcy was losing hope that she would ever get through to Josh. Of course she could hardly tell him that the "French asshole" was one of the many reasons why she would never, ever get back with him. "No, Josh, I really wasn't. I don't want to kiss you, I don't want to date you, right now I don't even want to remain friends with you. It's over, and if you try anything like that again, I will report it."

She really should report his behaviour now but given that Mr Grayson had blamed both of them, probably no one would believe her.

Josh looked numb. Marcy found it hard to care. She was too miserable about the memory of Mr Grayson's face, completely despising her. She really hoped she would get a chance at rehearsals that night to explain.

* * *

But it was the worst rehearsal ever. Gray completely blanked her, and was completely focused on his role and talking with his fellow actors about their scenes.

Marcy tried to approach him but he dismissed her. Not coldly, so that anyone else would notice anything was wrong. Just politely, but with zero warmth or friendliness.

Even worse was that she hadn't had a chance to tell Revel about it, and Revel was very late for rehearsal and then was on stage practically the whole time or busy with her lines. Everyone was super serious about trying to remember their roles. After tonight they couldn't use scripts anymore, and suddenly it was starting to feel like Opening Night would come all too soon.

When they had a break half way through, Gray disappeared and Marcy had no idea where. She finally got a chance to speak with Revel who guessed instantly that something was wrong.

"You two have a row?"

"Far worse." Marcy told her about stupid Josh and his stupid kiss.

"That's easily fixed. It's just a misunderstanding. Go and talk to him."

But Marcy had tried this. "He's avoiding me, he's just giving me the brush off every time. I don't even know where he's gone now."

"He said something to Martin about needing to make a phone call," Revel told her.

Marcy was sure this was just another way of avoiding her.

"Have you tried texting him?" Revel asked.

Marcy had. She had sent "We need to talk" and "it's not what you think" but he had ignored them. They did, admittedly, sound like just the kinds of texts one would send if they had cheated.

The problem was that Gray had no idea of the history of Josh and her. Marcy felt so stupid that she had never told him about all that, because if she had, he would surely have realised the activity he witnessed was completely one way. It had just never come up. Neither of them had mentioned exes.

Marcy had also been a bit embarrassed about the whole Josh thing. It had all seemed so childish and so high school compared to Gray. Plus all the Brittany Paige-Mean Girls stuff. It just drew attention to the fact that she was still a high school student, which she preferred to forget when she was with Gray.

If she would ever be with Gray again. She was even supposed to be staying with him that night, and told Revel.

"It's probably his ego, even if he realises he's been an idiot he'll need some time to brood. You're welcome to stay over at mine if you like," Revel said. "I'm not singing tonight, though it would still be cool if I were."

"Thanks. I'm not sure if I'll be great company though."

"No problem. Grandmother's home made raspberry wine will knock us both out to a nice deep sleep. It smells like candy, kicks like a horse," Revel told her. "It's perfect for banishing a dark mood."

They were interrupted by Mrs Helberg hustling everyone back to the stage for the rehearsal of the second half, and Marcy had no future opportunity to talk with Revel or Gray. Len was now really relying on her as Assistant Director, so Marcy spent all her time in the audience stalls next to him with no opportunity of sneaking backstage and cornering Gray.

Marcy wasn't surprised to see Gray leave immediately afterwards, not even giving her a chance to say goodnight. He must absolutely hate and despise her. Her heart was sinking deeper and deeper into a pit of black despair.

29. Tea & sympathy

"You'll have to confront him at school next week. Given he's still in a mood about it I wouldn't bother calling him this weekend, unless he calls you of course. Let him stew and get over it. It will all have blown over by Monday."

Revel had been right about her grandmother's raspberry wine knocking off the edge of Marcy's misery. But Marcy wasn't so sure she was correct about Gray. She couldn't get his face out of her mind: the white anger, and then the way that he had treated her like a total stranger.

"It's not just anger," Revel said. "It's also fear. He's realising what you mean to him, and the risks he's taken. The risks that you're both taking."

"Do you think it's too dangerous?" Marcy asked.

"No way. Life is about risk. You have to fight for what you want."

Marcy found herself wondering what battles Revel had had to fight for herself. She wasn't quite sure if Revel's grandmother knew about all the different activities she did: singing in a bar, the modelling. Rowena seemed both old-fashioned as well as laid back. She acted towards Revel as though she were an adult, not a child.

Sure, they were all pretty much reaching adulthood now, but Marcy sensed it might always have been this way between Revel and her grandmother. It would explain why Revel always seemed so much older.

Revel poured Marcy some more wine. "We should probably put a lid on it soon, it hits you like a lead weight the next morning."

"Your grandmother doesn't mind you drinking?"

"Not that she's ever said. Neither of us drink that much. This moonshine is supposed to be a tonic," Revel said.

It was a tonic. A beautiful, numbing tonic. But Marcy was just getting to the head-swimming stage. She would feel bad enough waking up without Gray next morning, let alone hungover. So she took Revel's advice and decided she'd had enough.

But emboldened by the wine she had drunk, Marcy felt able to ask Revel about her own situation. "So how are things with you? You mentioned that you and Nick are kind of on-off."

"Yes, from time to time. It's a convenience thing really. Truthfully there's another guy that I would be more into, but it's had to stay casual as he's in LA," Revel told her. "He's a musician."

Revel fished out a photo from her purse. It showed her and a guy with longish blond hair in a photo booth. He looked nice, like a surfer. Maybe about nineteen or twenty. "His name's Jeff. We try to catch up when we can, but a full-on long distance is too hard right now."

"How did you meet?" Marcy hoped Revel didn't mind her asking.

"At a festival. Jeff was playing there with his band. They're planning to tour this winter."

"Will you be able to go and see him?"

"Depending on the venues. Hopefully."

Even though she now knew more about Revel's love life, Marcy still didn't feel that she knew Revel any better. Revel was really nice but something about her remained enigmatic. All in all she felt hugely thankful to have her as a friend. Addy being in New York was just too far away for moments of crisis like these.

* * *

The next couple of days were as awful as could be imagined. Marcy waited and waited and hoped for her phone to ring, but Gray remained silent.

She tried to distract herself with doing homework. In the end she decided to turn her phone off and not let herself look at it until Monday morning. At least then she wouldn't face more stress or disappointment beforehand.

Marcy was half way through some French homework of all things - it totally reminded her of Gray but it absolutely had to be done - when her mother called her. "Addy's on the house phone. Is your mobile off?"

Grateful and relieved for the interruption, Marcy went to take the call. There was an extension in her parents' room so she used that as at least it was more private.

"So what's happening?" Addy was all eager to hear about everything going on in Marcy's life, and it was quite painful to have to tell her what had happened.

Addy was furious on Marcy's behalf. "I can't believe Josh would do that! It's like assault, you should report him. And no offence but Mr Grayson not giving you a chance to explain, that doesn't make him look very good, does it?"

It didn't, and that was something that Marcy was struggling to get her head around. But she remembered what Revel had said about fear.

"It may be more than that. He may have decided the whole thing is too risky and we should cool it." Just saying the words made her heart sink because it did sound very possible.

"Don't lose hope. Maybe he's just brooding."

"Maybe." Gray hadn't seemed the brooding type though, at least not the type to sulk or anything like that.

They changed the subject to Addy's life, where there was heaps to talk about. Addy seemed to be surrounded by cute available guys, she had also spotted - or thought she had spotted - celebrities on trips to places like Fifth Avenue, and the whole New York thing just sounded amazing.

Marcy just wished she could skip high school. That it could be over already: Brittanny and her stupid gang, the whole drama with Gray, the whole last year of studying and then exams and having to put on a brave face. If only she could be in New York right this moment, hanging out with Addy, millions of miles away from her current reality.

"So is school in New York harder?" she asked.

"Yes and no," Addy said. "It's pretty much the same. It's weird being the new girl in the last year, but there were a couple of other new people as well. We also have the hottest science teacher, enough to tempt me into following in your footsteps, except it turns out he's gay."

Marcy laughed. "It would be a lot easier if Mr Grayson was gay. Or a monk or something."

"You could always become a nun. You'd never have a bad hair day, wearing a wimple."

This was true. Somehow Marcy didn't think it would be quite her style though. Though she was quite prepared at that moment to swear off men forever.

For now, she had to pluck up her courage. She was going to face Gray and confront him, and she was going to do it tomorrow.

30. Confrontations

On Monday Marcy decided to take the bull by the horns. She simply didn't care any more what any of the supposed in-crowd thought of her.

So she marched up to Brittanny and Gretchen before class started. They were doing their usual thing of exaggerated eye rolling and trying to look down on everyone. Marcy had noticed that Gretchen tried to dress like Brittanny but never managed it so well.

Not that Brittanny ever really looked that great. She might have a good figure with all her cheerleading, but even designer clothes couldn't actually turn her into a model. Always having a sour, sneering expression didn't help.

When Marcy thought of how stunning Revel looked in her photos the comparison was laughable. All the more so because Brittanny despised Revel and thought her ugly and uncool.

"A word, please," Marcy said.

Both girls looked startled. Before Brittanny had time to gather herself together and attempt a put down, Marcy spoke, addressing Gretchen directly. "If you could please call your little boyfriend off from harassing me, I would be very grateful."

"If you mean Josh, he's not my boyfriend..." Gretchen began to say.

"So far as I'm concerned he became your problem when he decided to date you, not me. And you're absolutely welcome to him. Given I'm not managing to get the message through to him, if you could request that he no longer pester me for dates, send me unwanted gifts, or sexually assault me at school I would be very grateful. Thank you for your time."

Marcy turned and left, leaving Brittanny and Gretchen open mouthed. If nothing else, it would spell out to them that she had absolutely nothing to do with Josh dumping Gretchen.

It would also infuriate Gretchen to think she had been dumped by someone that Marcy wouldn't even go near.

Above all, Marcy was amazed at how easy it had been to put them in their place. Once you stopped caring, you could do anything. It was like a super power. When she thought how many years she had sought Brittanny's approval, tried to keep on her good side, tried to keep her head down and not be outcast, she felt frustrated with herself. What a waste of time it all was.

* * *

The next confrontation was considerably harder. Marcy spent the whole of French with her stomach turning over from nerves, trying to act normally. She avoided catching Mr Grayson's eye at all.

At the end, she deliberately lingered as the others left. She could tell that he didn't want her to stay behind, but that he also expected it.

She took a deep breath. "I really need to talk to you."

"Marcy, we have nothing to talk about." He was trying to appear formal but she could tell it was an act, at least partly.

"You owe me the chance to explain. What happened by the lockers was not my choice. Josh basically assaulted me. We did date, some time ago, but it was over during the summer. Now he won't take no for an answer."

Mr Grayson did look a bit shamefaced. "You don't owe me an explanation." He dropped his voice. "I know I overreacted. But that's why this has got to stop. It's not right, it's too dangerous and too complicated."

Marcy felt like she was clinging onto a rock face with her finger tips, gradually losing her grasp.

"I don't see how it's complicated. No one knows," she said.

"I know. I also know that I can barely control myself around you. It can't go on. I had no right to get mad last week. You should be dating guys like that, your own age."

The first thing was one of the best things he could have said. Because he was still using present tense. But the end was the worst thing he could have said so Marcy felt wretched. He was putting her in her place as a student, trying to emphasis the gap between them.

"That didn't bother you before."

"It did, I just tried to kid myself it didn't."

My Grayson looked so gorgeous today. The worry and the sleepless look he had made his features even more defined. It also made him look older and more remote. This only made Marcy want him even more.

"What about theatre group?" she asked.

He pushed his hand through his hair. Marcy wished she could run her own fingers through it. "What about it?" he said. "Nothing needs to change, we rehearse, we go home."

But not together, was his implication.

"Then do we act friendly? Or pretend not to know one another?"

Mr Grayson now looked frustrated. "Everyone knows that we know each other, that I'm your teacher. It's no big deal. We just act like any other teacher and student, which is what we should have done from the start."

"So I'll call you Mr Grayson, then?"

He flinched at this. "If you prefer."

Marcy didn't prefer it at all. She decided she probably wouldn't call him anything. If she really needed, she could probably just call him Sky. Len tended to call the actors by their character names even when they were offstage: Mrs Helberg in particular adored this practice for some reason.

"Everything that happened then, we just forget about it?"

Again Mr Grayson looked uneasy. Marcy figured he must at least feel bad about things. "It's for the best." He looked into her eyes and for a moment it was like how he used to be, when they were alone. His gaze was a little softer. "I am really sorry for what happened. I do care about you, Marcy. But it needs to be no more than a professional, student teacher relationship."

The way he said it could have been meant just as a friend but Marcy hoped, really hoped, that he meant that he still cared in a deeper way. She had really felt like he did before, and surely he couldn't have got over it all that quickly? Not if seeing her with Josh had made him that mad.

"Very well, Sir." She emphasised the "Sir" just slightly, and Mr Grayson flinched once more. Marcy couldn't believe that there was such a huge wall between them already. Just a week or so ago she had been in his bed, in his arms, and now he was completely off-limits.

She just wasn't sure whether she should accept things. Maybe after time he'd change his mind? If so, should she try and encourage that? Or should she back right off and just let things be?

31. Backstage behaviour

A subtle but sustained plan of re-seduction was the recommended strategy by both Revel and Addy. "You can't let this one go!" Addy had shrieked at her down the phone.

Ever since Marcy had finally managed to send Addy a photo of Gray, which she'd found online, Addy had been the relationship's number one supporter.

Revel also thought that Marcy shouldn't give up. "Be patient. When he's high on adrenalin and a few drinks at the first night party, his defences will be down. That's when you swoop."

Marcy had never swooped in her life so had no clue how she might go about it.

By rehearsal that Friday she was coping much better with Mr Grayson's newly formal attitude. They didn't have much occasion to speak to one another on the Tuesday, and he had left straight away, telling Martin he was off to the gym.

On Friday Marcy felt more relaxed, though she still missed him like hell. She spent most of the downtime - there was quite a bit that day, as they were having something of a technical rehearsal - chatting with Martin and Revel.

Martin had just been telling them a very suggestive anecdote about a leading lady in a previous play who sounded uncannily like Mrs Helberg, when Revel excused herself for the bathroom. They had all been laughing, and Martin continued to crack a couple of jokes which Marcy found funny.

She saw Gray glowering over at them from a distance, but didn't think anything of it. It wasn't like they were making a huge amount of noise or anything, and it was in a break.

Later, Marcy was backstage while Revel and the Hot Box girls were rehearsing A Bushel and a Peck, quite a long scene which involved Martin as Nathan, but not Sarah or Sky.

Marcy was just watching the moves, admiring how it was all coming together so well, and how sprightly many of the older ladies were at dancing. Many of them clearly had many years experience in tap and other dancing. It probably kept them fit, Marcy thought, and vowed to improve her own exercise routine.

She'd also seen how useful it was when a director had some dance knowledge. Len was able to work with the choreographer much more efficiently because he could suggest alternative moves to get them round obstacles, or to get an actor to a certain place on stage to deliver a line at a certain time.

I have so much to learn, Marcy thought. Even if she didn't plan to write or direct musicals, this stuff would still be really helpful. Her experience with this play had also made her realise that she would like to be a writer-director if possible. It might never happen, but there was no harm in aiming high.

As she thought these things, she was suddenly pushed roughly up against the back of the theatre wall.

Hands gripped her shoulders, pinning her against the bricks.

Then before she could gasp out in shock, lips were on hers. Gray's lips.

Hot, hard, relentless.

Despite her inner turmoil Marcy wanted to melt. She was stunned but absolutely flipping out, in a good way. She yielded so Gray could take full possession of her mouth - not that he was giving her a lot of choice - wondering what on earth was going on with him.

It was like old times except more urgent. And also like a kind of relief. She had longed for him to kiss her, to make everything ok again.

Gray broke off and swore. His hair was dishevelled, he looked haunted and angry.

"I can't stand seeing guys flirting with you."

"What...?" Before Marcy could say anything, he was kissing her again. Ravishing her. She breathed in his wonderful male aroma, he was wearing her favourite aftershave. She could picture the bottle now in his bathroom cabinet.

Which made her think of his bathroom. And then his bedroom. And then his bed... if only they could escape there now. She didn't even care what was going through his head, she just wanted to be alone with him and to shut the world and everyone else out for a while.

Judging by the hunger she felt from him, he felt this even more so.

Then Gray was releasing her, apologising to her.

"I don't know what the hell I'm doing. This whole situation is driving me insane."

He was looking at her now and she could see the deep tiredness in his eyes.

"I miss you so much," she said.

Now he was gentler with her, brushing hair from her face, gazing into her eyes.

"I don't know what to do. I can't get you out of my head, I can't even stay away from you like I want to."

"Do you want to?" she asked.

She could see the answer in his eyes before he spoke. "Not really. What I want is to be with you. But without having to sneak around and live in fear of the consequences all the time."

Marcy felt the same. "It's just a few months though. Can't we just stay careful?"

Gray looked conflicted. "It's not only getting caught. It's the fact that it's not right."

This was exasperating Marcy. "I'm above the age of consent. It's not like it's illegal."

"It's grossly unethical. And legal or not, how do you imagine your parents would react?"

This was something Marcy had thought about but tried not to think too much about. They would be shocked, she knew, and disappointed. Probably angry. She thought in any other circumstances they would really like Gray.

"A year from now, when I'm at college, I think they'd be totally happy."

"But we're talking about now, Marcy." He was starting to look resolute again and Marcy felt her heart begin to sink once more.

She tried another tactic. "Do you want me?"

He was taken aback for a moment. "Want you?"

"I mean if we were alone. At your place, right now."

Gray half laughed, half frowned. "What do you think? Yes, I want you Marcy. This whole thing might be a lot easier if you looked more like Cora Helberg, and less like…" he tailed off.

"Less like…?" she wasn't going to let him off the look.

"Less like the most beautiful and intelligent girl I have ever met, with the hottest body, the memory of which drives me wild night and day. Does that answer your question?"

It more than answered Marcy's question.

"Then I'm coming back to your place tonight?"

"I don't think so." But he looked undecided. He was wavering.

Marcy didn't want to beg and plead. "Either way, I'm watching Revel sing later. So maybe I'll see you in the bar."

Gray was silent for what seemed like ages. "Maybe."

She was sure she'd won. He wouldn't like the thought of her being chatted up by other, older guys in there if she was by herself. She knew he would come to at least keep an eye on things.

Now she just had to get to the end of rehearsal, and then figure out how to break down his defences just a little bit more.

32. Temptation

Sure enough, Gray decided to come to the bar that night to watch Revel and her band. Martin also accompanied them which was a bit annoying as it meant Marcy had to keep a bit of distance from Gray. Martin wasn't supposed to know they were together on any other level than colleagues at theatre group and staff and students at school.

The town was buzzing this Friday evening. Even though the nights had really drawn in and winter wasn't far off, it was still pleasant to walk in. Cool, of course, but not yet cold. Not that chill-to-the-bones feeling with a mean wind.

Marcy wondered how the four of them appeared. They possibly looked like two dating couples. There was every chance that someone from school might see them, though it wasn't far from the theatre to the bar.

At least no one would be inside, because you couldn't get in without ID or being on the list, as Marcy was.

Revel left them to take her place. She had quickly changed at the theatre into a different outfit and fixed her make up, but it wasn't a huge change. The band was pretty casual.

They found a bar table to stand around near the front. "What are you drinking?" Martin asked, offering to get the first ones for them all.

Marcy was keen for Gray to get a little bit tipsy so his better judgement would dissolve and he would invite her back. But he was very serious and steady all night, sipping his beer agonisingly slowly in Marcy's opinion.

He was obviously lost in thought: even though he was watching the band he looked distant and barely spoke to Martin or her.

Maybe it was time for a more provocative tactic. As usual there were more men than women in the venue, so it wasn't hard for Marcy to return someone's gaze as there were plenty of guys eyeing her up.

She knew it would drive Gray wild if someone actually approached her.

So that was exactly what she planned to encourage.

When the band took a break and it was easier to hold a conversation, Gray turned to Marcy. "It's getting late. You should probably be getting home."

"It's not that late. And there's no school tomorrow."

"That's not the point."

They couldn't continue the discussion as Martin had just returned with more drinks. Marcy hoped he didn't pick up the tension in the air.

She was feeling a kind of déjà vu anyway. it was like that earlier night in the bar when she'd bumped into Gray and he hadn't been able to keep his hands off her. But Martin hadn't been there that night as he was now, and his presence was a huge obstacle.

So what was a girl to do?

Let Gray figure it out!

When the music started up again, Marcy deliberately returned the look of a guy at the bar with as alluring a smile as possible. He had curly hair and looked about the age of a college student. No surprises, he soon came over and started to chat to her. She felt a twinge of guilt, but she was careful to keep the conversation light and not be overly flirty with him.

Just talking to the other guy was enough, of course. She could practically feel Gray's eyes boring into her, even though she wasn't looking at him.

They had been chatting about the usual kinds of introductory things when Marcy felt a hand at her elbow.

"Excuse me." This was addressed to the curly-haired guy. "I think it's time we left." This was directed at Marcy.

The guy looked annoyed. "Is this your boyfriend?"

Marcy was about to try and respond when Gray cut in. "I'm a friend, and we need to go." He was as polite as he could be given the abruptness.

Marcy shot the guy an apologetic look and let Gray usher her towards the exit. She should have been furious, of course, at someone interrupting her conversation and herding her out.

But since it was her plan, she was delighted.

"I'm just escorting Marcy to her car," Gray told Martin as he left. Martin nodded, he didn't seem to find it remarkable in any way. After all they had all become friends through the theatre group and had given one another lifts here and there. Or if he did suspect anything, he kept it to himself.

As they left the bar the coolness of the night air made Marcy's skin tingle.

"I didn't drive, by the way."

"What?" Gray was still too wound up to process this.

"Revel and I walked here. So I really don't need an escort."

"Then I'll drive you home."

The hell he would, Marcy thought. Unless he meant to his home. No way was she going home alone, returned to her doorstep like some kid with an early curfew.

She said nothing, but walked with him to his car. As ever, Gray held the door open for her and waited for her to get in before closing it. It was one of those habit of old fashioned courtesy that she loved about him.

Marcy sat back in Gray's car, enjoying the familiarity of it. She could sense he was still furious - with himself, more so than with her - and that he was wrestling with himself over what to do.

She made it easier for him.

"You're not actually going to drive me home, are you?"

"It's what I should do." His eyes were fixed on the road ahead, he was concentrating on not even looking at her.

"You know that my parents aren't expecting me home tonight? I was supposed to be staying with Revel."

"I'm sure they won't mind the change of plans."

Actually, Marcy thought, though they probably wouldn't, there was every reason why they should. They might have planned their own quiet dinner-and-date night. While she shrank from the thought of her parents doing THAT - for she had surely been delivered by the stork, anything else was unthinkable of one's own parents - it was possible they might be enjoying a night alone.

She mentioned this to Gray. "It might interrupt their evening."

It was enough to tip him past pushing point. "OK. We'll go back to mine. I'll take the couch."

Marcy smiled to herself. They both knew that wasn't going to happen.

33. Giving in

They entered Gray's apartment.

They stood there.

And then he was all over her. They were both all over each other.

The forced separation, the tension, the games. Gray was angry with himself for losing his internal struggle, and angry for having it in the first place.

Marcy was frustrated at the weeks of misery and trying to cope with Gray's rejection.

Now they were crazy one another. It was like a fight as much as it was making out.

His mouth was hot and hard on hers, his hands were grabbing her, twisting her clothes off.

"Did you do that on purpose?" he asked her, when they paused for air.

"Do what?"

"Flirt with that guy to make a point?"

"Did it make a point?"

Gray's response was to kiss her again, hungrily. "You know that it did."

"Are you angry with me?" Marcy asked.

Gray looked into her eyes. "I'm angry with the situation. And at my own lack of self-control. And at that moron who was trying it on with you. But not with you, no."

Marcy smiled. She reached up and drew him to her again, putting her lips on his. "Wouldn't it be simpler all round if you had let him talk to me?"

She felt Gray tense and grip her harder, which was her intention.

"No goddamn way. No flop-haired idiot like that is laying a finger on you. And I'm going to show you exactly why."

He scooped her up before she could protest, and carried her into the bedroom where her practically threw her on the bed.

"I vowed I would hold off from this. But you've been winding me up all night."

* * *

The heat in Gray's eyes made Marcy a little afraid.

She wanted him, her body had ached for him so many times, but he'd never been quite this resolute before.

She wriggled herself up to a sitting position but Gray pulled her back down and slid her underneath him, laying on top of her.

They were both fully clothed but she could feel his hardness through his jeans as he pressed against her.

His lips were on hers, hard and demanding. Forcing her mouth open.

Then on her neck, sucking and nearly biting; she feared he would leave a mark. But a part of her wanted to be marked by him, the thought made her stomach go liquid.

Gray's hands slipped between them and over Marcy's body. He was unbuttoning her blouse, exposing her skin.

He pulled the fabric of her bra down, and swore. "I've wanted this so badly."

Then his mouth was over her breast, his tongue swirling around her nipple, making her writhe up against him. She loved the hotness and wetness against her skin, his urgency.

Marcy reached under his shirt to feel the hard, hot muscles of Gray's back.

Then his mouth was back on her neck again, this time drawing in her skin so firmly that she knew he would leave a love bite.

"You'll leave a mark..."

He broke off. "Then I can look at it and know you're mine." There was a harsh edge to his voice.

156

His possessiveness caused a jolt through her.

"I thought you wanted to be discreet?"

"Discreet? By the time I'm done with you, you're barely going to be able to walk."

Marcy gasped as Gray roughly tugged her jeans down.

Then he gripped her hips and twisted her around, so he was behind her. They hadn't tried this position before and Marcy felt nervous.

She felt his hands on her buttocks, opening her and positioning her ready for him. At some point he must have tugged his own pants down.

"This is what you get for your behaviour earlier. You pushed for this, Marcy."

Then Gray drove into her in one long, hard thrust. So deep it was nearly painful. She was stretched around him, he was completely filling her.

For a moment he just stayed inside her, at full length, allowing her to get used to the size of him filling her.

Then as Marcy caught her breath he started to slam into her. She shifted a little to soften the angle. She loved the way he was taking her, owning her.

He planned to show her no mercy.

He had never felt this hard before, nor gone on for so long. She felt quite dizzy with it all, her hands clutching the sheets.

Suddenly Gray slowed. Grasping her, he managed to pull her back onto him, then manoeuvred her around, raising her leg past him and twisting her body towards his so they were eventually face to face, on their sides. He stayed inside her the whole time.

His hair was damp from the exertion so far and he slowed the pace. He looked into her eyes, not saying anything, just making long, smooth, deep strokes into her, his face intense with desire.

In this position he could also touch her wherever he wanted, and he did so. His hand moulded her breast, his thumb and forefinger squeezing her nipple, firmly but not enough to cause pain, only pleasure.

Then his hand slipped down between them, into the hot wetness where they were joined. He flicked a finger up against her, instantly finding her most sensitive place.

"I want you to come for me, Marcy." His eyes never left her face and she felt herself blush amid her own desire for him.

He hadn't consciously watched her before. Now he was fixed on her, wanting her to submit to his complete control of her body.

Marcy wasn't sure if she could lose herself under his gaze. But his fingers were relentless. The sensations from them were blending with the deeper feelings inside her, where he continued to push into her.

She tried closing her eyes. "Open your eyes and look at me." It was an order.

She was suddenly reminded of him in class, her teacher, instructing them. An authority figure. Something in his gaze was the same now, and it was enough to escalate the tension in her body.

Mr Grayson is inside me, making me come for him.

The thought was enough to bring her to the edge.

She was at her teacher's home, having sex with him, completely forbidden, and no one but the two of them knew.

And he was commanding her.

Marcy felt his thumb press more firmly against her and she couldn't stop herself crying out as a sweet, sharp pang started building and spasming through her core.

She managed to keep looking at him, the image of him in the classroom not leaving her, driving her even more wild.

As it all subsided, and her body had that lovely warm glow, he rolled her back onto her back and took his own pleasures. It was almost instant, he had been holding off so when he came, it was nearly violent.

They were both so exhausted - Marcy felt light-headed - that he collapsed on her and they lay there without moving, and she couldn't even remember him moving off her before she fell asleep.

* * *

She had him back. They were back together.

When Marcy woke it took her a moment to realise where she was. But then she realised that Gray was next to her, sleeping, his face looking both gorgeous and peaceful.

158

Marcy lay there, basking in relief and happiness. She was also a little scared, because each time they did this it felt like things were getting deeper and more beyond their control.

But for now, she would just enjoy it. Shut the world out.

Eventually he woke and gave a sleepy smile as he saw her lying next to him. "Good morning."

"Good morning," Marcy replied.

Concern passed over his face. "I wasn't too rough with you last night?"

She felt herself blush. "I loved every moment."

"Good." He looked relieved, and lay there for a few moments. Then he spoke again. "I'm not really sure what came over me, I've never gotten that carried away before. I really don't want to hurt you."

"You didn't, so it's fine. I promise," Marcy said. She thought she should be a little braver and honest. "I actually liked it. A lot."

Gray gave a more suggestive smile. "Then we'll have to repeat the performance some time."

They stayed in bed, feeling glad that it was Saturday and there was no pressing need to get up early. It was still pretty early: a few minutes past seven according to Gray's alarm clock.

Thinking about the time made Marcy think of school mornings, and then of what had gone through her mind the night before: thinking about him in the classroom and getting even more turned on. She felt kind of guilty about it.

He sensed her change of mood. "What's wrong?"

"It's nothing." Should she confess? She wanted to try and be open with him.

"You're worried about something?"

"No, it's just... last night. The thought of you being at Springdale kind of turned me on."

He laughed. "You mean me being your teacher?"

"Yes." Marcy buried her face in the blanket to cover her embarrassment. "It didn't before, it was just last night."

"Want a confession back?"

She absolutely would love a confession back.

"The thought of you being in my class and me getting to discipline you for misbehaving is the hottest thing in the world."

Just Gray saying this made Marcy throb and want him all over again. But after last night she wasn't sure if she was physically capable of anything, or if he was.

"You know something else?" he asked her.

"What?"

"You're incredibly cute when you blush." To prove it, he leant over and kissed her, a tender, lingering kiss.

Marcy wondered if anyone in the world anywhere had ever been as happy as she felt right at that moment. She was glad she had managed to confess her fantasy to him, it was probably healthier to be open about these things.

"So what happens next week?" She meant at school. Was last night a lapse, and would he want to call it off all over again.

Gray rubbed his face. "I don't know. Staying away from you doesn't seem to work out, does it? We'll just have to take each day as it comes and be incredibly careful."

It was all Marcy needed to hear. That he wasn't going to end it all again. For now at least, it was back on.

34. Suspicion

"So Mimi claims she saw something that absolutely can't be true. But Mimi wouldn't lie, would she?" Minette "Mimi" McCarroll was another of Brittanny's horrible crowd.

Small and dark haired and sneaky. Marcy had never liked her, though she'd always tried to be pleasant.

Marcy ignored Brittany, but Brittany wasn't going to let it drop.

"The saddest, ugliest girl in school - which is you, by the way," Brittany said, with a fake-sweet smile, "leaving a bar and getting into a car with Mr Grayson."

Marcy's blood ran cold. "Really?"

Brittanny narrowed her eyes. She looked both triumphant and irate. "You don't deny it then?"

Mimi worked at the pizza place opposite the bar, Marcy remembered that now. She kicked herself inwardly. Stupid, stupid, stupid not to have remembered something like that.

But she tried to keep her cool. "I don't see what your point is."

"My point?" Brittanny gave an ever faker laugh. "You don't think it's just a bit like completely utterly inappropriate to be leaving a bar with a teacher? Like, major, massive, big trouble inappropriate?"

Was she hoping to blackmail Marcy? Or just to gloat and then go and sneak anyway?

Marcy drew out the final folder she needed, closed her locker and turned to face Brittanny.

"You do know we're both in the same theatre group?"

Brittanny scowled, since she didn't know. "Theatre?"

"My mom's neighbour got me into this theatre group she runs. Mr Grayson happens to be a member as well. Friday night he was just giving me a lift home."

It was clear Brittanny wasn't quite sure what to believe. "A theatre group in a bar?"

"Some of us just went there afterwards for a drink." She wasn't going to get into explaining the whole Revel thing.

Brittanny was silent. Her lips were pursed in an angry way. Marcy sensed that Brittany was also wrestling with herself. She had her own huge crush on Mr Grayson and would have given her right arm to be in a theatre group with him. Which was a key reason why Marcy and Revel had kept the whole thing under wraps.

It must be pretty awful for Brittanny to realise she could have had all this extra time with Mr Grayson, but she'd missed out. She was now burning with curiosity but couldn't bring herself to admit it by asking Marcy about the group.

So Marcy took pity on her. "We're putting on Guys and Dolls. I can get you tickets."

Stung by Marcy having access to something she didn't, and feeling excluded by the fact that she - Brittanny - would only be just another onlooker, Brittanny got spiteful again.

"My parents take me to Broadway to see theatre. I don't think I could sit through your amateur production, thanks anyway."

"Your loss," Marcy said. "Mr Grayson's pretty great. He has the lead role."

Brittanny was silent again. She obviously wanted to see him in it, but did not want to lower herself by accepting a favour from Marcy. "I suppose you're Sarah? Now that would be something to watch - something awful."

Marcy laughed. "Hardly. I'm helping out backstage. The lead roles are all taken by really proficient actors and singers. It will be better than you think."

Brittanny had nothing left to say so she turned and left, her mood furious and her day ruined. From attempting to get one over on Marcy, she was the effective loser.

Still, Marcy was shaken. Being seen leaving a bar with Mr Grayson was a big concern. Regardless of Revel putting her on the

162

guest list she wasn't legally old enough to go in there, and her parents had little idea where she was hanging out.

They would have to play things a lot more carefully in future. For the first time it had also brought it home how much risk it was for Mr Grayson, more than for her. He stood to risk his job and maybe his reputation as a teacher. At most, Marcy would be reprimanded and grounded. Even if she got kicked out of school she'd still manage to graduate somewhere.

The euphoria she had been feeling about being back with him was fading. She sensed storm clouds ahead.

* * *

After French, Marcy hung behind to speak with Mr Grayson. She didn't want to draw attention to their relationship but she had to tell him about Minette spying on them. Well, not really spying, it wasn't her fault she had seen them. She was such a sneaky little thing to have gone blabbing to Brittanny though. Marcy could just imagine how that conversation had gone.

Though I would have done the same with Addy, if I saw Brittanny out on the town with a teacher, Marcy thought.

"I'll be quick, I just needed to tell you something," Marcy said.

He smiled at her. "I have a free period next, there's no rush."

"Someone saw us leaving the bar on Friday night. Minette McCarroll, she works opposite in Joe's Pizza."

Mr Grayson frowned. "Has she been spreading it around?"

"Yes, but I think it's okay. I got the third degree from Brittanny so I've told her it was after a theatre meeting. So she knows about the show, but I guess she would have found out anyway." They should get flyers up soon, Marcy thought, to corroborate her story.

He was silent for a few moments. "We really are playing with fire, aren't we?"

Which was partly what made it so exciting. But also stressful.

"I think it's riskier for you than it is for me," Marcy said.

They both stood there for a while, looking at one another. Images of Friday night were going through Marcy's head. Mr

Grayson was so sexy. Just thinking about what he could do to her body made her want him to take her then and there.

Mr Grayson had heat in his gaze as well. "Right now I have the strongest urge to throw you over a desk and make love to you until you beg for mercy."

Marcy felt herself grow hot at the thought. He had never used the phrase "making love" before and it was doing weird giddy things to her stomach. She knew it was just a phrase, but still. It was a phrase that she would replay in her thoughts a million times.

Trying to keep her cool, which was hard, she smiled. "That would give them all something to talk about."

Now he laughed, the physical tension between them easy.

"It would. We need to be more careful, I guess."

$$* * *$$

At the end of the day Marcy got a text message from Mr Grayson.

Can you meet me this evening? My place. We need to talk.

Uh oh. That sounded kind of ominous. But after today, Marcy was sort of expecting something. She just hoped it wasn't to call it off yet again. She didn't think she could bear to lose him.

OK. 7pm?

She waited for a reply, which came straight away.

Sounds good. See you then.

Marcy supposed she should really delete his messages to be even more safe, but they were so precious to her. He deliberately didn't text her too much in case someone saw. So all the ones she had were pretty safe and not incriminating. But if you read them all together, it would look incriminating.

At least if you knew that "G" was Mr Grayson, her French teacher and not just some high school guy.

What did he want to say to her?

35. Self control

"I don't want to end things with you. Hell, I couldn't if I tried. When I did try, it drove me nearly insane."

Marcy was at Gray's. He had greeted her with a kiss but wasn't immediately all over her so she knew something serious was up.

"The thing is, us being together is just too risky. I've been giving it some thought, and I think we need to put it on hold."

Marcy's heart sank. Gray saw her face fall. "I still want to be with you. But for now, until school finishes, we should just keep things professional at school, and just be friends outside school."

"So what exactly does that mean? The end of the year or the vacation?"

There was sadness in Gray's eyes as he spoke. "We should really wait the year out, and then see."

A lot could happen in a year. What if he started getting close to some other girl? "Would you date other people?"

"I don't plan to. But I won't hold you to living like a nun, you should be free to do what you want. I will admit, the thought of you with other guys kills me but I can't stand in your way."

Marcy had absolutely no desire to see anyone else. But not-being with someone she cared about so much for all that time seemed unbearable too.

And pretty impossible, particularly if they kept spending time together outside school at the Springdale Theatre group. There were already early murmurs that Mrs Helberg had a plan to stage Hello, Dolly! in the new year. No prizes for guessing that she would take the starring role of Dolly of course. But she apparently had her eye on getting Gray back - and Martin - for the male leads.

"So can we still hang out after theatre?"

"That's probably what we shouldn't do, any more," Gray told her. "For now, anyway."

It was as though there was a big cold black cloud wrapped around her heart. Somehow this was worse than him getting angry over Josh and breaking it off with her, because this time he had really thought about it. It was a decision made in calm, not anger.

Because of this, she knew there was no point challenging it. It also wouldn't be fair to try and seduce him out of the decision - though she was pretty sure she could manage that if she really set her mind to it.

But not even kissing him, ever. Or at least for months and months. How could she cope?

"Can you kiss me one more time? As a goodbye?"

Gray gave a sad smile and immediately took Marcy in his arms. It was a tender, beautiful kiss. His lips were firm but gentle on hers, warm. Their mouths parted and the kiss deepened.

Marcy was trying to concentrate on every detail of what it felt like to be pressed up against Gray. How his body felt, the warmth of him, his amazing, intoxicating male smell. She would have to live off this memory for a long while.

The touch of his hands on her hair. The feel of his skin. His height, how his broad shoulders made her feel protected.

The heat grew between them and she looked up at him, a question on her face.

"Could we - you know - just one more time? One last time, just for a proper farewell?" So I won't forget you, she thought. So when I'm an elderly spinster of eighty I'll have one more happy memory.

Because a part of her was convinced that Gray would forget her and move on, and she would never get to feel this way again.

Gray looked torn. "It's not that I don't want to, but…"

"I understand." She really did. He was right, she guessed. Being sensible started now.

"Come here." Gray took her in his arms again. "Okay then, one last time. Which I would prefer to make last all night, but I'm guessing you have to get home at some point."

He took her to the bedroom and made love to her, at least that was how it really felt. It felt like more than just sex.

166

He was tender, passionate, intimate. They both drew it out as much as they could. It was weird, doing it for the last time, or the last time for a good while. Marcy wanted to savour every moment, as did Gray.

Afterwards they showered together one last time and Gray made them both coffee.

"Think of it as though one of us is going overseas," he said. "If I was in the army or something we'd have to do this all the time, and be patient for months."

Being around Gray it was hard to be patient for a minute. Marcy didn't know how she was going to manage until next summer. Most of all she was scared that it would all fizzle out. That he'd eventually meet someone else and want to date them.

She was also a little anxious about herself. After a year of interacting with Gray solely as her teacher, maybe he'd start to become Mr Grayson only, and not Gray any more.

"Do you think we'll survive this?" Marcy asked. Then she felt kind of presumptuous in the way she had phrased it. As though they had something important enough to be worth surviving. They hadn't been dating that long, all things considered. It meant a huge a lot to her, but did Gray feel the same?

He wasn't fazed by her question. "I hope so." His green eyes looked into hers, intense, and she felt suddenly nervous.

Gray took her hands. He gazed at her. "I really care about you, Marcy. This isn't just some fling. If it was it would be easy to end it. Or even to take the risk. But you mean too much to me for that. I don't want to wreck your life."

Marcy swallowed. Gray had never said anything quite like this before and she wasn't sure how to respond. "I care about you too" just sounded so lame to say back though.

"I feel the same."

"Good." He cupped her face in his hands and kissed her. It was a long, lingering kiss.

This is the guy I want to be with, Marcy thought. The only guy in the entire world for me.

Somehow, some way, we have to get through this.

36. Pushing in

To Marcy's and Revel's amusement, Brittanny Paige actually tried to join the Springdale Players. She managed to find out when and where the next rehearsal was, and invited herself along.

She was clearly desperate to try and hang out with Mr Grayson.

Brittanny had dolled herself up and looked ridiculous, Marcy thought. So much so that she almost - almost, not quite - felt sorry for her. Brittanny was wearing a super tight short skirt and heels and a low cut top, which looked really silly given what a cold night it was.

Such a try-hard. If only she realised that Mr Grayson truly couldn't stand her.

Brittanny feigned a friendly greeting to Marcy, who was standing with Len, when she arrived.

"So I thought I might try out for your theatre group." Brittanny looked a little embarrassed and defiant as she said this.

Marcy tried to hide a smile. "You should probably talk with Mrs Helberg then."

"Is she directing this show?" Brittanny asked.

"No, Len is." Marcy introduced them.

Brittanny tried to turn on her charm. It was such a bad piece of acting that even if Len wasn't an experienced director he would have seen straight through it.

"Hi, I'm Brittanny. I'm really interested in acting, and I wondered if you still had roles available?"

Len raised his eyebrows, taking in the wannabe-vision before him. "Not for this production, no, we're well on the way to opening night."

"Like if someone's sick, or an understudy role?"

Len looked bemused. "Are you a friend of Marcy's?" he asked her.

Don't put this on me, Marcy thought. She didn't want to be associated with Brittanny.

"We're both at Springdale," Brittanny replied.

"As I said, I'm afraid there's nothing available for this production. If you're interested in future productions, you should talk to Cora." He waved Mrs Helberg over. "A possible new recruit for you."

Mrs Helberg came over, and was rather taken aback by Brittanny. "Can I help, dear?"

Brittanny repeated her request. "I'm really interested in acting and would like to join up." Her eyes flicked round the stage, clearly trying to spot Mr Grayson. But he was backstage in the dressing rooms, where some preliminary costume fittings were going on.

"I'm delighted to hear it. We could always use extra hands backstage," Mrs Helberg told Brittanny.

"No, I mean I'd like to act, not do off-stage stuff," Brittanny said.

Now it was Mrs Helberg's turn to frown slightly, as Brittanny's tone when she said "off-stage" had been kind of negative.

"We need willing workers for all aspects of theatre production. For example Marcy here has made herself invaluable assisting Len with direction."

Marcy felt herself glow from this. It was the first direct praise she'd had from Mrs Helberg.

At that moment Revel came onstage, wearing the semi-finished costume for Miss Adelaide's first scene. "Betty wasn't sure about the length," she said to Len, giving a twirl.

"It looks fine to me," Len told her. "If you can manage the dance moves comfortably in it, I'm happy."

Brittanny was open-mouthed. Forgetting herself, she said rudely to Revel: "what are you doing here?" She made the "you" sound incredulous.

Revel shot an amused glance at Marcy before turning her attention to Brittanny. Before she could answer, Mrs Helberg spoke for us.

"Revel is one of our leading ladies." Her voice was a little clipped, which Marcy knew meant she was annoyed. Mrs Helberg had taken a dislike to Brittanny.

Brittanny was still stunned. It had been bad enough discovering that Marcy was spending all this after school time with Mr Grayson. Now to find out that ultimate social reject, Revel Holmes, was a part of this was almost too much to take.

"I'd invite you to stay and watch," Len said, "but we have a custom of not allowing previews before the dress rehearsal." It was his way of firmly but politely getting rid of Brittanny.

Being shown the door in front of Marcy and Revel, and not having managed to get a single glimpse of her crush, so infuriated Brittanny that she couldn't find words. Which made it much easier for Mrs Helberg to escort her out, providing her with a flyer for the show as she did so. They had just arrived from the printer that afternoon.

Marcy and Revel fell about laughing once Brittanny had gone. "Did you see her face?!"

"She'll be nastier than ever in school tomorrow," Marcy said.

"Let her do her worst. She's got nothing on either of us," Revel replied.

* * *

Gray was relieved that Brittanny had been shown the door. Even with things on hold between him and Marcy, the last thing either of them wanted was Brittanny sniffing around.

"I guess we were right to be careful," Marcy said.

"Yes, things could have gotten dangerously complicated, fast."

They were both trying to act professionally around one another. Fortunately it was more relaxed and friendly than the time when Gray was actively trying to distance himself. Marcy still gloried in every moment she got to spend with him, even if it was platonic for now.

Revel thought the pair of them were being over cautious. "Life's too short," she said. "I mean I get why you're doing this, but what's the worst that could happen?"

The problem was that for Revel, getting kicked out of school wouldn't be the hugest disaster. She knew what she wanted to do with her life and she would get there regardless. She worked as hard as she needed to, but school was kind of like a casual job for her.

"It's his entire career though."

"Look at the guy. Why the hell is he burying himself in a high school with his looks and talent? He obviously enjoys acting, he could just try that instead."

But not everyone was so driven towards the stage as Revel was. Even with her talent and heritage it was a precarious career.

"He's such a great teacher though," Marcy said. "Maybe it's like a vocation for him."

"Maybe."

Marcy could tell that Revel wasn't convinced but she dropped the subject and asked Marcy about her play instead.

"How is it coming along? Are you nearly finished?"

"I'm getting there." She had had more time to focus on it recently. Whenever she found her thoughts wandering to Gray she snapped herself out of it by writing or editing another scene.

"Have you decided on the ending? A comedy or tragedy?" Revel was genuinely interested.

It was going to be a bit of both. Marcy planned to end it with a sense of hope, but she felt its message would be stronger if it had some grief and loss in it. "Sort of happy, or the potential to be happy."

Which was how she felt about the situation with Gray and her right now. It was sort of okay, and hopefully would be much more than okay if they could survive this next year.

37. On show

As often happens with a theatre group, the cast members were getting closer and friendlier. A real sense of teamwork and camaraderie was developing, and Marcy was enjoying the rehearsals for the social element almost as much as the theatrical.

There was a bit of sniping and backbiting, but that was normal with nerves growing jittery as First Night approached.

Marcy and Revel had come to adore Betty. She had worked briefly as a dancer and showgirl in her youth - "many, many years ago now, dears" - and had a host of wicked stories to share.

They had also become firm friends with Thaddeus and Phyllis, who it turned out were not a couple but "companions", as they liked to term it. They were both widowed, unlike Betty who had divorced three husbands and had a large troupe of gentleman friends. She preferred to call them her "dancing partners".

Marcy found it encouraging that all these older people still had romance in their lives. Not that she wanted to wait until she was seventy to start dating again, but it made her feel less like she was running out of time with Gray calling things to a halt. Hopefully a temporary one.

Len was also a valued colleague, Marcy was learning so much from him. She also recognised how much work Mrs Helberg did in keeping everything together and managing the company as a whole. Even without the fact that she got to see Gray more often, she was very glad she had joined the group.

Len had also arranged for a cast recording. "In case anyone gets laryngitis," he told them. "And a great Christmas gift, for those who enjoy showtunes."

"Nick's photography exhibition is finally on," Revel told Marcy as they walked from Springdale High to the theatre. "I thought we could invite some of the cast members to the opening."

Marcy felt hugely embarrassed because one of her photos was among those being displayed. But she squashed down her discomfort. After all, Revel had half a dozen portrait shots in there.

"Sure, why not?" What was the worst that could happen, after all? It wasn't like it really mattered if people thought she looked dumb in her picture. And Gray had called them beautiful. In front of Brittanny, no less.

"It's Saturday afternoon. There'll be wine and canapés, the usual."

Marcy had never been to an exhibition opening before so she had no idea what was usual. Or what to wear. She had an idea that people dressed very smartly to visit galleries, but Nick had seemed such a casual kind of guy. Not the type to even own a suit.

"Is there a dress code?" she asked.

"No, just whatever."

If Gray was going to be included in the invitation Marcy wanted to look a little bit nice at least. And hopefully older. She was still worried that if he kept forcing himself to view her only as a high school student, then that's all he would eventually see.

The other cast members were delighted to be asked to the opening. Mrs Helberg was particularly pleased as Revel had arranged for some of the Guys and Dolls flyers to be handed out there.

Everyone was hoping for packed audiences, particularly as a reporter from the Springdale newspaper had come down to do a preview. A local magazine for retirees had also featured Betty and the dancers in a story on "keeping fit in your golden years" which they were hoping would draw a few more people in.

Loads of students from Springdale were also planning to come. Mr Grayson was such a popular teacher, and so many girls still had crushes on him that they were eagerly trying to get tickets.

The show was becoming so overwhelming that it was almost a relief to have another diversion. Marcy deliberately put on the sexiest outfit she could get away with at an afternoon event: a slinky, fitted dress that she'd once worn to a winter wedding. Everyone else had decided to dress up to make more of an occasion of it.

* * *

Marcy was still super nervous when she arrived at the gallery. Her parents were also coming, and they would meet Gray for the first time. Albeit just as Mr Grayson: as they had no idea of Marcy's considerably closer acquaintance with her high school French teacher.

She was terrified they might sense something, even though both she and Gray had managed to be on their best behaviour. Sometimes she would catch him looking at her in French class and she would look back. There was an unspoken understanding there, even though there wasn't meant to be.

"What beautiful photos!" Marcy's mother said as they entered. She had already seen the two prints that Nick had given Marcy, but it didn't compare to seeing the huge, blow-up photo of Marcy on the wall.

There were six of Revel, all arranged along one wall in a series. Revel was standing near them, with another photographer taking a picture of her and her photos. Marcy was also surprised to see Revel's grandmother there, looking very elegant and proud.

Marcy was never quite sure what Revel's grandmother knew of and what she didn't in terms of what Revel got up to, but she seemed to be okay with the modelling at least.

"Hello Marcy."

Her world swam. It was Gray, looking absolutely amazingly good looking in a well-cut suit.

"Hi... Mr Grayson." She nearly slipped up but covered it. "These are my parents. Mom, Dad, this is Mr Grayson, who teaches French at Springdale High."

Marcy's parents were happy to make his acquaintance. "We've heard so much about you," Marcy's father said.

Marcy felt her face flame up. What? She was sure she had barely mentioned him. She could see a smile in Gray's eyes.

"From Cora Helberg," Marcy's mother went on to explain. "She seems very excited to have secured your talents for the Springdale Players. She's our neighbour," she told Gray.

"Marcy's showing a lot of directorial talent herself," Gray said.

"She's always been very keen on the theatre. We were looking at possible theatre management and playwriting programs for her next year."

Marcy wanted the floor to swallow her. It was like being a little kid again, with your parents talking about you over your head with other grown-ups.

"I'm sure she'll get the grades, if her performance in French this semester is anything to go by," Gray said. His eyes just flicked to Marcy on the word "performance" and she knew he was thinking of quite another kind of performance.

In my head I'm glaring at you, Marcy thought, since she couldn't actually react openly.

Her parents were blown away by the photo of Marcy and her father ordered prints for themselves and for Marcy's grandparents.

Later on her mother couldn't stop going on about Gray.

"What a nice young man your French teacher is. And so handsome! I expect he's broken plenty of hearts at Springdale. He was certainly very nice about your progress."

"Yes, he's a great teacher," Marcy said. In more ways than one.

38. Dress rehearsal

"It'll be all right on the night."

Everyone kept saying this, but Marcy had her doubts. The dress rehearsal was turning into an unmitigated disaster. Whether from nerves or whatever else, people forgot their lines, came on from the wrong sides or didn't come on at all.

Some of the costumes got mixed up and lost, and the Hot Box girls messed up all their moves and Betty nearly sprained an ankle when someone fell into her and knocked her over. Martin managed to trip up and bring down a piece of scenery with him, which had to be urgently repaired.

Marcy was surprised at how calm Len seemed throughout. He took everything in his stride.

Alan, the stage manager, also seemed to take the damage to his set quite calmly. He just fixed it all up and they were good to go again.

Mrs Helberg had just a touch of the diva about her that evening, fretting about "the critics". If Variety and the New York Times were sending reviewers she couldn't have been more stressed.

She tried not to back-seat direct, but couldn't help herself a few times, berating a couple of the men who had stood in the wrong place and blocked her own route across the stage.

Revel in contrast was completely laid back, enjoying the chaos even. While Marcy was run off her feet trying to soothe nerves and egos and fetch and carry a million things that had got lost, Revel took it all in her stride.

"It's going to be a success whatever happens," she said. "Either it will be okay and people will love it, or it will be such a disaster that they'll flock to see it for the comedy value."

Everyone looked amazing in their costumes, even Mrs Helberg, though she didn't exactly look like a young ingénue. Marcy's favourite scenes were the dancing ones because Betty and the other ladies were such fun to watch. And as ever, Marcy felt a tear in her eye when Thaddeus sang his sweet ballad.

When it was over there was a mixed sense of relief and anxiety.

Len tried to soothe the actors' nerves. "Everything that went wrong tonight is something you've all done perfectly countless times before. You can do it, and on opening night everything will be fine."

Marcy was just so glad she didn't have to get up there and face an audience. She hugely admired the others for being able to do so but she would have died of nerves.

* * *

After the dress rehearsal everyone went for a cast meal at a restaurant in town. Of course it would be the pizza place opposite the bar, and of course Minette McCarroll would be working that night.

"Hi Marcy," she said, with false friendliness. "Can I take your order?"

Minette's gimlet eye would mean that Marcy would have to be really careful talking with Gray. Even if nothing was officially happening now, a spiteful rumour could still cause a heap of woe.

She was sitting just across from him, which hopefully looked less incriminating than if they had sat next to each other. Also she hadn't thought she could sit through a meal, with his thigh pressed against hers on the bench, trying to deny the attraction.

"So Brittanny tells me you're all in some theatre group," Minette said. "These must be your theatre friends." She managed to say the words with a kind of patronising, spiteful emphasis.

Marcy tried to ignore her, and Revel spoke instead. "That's right. I think you know Mr Grayson from school though, right?"

Minette looked a little embarrassed. "Hi Mr Grayson."

"Hello Minette." His cool, green eyed glance gave nothing away. If Minette was planning an evening of spying and sneaking, she wasn't going to get any material here.

Len took the lead in ordering food for everyone, since Mrs Helberg was still a little overwhelmed and unusually subdued from the exertion of the dress rehearsal. Marcy felt a little sympathy for her. It was Mrs Helberg's big thing, the Springdale Players, and she had a lot of personal pride invested in it being a success. Not to mention she had to carry the performance, being in the lead role.

Although she had found Mrs Helberg very bumptious and overbearing to begin with, Marcy had come to like her more and more over the course of the rehearsals.

Revel also admired her. "She's very committed. You have to appreciate how much she puts into all this, even if she drives you mad at times."

"So what's next for you after Springdale High then?" Gray asked Revel. The four "young people" of the cast - Marcy, Revel, Gray and Martin - were grouped together on one end of a long table. "Broadway?"

Revel grinned. "Maybe. I want to go to Juilliard so we'll see what happens."

Gray already knew what Marcy had planned so didn't need to ask her about it. But Martin spoke: "Revel tells me you're writing a play, Marcy. Is it something we could perform in future?"

Marcy blushed. "It's not a musical, so probably not. It may take ages to finish."

"It could always be scored though," Revel said. "I mean you could have a musical version of it as well."

Marcy wasn't sure if it would work.

"It did for Oklahoma," Revel said. "And Hello, Dolly. And West Side Story, if you consider it was based on Romeo and Juliet, though I guess that is a pretty different treatment."

Maybe in five hundred years someone would turn Marcy's play into the next Sound of Music, but right now she couldn't really see it.

* * *

178

Marcy had been keeping Addy updated on the whole saga with her and Gray. Addy viewed it as a kind of real life soap opera.

"So what's the next episode in the Gray and Marcy reality show? Has he given in to his feelings yet again?" she asked Marcy as they Skyped later that night.

"No, nothing's happening. We're just doing the friends thing still as it really was too much risk otherwise." Marcy told Addy about Minette.

"Yeah, I guess there are eyes everywhere in Springdale. Nothing gets to stay secret," Addy said.

Marcy told her about the disastrous dress rehearsal. Addy drank it all in avidly.

"I'm now desperate to see it. I can't imagine anything more fun than you and Revel prancing about and knocking over the scenery in front of half of the town."

"I'm not actually in it," Marcy reminded her. "Though if Martin does bring down the set again I guess everyone backstage is going to get their turn in the spotlight."

"Of course my main reason for seeing it is that I'm desperate to see your Mr Grayson. To see if he's actually as hot as his photos."

He's hotter, Marcy thought. Way, way hotter.

"There's no chance you could fly down?" she asked.

"I'm tempted. So, so tempted. But what with school and trying to save up for Christmas, so we can have a blast when you visit, it's probably not going to be possible."

The thought of seeing Addy in just a few more weeks lifted Marcy's spirits. She had missed her so much, and even though Skype was great there were certain things that you really wanted to talk about person-to-person.

39. Curtain up!

First night was one of the most crazy and wonderful nights ever.

Everyone was pumped up with adrenalin and the whole performance just sparkled. The four leads were flawless and nothing went seriously wrong.

They were playing to a packed house, which was great, as well as an audience that was hugely appreciative. They laughed, clapped and cheered so strongly that it carried the show along.

To Marcy the whole night was golden. The darkness of the auditorium. The dazzling bright lights on the stage: how the actors dared go out there was anyone's guess. She had so much admiration for their nerve.

She loved greeting people when they came off stage after a big scene, buoyed up with all the emotion. Helping them change costumes, get the right props, touching up their make up. Marcy had turned out to have a bit of a talent for greasepaint after Betty had showed her a few tricks.

There was actually an encore. They hadn't rehearsed this as it had been somewhat overlooked, what with the usual last minute panic and the nightmares at the dress rehearsal.

"Whole cast: Guys and Dolls Reprise again," Len called from the wings. "After the first verse and chorus we'll have an interlude. Revel and Betty - do your Hot Box tap duet - then back for a final chorus."

The tap dance had been an absolute show stopper so Marcy thought it was a great idea to repeat it. And it was. The audience were even crying out for a second encore but by then everyone was exhausted and needed to wrap things up and get home.

Afterwards everyone was hugging everyone else, happy and relieved that it had been such a success. Mrs Helberg was even sharing out bunches of flowers that had been delivered to her dressing room, or rather the one all the female cast shared as it was only a small theatre.

"The best show this little theatre has seen in years," Thaddeus said. "A real roof raiser, even if I do say so myself."

Mrs Helberg was absolutely thrilled with the success. "And we mustn't forget all those vital people behind the scenes," she said, smiling kindly at Marcy and the other stage hands. "Tonight wouldn't have been possible with all of you."

There wasn't a huge celebration that night as everyone had to get home and save their energy for the week ahead. But Len and Alan had been planning an absolute blast for the Closing Night party, which after tonight would be very well deserved.

Even if the rest of the week was a catastrophe, it would be okay. Because they knew they could do it, and they'd had one perfect night.

* * *

Then a couple of days later: disaster actually struck.

Guys and Dolls was playing for a whole week, including a special matinée performance one afternoon. The audience for this included a lot of people from retirement homes who were given free tickets as a community gesture.

"It's one of the best audiences," Betty had said. "They're always so appreciative, and they love the Golden Oldies."

But then a relative of Mrs Helberg's died suddenly, and the funeral was the same afternoon as the matinée. Neither event could be rescheduled, for obvious reasons, and Mrs Helberg's priority had to be the funeral service.

The bad news was revealed just after the cast arrived at the theatre to get ready for that evening's performances.

"What the hell are we going to do?" Martin asked.

There was a vague understudy plan in place where Betty would understudy for Revel as Adelaide and Revel for Mrs Helberg as Sarah. In practice though, no one was expecting such a thing to happen. Shifting two major roles and losing the lead Hot Box dancer would cause huge disruption to all the routines, and there was no time to rehearse.

Thaddeus suggested putting Betty in the lead role as Sarah and making do when it came to the dancing scenes. It might even be possible for Betty to double up in a scene that didn't involve Sarah.

"I do have an idea," Revel said. She turned to Marcy: "You're going to hate me, but honestly this is the best thing for the show."

Marcy felt a sinking fear in the pit of her stomach.

Revel addressed Len again. "Marcy knows all the lines backwards. Put her on as Sarah. It's only for the matinée, even if a few prompts are needed the audience will be kind, from what Betty says."

"Oh they will indeed," Betty said. "They'll applaud all the more knowing an understudy is trying her best." She smiled brightly at Marcy.

"But I can't sing," Marcy said. "Not properly, I mean."

"That's okay. We can use the cast recording of Sarah's songs," Revel said. "It will look fine, trust me. And it's just for one performance."

Everyone started to exclaim at what a great idea it was, and how it would really save the day, and Marcy felt completely stressed and miserable. Like she was being pushed into a corner. She caught Gray's eye and saw sympathy there.

"It's all right, you'll be fine," he told her. "We can all run through the lines with you."

Thaddeus offered the same, as his character had several scenes with Sarah. As did Revel.

Everyone was now looking at Marcy, anxious for her to accept. It was the thought of letting them all down, and making Gray think that she lacked courage, that got her over the line.

"Okay, I'll try. But you'd all better make sure the New York Times reviewer doesn't show up that day."

Marcy got so much overwhelming relief and gratitude after agreeing to stand in for Mrs Helberg that she started to get even more stressed about how much hope they were investing in her.

How could she stand up in front of all those people? She would be sure to mess up and let everyone down.

Revel took her to one side later on. "I am sorry. But it was the only way. Everything else they were suggesting would have been disastrous, and this way it really won't be that bad. You look the part, at least. Most of the old dears in the audience will find the sight of you and Gray so sweet together that they wouldn't notice if you suddenly switched to Macbeth half way through."

Her and Gray. Doing a love scene. This hadn't even crossed Marcy's mind yet.

Betty also had a quiet word. "A couple of pins and the costumes will be peachy. Just don't tell Cora how much I've had to take them in from her size!"

Mrs Helberg was also very thankful to Marcy. "That's real team spirit, my dear. I'm very grateful to you." The relation that had died was elderly and had been ill for a while, so it was considered a "happy release" and Mrs Helberg wasn't overwhelmed with grief. But she also couldn't miss such a solemn event.

At least Sarah didn't have to do too much dancing. With Mrs Helberg in the role this had been scaled back, another reason why it made better sense for Revel not to switch roles.

"Thanks for stepping up," Gray said to Marcy later, just before he had to go on stage for his first scene. "You really have spirit."

He smiled at her and there was a look in his eyes that was more than just friends.

Marcy felt a warm glow. Suddenly it all seemed worthwhile.

40. Love scene

Marcy felt increasingly sick as the matinée approached. It didn't help that she had gone over her lines a gazillion times.

Her parents were really excited for her and were coming to watch the show again, having already seen the opening night.

Everyone else was also over the moon about it. Ben, her boss at the café was coming to watch specially, as was Great Aunt Esme. Addy was frustrated beyond belief that she couldn't fly down.

"Your big night! I am so mad I can't be there!"

Revel was the only one who really understood what Marcy was going through and how conflicted she felt about it. And Len too, to some extent. He gave her some advice which she never forgot.

"This is your first and best chance to see things from the other side, if you never do this again. You will be a much better writer and a more empathetic director if you've put yourself through this. I know it feels like an ordeal, but in terms of what you want to do with you career, it's gold."

It was this, more than anything, that steadied Marcy's nerves. She started thinking of it as a learning experience, as a kind of experiment.

Make up and costume were just a blur. She was sitting in the female dressing room at one of the mirrors, marvelling at how anyone would do this voluntarily, when there was a knock at the door.

It was Gray, with a huge and beautiful bunch of roses.

"Flowers for my leading lady. For luck."

He was gone before Marcy had a chance to blush.

"What a very sweet young man that is," Phyllis remarked. "Such a lovely gesture."

"Isn't he so?" Betty said. "Now if I was ten years younger..."

"...you mean fifty," Phyllis said.

Betty winked at Marcy. "If I was your age he'd be just the kind of beau I'd set my cap at."

Marcy saw Revel practically choking with laughter and trying to suppress it.

"He's my teacher," Marcy said.

Betty and Phyllis shot one another a knowing glance.

"Well if he wasn't, I'd go so far to suspect he was sweet on you," Betty said.

Revel started coughing and hid her face in a tissue.

Marcy just hoped her greasepaint was thick enough to mask what she was sure would be her bright scarlet complexion.

To her relief the conversation was broken up by the call for the first scene, which Marcy was involved in. She closed her eyes, thought "now or never", and made her way to the wings.

When the curtains first opened Marcy was utterly dazzled. She felt like a deer in the headlights. She had sort of seen this viewpoint from the wings: the brilliance of the footlights, the black void of the auditorium, but it was another world once you were actually on stage.

Fortunately the first scene was a kind of ensemble so she had a few moments to get used to things, not having any solo lines. She got her bearings, tried to get used to the strange sense of void beyond the lights, and then let the script take over.

Once things finally got going it was all a bit of a blur. Everything went at once very quickly and very slowly. Marcy didn't enjoy it - each time she left the stage it was a shattering relief and a huge ordeal to step back out there - but somehow she got through it. Everyone was very kind to her but were careful not to overwhelm her.

The lip syncing was probably the easiest bit as she didn't have to think so much. She knew all the songs backwards so all she had to do was mouth the words while Mrs Helberg's powerful voice rang out from the audio track.

Marcy was most nervous about her scenes with Gray as Sky, and above all the scene in which they had to dance. Revel had practiced it with her a few times but being in Gray's arms made her feel hopelessly clumsy.

Then of course they had to kiss. On stage. In front of millions of people, or so it felt.

It was only a brief stage kiss, and Marcy tried to remind herself that Gray had done this dozens of times with Mrs Helberg. But it was still his lips on hers, and for a moment the world stood still. If the audience thought her acting was particularly convincing at that point, no one was going to reveal that she wasn't really having to act. She was genuinely dizzy and uplifted, as ever, by Gray's kiss.

Finally it was all over, and she had Gray's and Martin's hands steering her and steadying her for the final bow.

She stumbled as she left the stage after the final curtain fell, and Gray caught her. He hugged her for a moment - it was something any of them might have done because they all knew what she had been through, getting thrown in at the deep end - but Marcy felt like drowning in his arms.

"You were absolutely amazing," he said.

When he let her go she saw Phyllis and Betty sharing another little knowing smile between them. They really were a pair of meddling old gossips, but they meant well.

They had an evening performance later on so most people left promptly to get some rest and recharge. Thank goodness Mrs Helberg would be back for that one.

Marcy found Len before she left. "You were right," she told him. "I can't say I loved the experience, but it's made me realise some things that I wouldn't have before."

"You did a fine job. If you want to go on stage in a future production, I'd be happy to cast you."

"Thanks, but no way! It's also confirmed to me more than ever where my place is in the theatre. I'm glad I did it though," she said. "Or rather that I survived it."

"Well good for you. You had some great chemistry with Sky up there, no one would have guessed it was your first time."

Probably because it wasn't exactly, Marcy thought.

"I'll see you later this evening," she told him. Right now she wanted to zone out. And that meant some ice cream, a couch and a movie.

41. Closing night party

After Marcy's ordeal at the matinée the rest of the performances were plain sailing. There was a mixed sense of sadness and relief as the final show approached. It went just as beautifully as first night, and the cast gave two encores.

Afterwards the Closing Night party was held in the theatre. It was a large event, with many friends and family invited. Most of the cast wore their costumes since they were pretty stylish, and it was the last chance they'd get to wear them. Most removed their greasepaint though since without the stage lights it looked a bit mask-like.

Not having costumes, Len and Alan swapped their backstage clothes for suits, while Marcy slipped into an ultra sexy dress which had seemed perfect when she tried it on, but she was anxious it might be a little bit too suggestive. It was black and slinky, clinging to her curves, with some lace around the top of the shoulders.

She barely noticed the reaction of the other male members of the cast, but she saw Gray do a double take. He couldn't keep his eyes off her.

The dress had served its purpose.

"It's been a great week, hasn't it?" Revel said, managing to slip away from a crowd of admirers. She was openly drinking champagne but no one seemed to mind. "That's an absolutely amazing dress by the way." Revel herself was wearing one of Miss Adelaide's nightclub outfits: it was red satin and designed to look flashy on stage. She carried it off perfectly.

Both Revel and Gray were getting a lot of attention from people who wanted to meet them and tell them how much they had enjoyed their performances. Revel handled it all with supreme grace and Marcy had a sudden vision of her in a few years' time, signing autographs for fans. She wondered if they would still be friends once Revel inevitably became a star. She hoped so.

Gray seemed a little more uncomfortable with all the praise but was still polite to everyone. Dressed in his 1920s gangster outfit, Marcy could see why people used the term "matinée idol" to describe him. Both he and Revel managed to look convincingly as though they were from another era.

Brittanny Paige and Gretchen had bought tickets to the final show, having already seen it during the week. They tried to get into the party but thankfully were refused. Alan had drawn up a guest list and wouldn't yield. "Cast, crew and named friends and family only I'm afraid girls. Thanks for coming, and we look forward to your support next year."

Brittanny was scowling while craning her neck trying to see where Gray was. Little did she know he was deliberately avoiding her.

"Hey Revel, Marcy, you can get me in can't you?" Brittanny was so desperate she was even prepared to swallow her pride and beg.

"Sorry, I used up all my invitations," Revel said. "And Marcy too."

This wasn't the case at all but no way did they want Brittany and Gretchen hanging around. In fact Mrs Helberg had invited Marcy's parents but they had a prior engagement, which was a bit of a relief to Marcy. She was hoping that she might get the chance to speak with Gray and didn't want her parents observing her too closely.

Revel's grandmother wasn't a fan of late night events so she had stayed at home as well. The result was that both Marcy and Revel were much more free to let their hair down.

"Poor Brittanny, being shown the door yet again," Revel said. "It's just not her year, is it?" There were rumours that Brittanny's long-suffering boyfriend had finally dumped her. Marcy was surprised he'd put up with her for this long.

"I guess not. I really hope she doesn't sign up next year though." Marcy was looking forward to being involved in a future production but Brittanny's presence would take a lot of the fun out of it.

"She won't. I'll tell Mrs Helberg it's her or me," Revel said. Since Mrs Helberg had found out who Revel's mother was, she had become even more delighted with Revel. Her earlier hesitation when Revel had first joined the theatre group was long gone. There was no way she would risk losing her newly-discovered star.

Martin came up to them, Gray just behind him. "Sad that it's all over?"

"A little. But it's always that way, isn't it?" Revel said. "Anyway, we have the next production to look forward to."

"Will you be taking part in that?" he asked.

"If there's a role. It depends what show they choose," Revel told him. "How about you?"

"Probably. This one has been fun."

"What about you, Mr Grayson?" Revel asked. There was an expression in her eyes that Marcy couldn't quite interpret.

He smiled. "We'll see. It's a big time commitment."

Marcy hoped beyond hope he would agree to another production. She trusted in Mrs Helberg's unfailing ability to get anyone to do anything. She would simply push and push - just like with Marcy's mother - until people gave in. It was the path of least resistance.

A little later Revel and Martin had drifted off to separate groups and Marcy and Gray were left talking. They were supposed to avoid being one-on-one, she knew, but they were in a room full of people after all.

"You look beautiful," he said, his voice lowered so no one could hear. "I know I'm not supposed to say it, but you truly do."

"Thank you. You too." He did look incredibly hot. For a moment they both stood there and Marcy was sure he was thinking exactly what she was thinking. However they were in public and had to be careful.

"That dress makes it really hard for me to keep my resolve," Gray said.

"Should I take it off?" she asked.

"If we were alone I would take it off you myself."

From the look in his eyes he wasn't joking. Marcy shivered, longing for him to drag her backstage and release some of the tension that was building up between them. The thought of all those empty dressing rooms was tempting...

But also far too risky. If Mrs Helberg found out that she was involved with her teacher it would get straight back to her parents and there would be hell to pay. Even though they had liked him, they would hardly see him as appropriate boyfriend material. "Mom, Dad, I'm dating my teacher." They would probably send her to military college in Antarctica.

"So will you be signing up for another one?" he asked.

Will it make any difference to your decision if I do? Marcy wanted to know. Instead she said: "Most probably. I don't think Mrs Helberg would give me the choice of not doing so, what with living next door to us. What about you?"

"I don't think she's going to allow me to quit either."

Marcy felt a surge of happiness at this. It gave her something to look forward to in the New Year.

"Will you be in Springdale for the Christmas vacation?" Gray asked.

"Not all of it, I'm going to stay with a friend in New York," she said. Was it her imagination or did Gray look slightly disappointed, maybe even worried? "Addy, my friend since we were kids. She left Springdale last summer," she explained quickly.

There was definitely a hint of relief in his eyes. He had thought she might be staying with a boyfriend, she guessed. "Will you be here?" she asked him.

"I'll probably stay with family for the Christmas weekend, but I'll be here the rest of the time."

Marcy was glad to hear this. Maybe there was a chance she might bump into him in town, or at the café. The next rehearsals wouldn't start until January, after the school term started. Otherwise she wouldn't see him for several weeks. Long enough for him to get over her, to forget her.

42. End of term

For the rest of term Marcy buried herself in schoolwork and finishing off her play. The experience on stage and off during her time with the Springdale Players had been invaluable.

She had a much better idea now of how it should all fit together, and what would actually work in a performance and what might not.

Plus she had all the inspiration she needed - and more - for the love scenes. Rapunzel, or the character based on her, had become a living, breathing person. And as for the Prince, who Marcy had chosen not to name... well there was only one face that came to mind when she envisaged him.

As she wrote it, Marcy couldn't help remembering Revel's suggestion to do a musical version. Revel hadn't read it, of course, and initially Marcy had thought it could never work. But now as the scenes came to life in her mind and on the page, she could see where songs might fit in.

It would be a very different kind of show to the play she had imagined, and she certainly couldn't imagine lavishly choreographed whole cast numbers as in Guys and Dolls, but still. She already found herself writing lyrics for a ballad called "Song of the Tower".

"Are you still busy with your assignment?" Her mother was calling up to her. Marcy had got carried away writing and had been shut in her room for hours. It was already dinner time.

"I'm done, it's all good," Marcy called back. She saved the file and came downstairs.

Things with Gray were the same as ever. She had got used to the weird limbo of not-being with him, and waiting and hoping that there might be a chance again when school was finally over.

For his part he was very professional: friendly without singling her out, which made her look forward all the more to Mrs Helberg's next production when she might get to spend time with him in a more relaxed setting.

Sometimes she sat in class and marvelled that she had ever been with him. How all the other students had absolutely no clue that until a few weeks ago, she had been sleeping with their French teacher. Brittanny would implode with the knowledge, she thought.

Coming into the kitchen she discovered that Mrs Helberg was there.

"Cora's popped round for supper. Barry has an event at his club tonight," her mother said, referring to Mrs Helberg's husband. He was a pleasant man but worked long hours in the city and didn't share his wife's theatrical passion, so Marcy didn't much of him.

Marcy's father came in and they began the meal. As usual Mrs Helberg was full of conversation about this and that. She was so sociable, it must have been a bit of a drag having a husband who wasn't.

"You'll be joining us again next year, I hope Marcy?"

Marcy had expected this. She knew there was no escape, but she didn't mind.

"I'd be happy to. I really enjoyed being a part of things." This was true. Even without Gray being there, it would have been an interesting and rewarding experience.

"Len may take an acting role next time, so we may need more of your assistance with directing," Mrs Helberg said. "Though of course you may wish to act as well? After such a commendable performance understudying Sarah. I do thank you for that, dear, it got us all out of a difficult situation."

"I was happy to help," Marcy said. "But I'd love to take on more directing work, if that's possible."

"By all means. Our next task, of course, is to get your mother involved. There's always room for more."

Thankfully for Marcy her mother remained resolute against joining the Springdale Players. "I'm afraid I have so much on, Cora." Marcy really couldn't trust her mother being around her and Gray every week and not guessing that something was up. If Gray was going to be there of course.

Marcy fished. "Will most other people be back next year?"

"But of course! I already have roles in mind for our new young people, all three of them should be available," Mrs Helberg told Marcy, to her joy.

* * *

The last week came all too soon. Not for everyone else: all the other students couldn't wait for the vacation. But it was a mixed joy for Marcy. There was the trip to New York to look forward to and she was excited to see Addy.

"I've got the whole week planned out," Addy told her. "Every hour of every day is packed with all the things that you absolutely have to do in New York."

Marcy knew from long experience that Addy's plans would disintegrate from the get-go. She never stuck to a plan. The mood to do something totally different would grab her, and she would immediately switch what she was doing. You never got bored with Addy, that was for sure.

Revel and Marcy also planned to hang out over the Christmas break. Revel had seemed a little distant, Marcy thought, since the show. Not unfriendly, just maybe preoccupied in her work. After all it had been a big commitment, so like Marcy she possibly had some neglected assignments to catch up on.

She barely noticed Brittanny and her bitchy squad. It was as though they barely registered any more. Josh avoided her, his aggressive ardour had turned to a mix of embarrassment and resentment.

All in all it was a peaceful close to the semester. Marcy had also printed off her now-completed play, and after wrestling with some self doubt, gave it to Revel to read.

"Thanks, I'll start reading it tonight," Revel said.

"Really you don't have to. Just skim through if you want, Whenever you have time."

Revel laughed. "You're not really selling yourself, are you?"

"It's hard as I have no idea if it works or not. I mean I can see it in my head, but I don't know if I've translated that to the page, if you get me," Marcy said.

"If you haven't, you can always tweak it. I'm sure it's great."

Handing over the script to Revel felt a bit like handing over her baby. But Marcy had to be brave. If it really was terrible, she may as well be told so now.

* * *

Marcy had to say goodbye to Mr Grayson in the last French lesson. She lingered behind when her classmates left.

"I just wanted to say goodbye and happy holidays. And an early Merry Christmas," she told him.

"You too. I've really enjoyed having you in my French class," Mr Grayson said.

She couldn't stop herself. "Just your French class?"

He looked at her, and she could see the amusement in his eyes.

"And in theatre group as well."

He wasn't going to budge. This would have to do. But maybe she should try one last time.

"I didn't manage to bring you a present. So do you want a Christmas kiss instead?"

She could see the heat in his gaze at her words. For a moment he swayed towards her, and she was certain his lips would come down on hers, soft and sensuous, then firm and demanding as always.

"You know that I do, Marcy," Mr Grayson said, his voice lowered. "God only knows how much. But you also know that we are not going to cross that line, let alone on school grounds."

At least she had tried. And at least she knew he still felt the same. Right now she felt she couldn't care less if the whole of the staff of Springdale walked on them. Indeed it would actually be joyful to see Brittanny Paige's reaction to her making out with their French teacher.

But that was not the way to win this.

"I hope you have a happy Christmas anyway," she said, smiled at him and left.

She heard him say her name under his breath as she left - "Marcy…" - but she didn't turn around. If he could display such exceptional self-control, so could she.

43. New York

New York at Christmas time: the most magical place in the world. Marcy had secretly been hoping for snow and the heavens answered her prayers, with thick white flakes falling as she and her parents landed at JFK.

Everywhere sparkled with Christmas lights, the shop windows glowed with presents, everywhere seemed to be red and gold and garlanded with fragrant pine leaves. Even the plastic foliage seemed to have the aroma of Christmas trees.

As promised, Marcy and her parents took in a show on Broadway. It felt like coming home. This is absolutely where I want to be, Marcy thought. This is my future. One day I'm going to sit here and watch famous actors bring my own script to life.

The leading lady had a slight look of Revel about her, though Marcy personally thought that Revel, even if less experienced, was even more talented. She found her mother shared her opinion.

"I do think your friend Revel has a very bright future ahead of her," she said. "She's quite as good as any of the professional performers here. The young man who teaches you French as well, it surprises me he didn't choose a career on stage. All that talent in Springdale! No wonder Cora Helberg is over the moon."

The next day they shopped and had lunch with Addy and her mother. Even though Marcy and Addy Skyped or texted pretty much daily, they were still ecstatic to see one another. They had so much to share. Addy was desperate to know all the gory details about Marcy and Mr Grayson, which she felt Marcy had been reticent sharing over the internet.

They walked down Fifth Avenue while their mothers stopped for coffee, laden down with festive purchases. The nearby boutiques had price tags several zeroes too expensive for their budgets. "I can't believe you live here," Marcy said. "Just imagine if we could actually afford to buy all this stuff. It's so exactly like Sex in the City."

"It would be, if I was getting any," Addy said. "Unlike you."

"I'm not either. It's all over, remember," Marcy said, referring to her and Mr Grayson.

"On hold. That's not over."

Marcy desperately hoped so, but anything could happen between now and the next term, let alone now and the end of school next summer. She was particularly anxious about New Year's Eve as people always seemed to end up kissing and falling in love with strangers then. What if some beautiful woman happened to target Mr Grayson?

There was something a bit strange about Addy in New York, Marcy felt. From time to time got the sense that Addy was hiding something from her. But what?

"Is there something not telling me?" she asked her.

"No, why?" Addy was the world's worst liar and looked defensive.

So there was something. "You know you can tell me anything," Marcy said.

Addy shrugged. "It's nothing. Honestly."

"I mean it. Like if you got pregnant, you know I'm always here for you."

Addy burst into shocked laughter. "I love how that's what you imagine I must be getting up to! I did take Biology you know."

"And you got the lowest grade of all your classes."

"That's because I had the worst lab partner," Addy said.

Marcy was mock indignant. "I was your lab partner."

"I know. It was your job to keep me from being distracted by Cody Marsh. And you failed, every class. What's he up to these days?"

"Still playing football, still a moron. Still dating Minette McCarroll."

Addy made a mock vomiting noise. "I seriously can't wait until we finally get to college. Honestly the guys in my New York high school are barely any better. I think I've outgrown them. I need an older guy, like you have."

"I don't have one at all. Not any more," Marcy told her.

"Yeah, well you never know what the future holds," Addy said. Marcy assumed she was imagining getting hit on by hot seniors at college. Or even hitting up hot professors herself. She would have too keep an eye on Addy if they both ended up at NYU.

* * *

Marcy's parents flew home the next day, while she stayed behind to spend the week with Addy. As expected Addy's precision organised, activity packed timetable rapidly disintegrated, though they tried to do the main things on her list. Such as the Empire State Building and the Statue of Liberty. Marcy felt like a total tourist but it was fun seeing America's icons.

They met up with some of Addy's new friends in New York who seemed like nice people. They weren't quite as intimidatingly Gossip Girl as Marcy had feared.

One of the guys was clearly interested in Marcy but while he was attractive, she just didn't return his regard.

Towards the end of the week there was a Christmas party at someone's house. Addy was making a big deal out of going, and Marcy got the impression there was a guy she liked there. She still felt Addy was being a little secretive.

Addy had received a couple of mobile calls allegedly from her mother, but she had seemed oddly abrupt when speaking. Plus there was a text message that she had immediately deleted.

Marcy would never have gone through her friend's phone, but she was a little sad that Addy couldn't confide in her. There was obviously something going on with her love life or this mystery guy she liked.

They were watching TV when it suddenly struck Marcy that maybe Addy wasn't seeing a guy after all. Maybe it was something quite different. She was pretty sure that Addy wasn't seeing a married man or similar, because she was sure she would have confessed it. After all, it was about the same level as dating your teacher, in terms of being forbidden. And at least you couldn't go to jail for adultery.

That meant it had to be something quite different.

The other thing.

And if so, Marcy really wasn't sure how to broach it.

"Addy, you know that I would be totally cool if you, you know..."

"Huh?"

"I mean if you were ever to tell me that you were... you know what I mean," Marcy said. She was making a real mess of this.

"I honestly have no idea what you mean."

How to phrase this? She changed tactic. "Emilie, that Canadian girl in my AP French class, turned out to be really cool."

"Oh?" Addy stuffed a handful of popcorn into her mouth. She didn't seem hugely interested.

"Brittanny was always very mean to her of course, because you know... But that really doesn't matter. I mean it doesn't change who she is."

"Who she is? Who is she, then?"

Marcy didn't feel like she was making any progress.

"You know, that she doesn't date guys. I mean she's still really nice. It makes no difference."

Addy turned to her, frowning. "Marcy, why are we having this totally random conversation about Emilie the lesbian? Is there something you want to tell me?"

"No! I thought maybe there was something you wanted to tell me," Marcy said.

Light was dawning. "You mean you think I'm struggling to come out and tell you I'm gay?" Addy said. She started laughing.

"So you're not then?" Marcy asked.

"God no. I mean life would be a hell of a lot simpler if I never again had to deal with guys in that way, but I can't change my wiring. Why on earth did you suddenly think I was a lesbian? Is it because my aunt's gay?" Addy clearly found it hilarious.

Marcy was really embarrassed now. She was glad Addy saw the funny side, but she was still no closer to solving the mystery. If there was one. Maybe she was just being really paranoid?

"I don't know. I just worried that if you were, you couldn't confide in me."

"Well, I'm not. However I did once look at a picture of Angelina Jolie, and decide that if I ever had to be, I'd probably go for her. Is that confession enough? And if you want more, I had a crush on that Mexican guy who was my chemistry lab partner last year, before I realised he was gay. And finally, I kissed Jayden Price - or rather he kissed me but I didn't stop him - at the Easter fair."

Marcy was shocked by nearly all of this. "I can't believe you never told me any of this. And does Brittanny know? And how did you not know Ricardo was gay? He had a photo of his boyfriend in his locker all year."

"You're hardly one to talk about gaydar, practically casting me on The L Word," Addy said. "And no, Brittanny didn't know, but I'm totally happy for you to tell her sometime. So long as you record her reaction on your phone when you do so."

44. Christmas party

Addy insisted on going shopping and both of them getting new dresses for the Christmas party.

Marcy protested that she really couldn't afford it, but Addy waved a credit card at her.

"Mom got a huge bonus and it's our Christmas present. One of the advantages of this job move was a tonne more money, so let's go for it."

Marcy felt awkward letting Addy's mom buy her clothes, but Addy's mom assured her it was okay. "It will be much more fun for Addy if you're both shopping for new outfits. Just enjoy yourselves!"

"You really do have the coolest mom ever," Marcy said as they hit Fifth Avenue once again.

Marcy found the perfect dress in one of the first boutiques they visited. It was snow white and sleeveless, with a skater skirt and a ruched, banded waist. There were scattering of crystals in a snowflake pattern over the bodice. It was also an exact fit.

"You have to get that, it's perfect," Addy told her. "You look like a Christmas angel."

But Marcy felt she couldn't buy the first dress she saw, not straight away. So she then spent the rest of the day looking at other clothes, agonising over whether to get it or not, and fearing that someone else may have already bought it.

Addy could read her mind. "Just go back and buy it. You haven't found anything else close to that."

At the back of Marcy's thoughts, which Addy didn't manage to mind read, was the feeling that the dress might be kind of wasted if Gray wasn't there to see it. She remembered his reaction to her outfit at the closing night party, and felt warm all over. And sad, thinking of how far away he was, and that they couldn't be together. For ages, if ever.

Addy herself was trying to decide between three different dresses. Being blonde, she could wear Christmas holly red, which Marcy was encouraging her towards. "The black is elegant, but you have so much black in your wardrobe. It won't stand out. And the green is nice, but it's a bit Christmas-only, isn't it? The red you could wear for New Year's and Valentines. Or any time, really."

So they went for the white and the red.

"You absolutely have to have new underwear. You can't wear a dress with old stuff. Let's go to Victoria's Secret."

Marcy was certainly going through her holiday money quickly. Fortunately there was a sale on. And Addy was right, if you were going to wear a brand new dress, it felt nice to have brand new lingerie to match.

"Now the hair salon," Addy announced.

"Are you serious? It's not like we're going to prom," Marcy said.

"Trust me, New York is dressy."

Marcy went with it. After all, it was always nice to get pampered. She just hoped the make up artist was actually an artist, and not the type to turn her into a painted clown.

Luckily the stylist was very competent. She did something amazing with Marcy's hair: twisting it up on her head and allowing a few auburn tendrils to cascade down.

"Your neck looks super long and swan-like with that style," Addy said. "Seriously you look like a model, except you're not tall enough."

Trust Addy to bring her back down to earth. "Thanks."

"You know what I mean," Addy said. "You have to be six foot or whatever."

Addy looked wonderful too; Marcy could easily imagine her starring in some TV show. Not that Addy had any desire to go into showbusiness, but in her new dress with her hair styled into glossy waves, she looked the part.

For her own part Marcy felt kind of like she was all dressed up with nowhere to go. She felt a little guilty about thinking this, as Addy was so excited about the evening.

Of course they did have somewhere to go, but since she wasn't interested in attracting attention to herself, she wondered whether all this effort was worth it. It would have been so much more cool if it was Addy and her getting ready for the Springdale prom, as they had always dreamed of, and then getting picked up by whichever hot guys they were dating.

Marcy could only imagine showing up on the arm of a teacher. The scandal it would have caused was almost funny. She could just imagine the principal's eyes bulging out of his head with shock and outrage.

* * *

Addy had been right about the party. It was held in a penthouse in Manhattan and was full of super glamorous people. Even if they were only high school age - though at least half looked as though they were college students - they clearly had generous allowances.

Addy introduced her to Taleisha, whose party it was. She was in Addy's high school class and looked like a supermodel.

"So glad to meet you, Addy has told us so much about you. I love your dress!" she greeted Marcy.

"Yours too, thank you for inviting us." Marcy saw Addy and Taleisha exchange a glance but wasn't sure what it was about.

There was so many new names and faces but everyone was very friendly.

Compared to parties back home, it was very out there. There was catered food and a bartender, mixing cocktails all night. A slushie machine with bright red and green festive-themed drinks. An actual live DJ. Even a bubble machine.

"Is this normal for parties here?" Marcy asked Addy.

"They're not all quite like this. Taleisha's parents are super rich, her father's some big shot on Wall Street. She's really nice though."

Several cute guys were giving Marcy the eye, but she wasn't in the mood for flirting.

"You should see the view from the roof," Addy said. "You can see the whole city."

They went up to the roof. It wasn't just the regular old roof that Marcy expected, there was a hot tub filled with people and a guy jumped in, fully clothed, as they passed by. There was an actual roof garden with colour-changing LED lights all around.

The view was spectacular. "Imagine living here!" Marcy said.

"You will, one day. Once you're a famous playwright and I'm doing whatever the hell I'm doing and living with you rent free, because I'm your best friend and when you find out your Christmas present, you're going to love me forever."

Addy had had a few drinks but not enough to be beaming at her quite like this, Marcy thought. What was she up to?

Just then she saw Addy grin in recognition at someone behind them.

"And here's your present now!" Addy said.

Marcy turned around.

It was Gray.

45. Christmas surprise

Gray stood there, smiling at her.

And right behind him was Revel.

Marcy was too confused to speak. "What…?"

She turned to see Addy grinning her head off at Revel. Light started to dawn. "This is some huge set up, isn't it?"

"Something like that," Addy told her. "I'll leave you guys to talk."

She went of with Revel, leaving Marcy alone with Gray.

They stood there for a moment, neither sure what to say.

"You look absolutely beautiful," Gray told her.

"Thank you. So… what are you doing in New York?" And what on earth was Revel doing there?

"There's so much to tell you. But until today I didn't know if any of it was going to happen. Let's sit down."

They sat down on a couple of chairs. You could see all the lights of New York spread out below, past the tops of other buildings.

"I probably should be letting Revel explain all this," Gray said. "Since it's really thanks to her that I'm here. To cut a really long story short, some old friend of her parents turns out to be a big time Broadway producer."

Given who Revel's mother was, this wasn't necessarily a big surprise, Marcy thought. Coming from a family like that there would be showbiz connection.

"Anyway, she got this guy down to Springdale to watch the show. Afterwards he called me up and wanted me to audition for some show he's producing. It's off-Broadway, but it's still a pretty major production. I thought it was a wind-up at first, but he was legit. So I flew up to New York, not really knowing what the hell I was doing, and it all went well, and..."

He stopped, and took Marcy's hand. With his other hand he brushed a tendril behind her ear. Then slowly he moved towards her - she sat there spellbound - and his lips were on hers.

It was sensual, sweet, exploring. It was the kiss she had longed for for weeks. It deepened as her lips opened for him, and his tongue entwined with hers.

Marcy breathed in his familiar scent. Her brain tried to connect this gorgeous guy kissing her on a rooftop with the man standing at the front of her French classes. They had been "just friends" for so long now that she had started to increasingly see him primarily as her teacher, so the fact that he was kissing her now was an extra thrill.

She figured no one here in New York knew who he was, it wasn't like Brittanny or Mimi was about to pop out of the hot tub...

Gray broke off. "And that's the last kiss I'm going to give you..."

For a split second Marcy's heart lurched in a horrible way.

"...as your teacher. Because as of next week, I'm resigning. The bad news is that I do have to move up here to New York again. The good news is that - if you think you still want me - there's nothing to stop us being together any more."

Marcy felt herself flood with relief. Gray still wanted her! After all that time, even with some huge and exciting opportunity, he wanted to be with her.

Her smile answered him before her words. "What do you think?"

He kissed her again. "Technically that's another teacher kiss, but at least I can't get fired now." He looked over at the hot tub. "If I had one wish it would be to empty that of people and take you in it right now. It's been way too long."

Marcy figured he probably couldn't see her blush given the dim light. She hoped not anyway.

"So Revel set this all up, with Addy as well?"

"It seems so."

No wonder Addy had been acting all suspicious, she was the world's most hopeless person at keeping a secret. And there was Marcy thinking that Addy was dating a girl or married man!

"Where are you staying in New York?" she asked.

"I'm in a hotel. Revel's friends - whom she's staying with - offered me a bed, but her uncle paid for a hotel. It's pretty nice. In fact I was wondering..."

"Mm hmm?" Marcy had a suspicion where this was going.

"...if Addy can spare you for a night, maybe you'd like to drop by?"

She could see the heat in his eyes, and felt herself grow warm.

"I think that could be arranged."

"I'm here until the day after tomorrow," Gray said. "I have to sign some contracts and other things on Monday and see an agent. Then it's back to Springdale, and packing up my stuff once again. Everything is just happening very quickly. The role I got, they had someone else lined up for it but he dropped out, which was good luck for me I guess."

"You don't mind giving up teaching?" Marcy asked, hoping it wasn't a stupid question.

"Yes and no. I love it - particularly when I have students like you - " there was a gleam in his eye " - but the money is seriously good for this acting thing. And there's nothing to stop me returning to teaching if this doesn't work out. It was too good an opportunity to pass up. It's not where I imagined my career would be heading, but sometimes you have to roll with it."

He paused, and looked serious. He looked directly at Marcy, his gaze searing into hers.

"And sometimes you need to roll with someone. To have someone by your side."

Marcy stomach flipped. He'd never looked at her quite like this before.

"What I'm trying to say is, I want to be with you Marcy."

His next words took her breath away.

"I love you."

After all this time, all the ups and downs they had had, the constant on-off, on-off, Marcy could hardly believe she was sitting here with Grey now, literally on top of the world, with him telling her that he loved her.

"Really?"

"More than anything. I've wanted to tell you for ages. That was why it was so hard, not being able to see you. You were never just a casual thing for me, Marcy."

This time she went to kiss him. Pressed her lips against the warm, firm shape of his lips.

"I love you too."

She saw the joy leap in his eyes. "It's okay if you don't, yet," he said. "I know this is a huge amount to spring on you. But if you think you could feel the same way, one day, then that's enough."

Marcy had to hide a smile. "Gray, I love you. I've loved you for ages. I never knew if you felt the same way."

"Well I did. I'm completely in love with you, Marcy. I've never felt like this about anyone before."

Then she was in his arms, and all the pain from the separation of the last weeks - all the doubt, the anxiety, the missing him - it all melted away.

"It may still not be easy," Gray said. "We'll have the distance - at least for a few months before you start college, if you still plan to study in New York. And there's your parents to deal with."

Oh god. Her parents. If only they had never met him as her French teacher, she could probably have kept the knowledge from them indefinitely. Now it was going to be something of a bridge to cross.

"I want to do this properly," Gray continued. "No more sneaking around, hiding out. There's nothing to stop us dating, we're both adults, and I want your parents to know that I plan to take care of you."

Take care of her… it made it sound really long term. Like she was truly, completely his. Openly and officially. Gray's girl.

46. Revel's revelation

Marcy could only imagine the reaction of people back in Springdale. Brittanny actually might implode. Marcy felt kind of childish for imagining her reaction, but it was going to be something to witness. Addy would probably insist she recorded it.

Her parents were a whole other issue though. She was already bracing herself for that one.

Marcy, Revel and Addy met the next morning for coffee. Marcy had stayed the previous night at Gray's, partly at Addy's insistence. "You're only going to be thinking of him all night so you may as well be him," she had said.

It had been one of the most incredible nights ever. Actually making love with the guy you were completely in love with, with no more obstacles or problems, was amazing. Marcy thrilled every time Gray said those three words to her as well.

"This will pale by comparison to Gray, I'm sure," Revel began, addressing Marcy, "but I have a confession of my own. I read your play, and it was amazing. Beyond anything I thought it would be. Anyway, I knew you would never take my word for it so I took the liberty of sending a copy to a composer friend of mine. He loved it, he wants to score it. He actually thinks it could be produced, maybe with a few changes."

Marcy was blown away. She was part over the moon with excitement, and part totally embarrassed that the first thing she had ever written had been shown, unedited, to a professional.

"Of course it's totally up to you," Revel continued, since Marcy was still lost for words. "And he's just a music guy, so any lyrics you want, that's all yours to write. Just make sure you give the witch an amazing solo, because that's my role one day."

"You wouldn't want to play Rapunzel?" Marcy asked, having already imagined Revel in a long wig. There was no reason Rapunzel needed to be blonde anyway.

"No. Character roles are more me. And the witch - as you've written her - is just awesome."

"I guess Mrs Helberg will have to wear the wig then," Marcy said.

Revel laughed. "I think it's going to be a little beyond her league, once it gets cast."

"I still get to come to the opening night party though right?" Addy asked. "And hang out with all your future celebrity friends?" She was only half joking. They were all swept up with the excitement of it all, and anything seemed possible.

Marcy still hadn't figured out how Revel had planned everything, or involved Addy.

"I sneaked a look in your phone when you went to the bathroom," Revel told her. "Addy's number was top of your favourites, then I went from there."

Addy glowed. "I'm glad I wasn't kicked off the top of the list for Gray."

Hearing his name made Marcy's heart flip all over again. "So what do you think of him?" She hadn't yet had a chance to ask Addy this, after Addy had met him for the first time the previous evening.

"So unbelievably hot. The photos really don't do him justice. I'm just kicking myself I had to move to New York just when a guy like that arrives in Springdale. He'd not even my type but I so would. If it wasn't for the fact he literally doesn't look at any girl but you, Marcy."

Marcy was loving all of this. She could quite happily have talked about nothing but Gray all day, but she knew it would bore her friends to tears. Just a little more conversation wouldn't hurt though.

"He wants me to tell my parents and everything. They've met him and they liked him, but obviously just as my teacher," she said.

"My mom wasn't fazed by it, if that's any help," Addy said. "She figures we're all eighteen, we can do what we like."

Maybe Addy's mom could adopt her, Marcy thought.

"It'll be cool," Revel said. "Once they get used to it they'll be relieved you've got a nice, responsible guy in New York, not some gang member. That's what you should tell them, anyway."

* * *

The last days of Marcy's trip to New York passed all too quickly. Revel flew back the next day, then Gray. The fact that she would be flying back to see him in Springdale was some consolation.

But she really wished she could spend more time with Addy. She was even more resolved that they both had to end up going to college in New York somehow. Things just weren't as fun without Addy around, being her usual wonderfully generous, crazy self.

"You'll be back before you know it," Addy said. "Gray won't want to wait until next September, you can bet he'll be flying you up long before then."

Gray had already said something to this effect, which had reassured Marcy. She simply couldn't cope with another Gray-drought after all they had been through. She wanted to be with him.

"Just make sure you come and visit me when you are here, or I'll never forgive you," Addy told her. "And if you ever have a row or something, you're always welcome to stay. Or just come and stay anyway."

Marcy promised that she would. She wasn't the kind of person to ditch her girl friends just because she was dating someone. Even if that someone was the hottest guy in the world.

"I'll take you up on that. If you bake me brownies."

"If you eat at least half of them, then yes I will."

* * *

Finally it was Marcy's own time to fly back. It was always horrible leaving a place, even though she was excited to see Gray again.

"Just remember to record Bitchany Paige for me when you tell her about you and Gray. Though I'll probably hear her shrieks of rage all the way up here in New York anyway," Addy said.

212

"I'll do what I can. I'll give you a detailed account, whatever happens."

"You're the best!"

Addy's mom drove Marcy to the airport and she and Addy hugged and said a tearful farewell.

As Marcy walked through security her phone beeped. She panicked momentarily, thinking it was Addy and she must have forgotten something in New York. Then felt a rush of joy when she saw the message.

Can't wait to see you. Have a safe flight.

It was so great that she no longer had to hide his texts. And "G" was once against restored to "Gray" in her contacts.

You too x

Marcy had kept every single one of Gray's texts. Even the awful ones from the time when he was trying not to be with her. They were all part of the story of their relationship, and she treasured them.

Now, thinking happy thoughts of Gray as she settled back in her seat and watched the lights of New York disappear, she started to brace herself for telling her parents. They weren't unreasonable people, they would have to come around somehow.

47. Telling parents

"Mom! Dad! I'm dating my high school French teacher!"
This might have been the simplest approach, but Marcy felt it wouldn't be the best one to take.

Essentially though that was what she was going to have to tell them. There was no real way to break this gently, but she did her best. She thought it would help to start with her mom rather than face an entire family conference.

They were in the kitchen and Marcy was helping her mother bake some Christmas treats. Every year she took a basket of pies, cookies and other goodies to an old people's home in Springdale.

"I kind of have something to tell you," Marcy said. Seeing the look on her mother's face she quickly continued: "I'm not pregnant, nothing like that. Or in trouble with the police or anything."

Her mother laughed. "I somewhat doubted you would be."

"I'm seeing someone. He's in Springdale right now, but he's moving to New York soon."

"Well, if you end up going to NYU, you two won't have to be long distance for too many months," her mother said, thinking that this was the issue. "So, do we get to meet him before he goes?"

Marcy took a deep breath. "You've already met him as it happens. He's at - he was at - Springdale High."

"Oh? You don't meant Josh, surely? I thought you were long over him. I can't think which other boys we've met."

"That's the thing. You remember Guys & Dolls?"

"I've hardly forgotten it, Marcy, it was only a few weeks ago." Her mother put another tray of cookies into the oven.

"You remember the guy who played Sky?"

"Opposite Cora Helberg? That nice young man who teaches French at Springdale?"

Marcy couldn't meet her mother's eyes. She tried to focus on some silver balls she was sticking on snowman cookies.

"He won't be teaching French any more. He got a job acting in New York. Some producer guy saw him and auditioned him."

Marcy's mom looked momentarily confused. "That's very exciting for him. But I don't see…"

And then she did see. And went slightly pale.

"Marcy, you don't mean…? Not your teacher, surely?"

"He's not my teacher any more though. And he's only a couple of years older than me." Six was kind of "a couple", she figured. In terms of significance anyway. "And you said you thought he was really nice."

"Nice as your teacher, Marcy! Not as your boyfriend! How on earth did this happen?"

Marcy had decided it was best to edit this part of the story slightly. In years to come, if she was still with Gray, or if she was forty or something and twice divorced with three kids and her mother no longer cared about this stuff, she could reveal the exact truth.

"We just became friends through theatre. And then I bumped into him in a party in New York. And he told me he wasn't going to be at Springdale any more. And then you know, mistletoe and everything…"

If Marcy's mother guessed that something had happened before, or that it was somewhat too much of a coincidence for Marcy to have randomly bumped into her teacher at the same New York party, she perhaps decided it was wiser to say nothing.

"I don't know what your father will say. Still, I suppose you are eighteen. At least if he's a long way away in New York it will give you both time to think about things and have some perspective."

Marcy flung her arms around her mom, sending up a cloud of powdered sugar.

"Thank you for not being mad! Honesty you will like him even more when you meet him again. He's really kind and responsible."

And totally sexy and hot and a brilliant kisser, but Marcy figured her mother didn't need to be acquainted with that side of him.

* * *

Later that week Gray came round for dinner. Marcy's mother had insisted. "If you're dating him and it's serious enough that you plan to keep seeing him when he leaves for New York, then I think we should meet him, Marcy."

This wasn't the real reason of course. The real reason was that Marcy's mother was still freaked out that Marcy was dating her former teacher, and wanted a closer look at him. To check he wasn't some kind of predator.

"I hope you're ready for this," Marcy told Gray in a hushed voice when she opened the door to him. "My father hasn't got his gun out but he may as well have."

"Your father has a gun?" Gray was mock alarmed.

"No, actually. He's not really the gun type. He's pretty cool, but they're both a bit on edge."

Fortunately Gray was just as charming, polite and open as when Marcy's parents had met him at the photography exhibition.

The meal started off with some tension, as everyone was careful what to say. The million dollar question was of course: "did anything happen while you were Marcy's teacher?" but fortunately neither of her parents asked it.

Instead they decided to take things from the present situation and see how they felt about Gray for themselves. As it turned out, they liked him very much.

"I just hope you'll both take things slowly," her mom said when they were in the kitchen preparing to take the dessert course out. "He does seem to be a very nice young man but he is a lot older than you. He may have expectations that you're not ready for."

Marcy assumed her mother meant sex and wanted to die of embarrassment.

"And I don't mean sleeping together," Marcy's mother continued, to Marcy's surprise. "I mean expectations about a more serious relationship. You need to think about what you're ready for. He's already graduated college, he's underway with his career. Don't be rushed, however much you like him. If he really likes you, he'll wait until you're ready."

Marcy hugged her mom. "I'm so glad you don't hate him."

"We could hardly hate him, Marcy. We raised you with sound judgement, I hope, so I wouldn't expect you to make terrible choices about whom you date. I just wish you were a little older, or he was a little less serious."

"Serious?"

"About you," her mother explained. "You can tell from how he looks at you. He's what we'd call a keeper in my day. But you're far too young to be thinking about anything like that."

Not according to Great Aunt Esme, Marcy thought. She really should introduce her to Gray. She had a feeling he would be exactly Esme's type.

Marcy hoped Gray's ears hadn't been burning too much when she arrived back at the table. But everything seemed fine. He'd been holding a conversation with Marcy's father about classic cinema. Marcy's father wasn't really a buff, but had had a passion for John Wayne films in his youth. It turned out that Grey liked them too. Marcy was just relieved they'd managed to bond over something.

Her parents stayed tactfully out of sight when Marcy said goodbye to Gray at the door. She was seeing him again the next day, he was taking her on a surprise date. They both would have loved to spend the night together but for her parents' sake it was best to show they were taking things carefully.

"Your parents are great, I'm glad I got to meet them properly. Thank you for having me over."

"Thank you for coming," Marcy said.

He kissed her. Their breath was frosting in the wintry December air.

"Sleep well. I love you."

"I love you too."

"Until tomorrow. Good night." He left, and Marcy started counting the hours until their date the next day.

48. The big reveal

There are great days and there are legendary days. And then there are the days that your bitterest enemy - the meanest girl in school who has done everything in her power to make your life a misery - finds out that you have the one thing she wants.

A lesser person might have gloated. But Marcy was so buoyed up with happiness and love for Gray that she even managed to feel sympathy for Brittanny Paige. After all, she was going to look like something of a fool.

Marcy hadn't been sure how she was going to let it come out at Springdale High that she was now dating their former French teacher. She knew that some girls - out of jealousy - would probably call her a slut. But with just half a year left until they all graduated, who really cared?

She now felt like Revel did about school, that it was simply something to get through and not overly stress about. In the grand course of your entire life, high school was pretty negligible.

As it turned out, Marcy wasn't the one who told Brittanny. She didn't have to.

In the short time left for the vacation, before Gray had to leave for New York again, he insisted on spending as much time with Marcy as possible. "I'm not wasting a single moment, god knows we've both waited long enough for this."

This included, with a gleam in his eye, suggesting the two of them go for a pizza at the restaurant Minette McCarroll worked at, on the last night before school started.

"Are you sure?" Marcy asked. Minette's friends often congregated in there as she gave them discounts.

"Nothing to lose," Gray said. "And I feel like pizza."

So strangely nervous, and feeling like This Was It, Marcy accompanied him to the pizza parlour.

Minette was indeed working there that evening and ushered them to a table with a hostile and suspicious glare on her face. "I thought your theatre thing was over?" she said to Marcy.

"It is, for now," Marcy said, ignoring Minette's obvious curiosity.

She and Gray ordered drinks. They were talking about nothing much in particular, just laughing and enjoying being together, when he brushed a strand of hair back from her face. Then his face fell serious and he leant over and dropped a kiss on Marcy's lips.

As ever she felt her stomach flip at his touch.

Then there was an almighty crash.

What the...?

Minette had witnessed the kiss, and had managed to drop an entire tray of drinks.

Marcy wanted to laugh but she felt bad for Minette, and tried to help her pick up some of the tumblers. Fortunately nothing had broken as the pizza place used plastic drink containers, though there were ice cubes and Coke sprayed everywhere.

After that Minette spent the entire evening casting Marcy and Gray sidelong glances, burning to know what was going on. She must be dying to call Brittanny, Marcy thought. How great to be a fly on the wall for that one.

* * *

Brittanny didn't even bother being subtle when she saw Marcy the next morning at school.

She accosted her by the lockers.

"Did you go out with Mr Grayson last night? Don't deny it, you were seen together."

"Why would I deny it?" Marcy asked.

Brittanny frowned. "Was this something to do with your theatre group?"

"No, just a meal. Rehearsals for the next production don't start for a couple of weeks."

"So let me get this straight. You were out last night, having a pizza with our French teacher, and he... you...."

"...we what?" Marcy was beginning to enjoy herself.

"Mimi claims she saw..." Brittanny couldn't bring herself to say it. She was pressing her lips together in a tight line.

"...saw, what? Us sharing a table? Us having a pizza? Us leaving together?" Marcy played dumb. She knew exactly what Brittanny wanted to ask. She could tell that Brittany was dying for it to be a lie.

"Mimi says she saw Mr Grayson kiss you."

"So?"

Marcy's nonchalance infuriated Brittanny. "So what the fuck is going on?" she asked.

Marcy decided to ignore this, and was aided in her strategy by the arrival of Revel. "Hey, happy new term. What have we got first period?"

"Chemistry," Marcy told Revel with a groan. "Not a great start to the week."

"No, not really," Revel agreed.

"Excuse me," Brittanny said, trying to push her way back in as Marcy stashed some folders in her locker and closed it. "Marcy and I were having a conversation."

"Were we?" Marcy asked, with an amused glance at Revel.

Revel grinned. "Don't let me stop you." She made no move to leave.

Gretchen had also come up by that point. "So is it true?" she asked Brittanny. "What Mimi claims she saw?"

Brittanny swore. "I'm trying to talk to Marcy."

"Is this any of your business?" Revel asked Brittanny.

Brittanny's mouth hung open. She was so used to being queen of Springdale and having knowledge of everything that to be challenged by Revel Holmes was a huge indignity.

"I don't think it is, is it Brittanny?" Marcy said, and turned her back on the bitchy squad. She and Revel left for class.

"Let her sweat it out until recess," Revel said. "She'll get madder and madder and it will be more fun."

* * *

Revel was crunching an apple and Marcy was enjoying some rare winter sunshine when Brittanny stomped by.

"So what's going on? Why were you having a meal with Mr Grayson?"

Marcy realised it was time to put Brittanny out of her misery. "Gray and I were on a date."

"Gray?! A date?! What the hell, he's our teacher!"

"Not any more," Revel interrupted. "He's quit."

"Quit?" Brittanny was horrified and furious at this. She still had her own massive crush on their French teacher.

"Yes, he's going to New York to act," Revel told her. "He got a role on Broadway."

This was a slight exaggeration, Marcy thought, since the production was off-Broadway. But it more or less amounted to the same thing. Besides, she was sure that Gray's star was going to climb. Revel and her producer friend were both convinced of it.

"What's that got to do with Marcy?" Brittanny asked.

Revel rolled her eyes. "You're a bit slow on the uptake, aren't you? Marcy and Gray - Mr Grayson to you - are dating. And have been for some time."

"Is this true?" Brittanny demanded.

Marcy was feeling a little bit sorry for Brittanny. She was making such an idiot of herself, storming about and getting angry at something that truly didn't concern her at all.

"Yes, it's true," she said. "We couldn't date while he was still at Springdale - " she crossed her fingers behind her back given this was something of an untruth " - but now he's quit we can do what we like."

"I suppose this getting cosy all happened at your stupid theatre group?"

"The stupid theatre group you wanted to join," Revel reminded her.

Brittanny refused to respond to this and continued her attack on Marcy. "So it wasn't about acting at all, it was about sucking up to Mr Grayson?"

"Actually if you must know, Gray and I became friends last vacation. Long before theatre group, and before he even started teaching at Springdale."

Brittanny was losing and losing. She tried one last threat. "Do your parents know?"

"Yes. They like him. He came around for dinner the other night."

"I just can't believe this," Brittanny was saying. "It makes absolutely no sense at all. I'm only humouring you that I believe you because of what Mimi says she saw. I can't imagine why he would even look twice at someone like you."

Revel finished her apple. "Believe what you like, Brittanny, as I said earlier it isn't really any of your business, is it?" She got up and left for the water cooler, leaving Marcy alone with Brittanny.

Marcy tried to be nice. "You know, Brittanny, there's only a few months of high school left. All this bitching and cliqueiness that you put on, what's the point? Why don't you just drop it and try to be pleasant? You have nothing to gain by being like you're being, whether you believe me or not. Gray - Mr Grayson - is no longer at Springdale, he is moving to New York, and we are dating. If you want to convince yourself that's a lie and insult me, that's up to you."

Then she got up herself and headed back to the next period.

Whatever happened with Brittanny now, Marcy had won, though she'd never really wanted a battle in the first place. She was genuinely sad that their final year of high school had to contain so much spite and bitterness.

But still, it all paled into insignificance when she thought of Gray. And not forgetting her wonderful friendships with Revel and Addy.

Really, life couldn't be better. A few months ago Marcy felt like her world was ending, and now everything was just beginning.

49. Together

Gray was amused when Marcy told him about Brittanny Paige's shock and outrage. It was their last night together before he left for New York and they were having dinner.

It was in the same restaurant as their very first date. Gray had managed to book the exact same table, and have flowers on the table for when they arrived.

It was perfect. He was perfect.

Marcy could hardly believe how lucky she was to be with him. Just the prospect of spending the next few months apart from him made her nervous.

"You'd better not forget me by July," he told her. "I know it's half a year away, but I will visit and I will fly you up. If you want to to come and stay with me."

"What do you think?" Her smile was answer enough. "Besides, I'll have Aunt Esme to deal with if I try and forget you."

Gray had visited Marcy's Great Aunt Esme, who was now completely enamoured of him. Marcy had been terribly embarrassed when they visited her, because she had treated Gray as though he and Marcy were practically engaged. Esme had also warned Marcy with disinheritance if she "ever managed to lose such a lovely young man".

"I'm glad I won her approval," Gray said.

"She practically wanted to adopt you," Marcy told him.

"Well, maybe I'll be her great nephew for real one day." Gray cast a glance at Marcy who blushed. She was sure he couldn't really mean what it sounded like, but it made her insides all warm to think of it.

She had better change the subject before she melted into a puddle of pink hearts and flowers. Fortunately at that moment the waiter came to take their orders which was a useful distraction.

After they had chosen, the conversation turned to New York and Gray's accommodation there. He was being put up temporarily in a serviced apartment before finding his own place.

"So you're starting rehearsals straight away?" she asked.

"Pretty much. I guess it's better to be thrown in the deep end and get it over with."

Marcy realised that Gray was actually a little apprehensive about the move. He always seemed so in command of everything.

"You'll be brilliant. I mean Revel thinks so anyway, and she knows this stuff."

Gray laughed. "Well if it doesn't work out, I think I may have burned my bridges with teaching at Springdale High. Now everyone knows about you and me. It doesn't exactly look great for a teacher, dating a student. Even an ex-student."

"Do you mind?" Marcy felt bad about causing problems for him.

"No, not at all. I love teaching, but students like Brittanny are a headache. Students like you, on the other hand…"

"…I'm not sure how far your teaching career would progress if you made dating your students a habit," Marcy said.

"Trust me, you are a one off. I did everything I could to try and stop feeling what I felt for you. That first day when I saw you in class and realised you weren't a college student, it was the worst day of my life," Gray told her.

"I'm sorry," Marcy said. "I know how mad you must have been."

"Mad? Well, maybe a little. No, the main thing was disappointment. Because I'd just met this girl who made me feel on top of the world, and suddenly she was out of reach."

Marcy never got tired of hearing how Gray felt about her. "On top of the world?"

"I think I probably fell in love with you on the lake, if you want a confession," Gray said. "Though I didn't realise it until later on."

On the lake. Summer ending, and Marcy's final year of school just beginning. She had so many hopes and expectations, and it had all turned out so differently than she had imagined. But so much better.

Their food finally arrived. It was a pepperoni pizza to share, the exact same thing they'd ordered the first time here.

"At least my parents are finally cool with everything," Marcy said. "I was worried at first, but they've totally come around. I think they're secretly pleased that we'll be long distance so it doesn't distract me from graduation."

"Once you graduate, I will be doing everything I can to distract you," Gray said.

Marcy shivered at the heat in his eyes. She could tell exactly what he had in mind.

"And I want you to meet my family. Easter, if that works for you?"

It definitely worked for Marcy. It was just too long away.

"I'd love to meet them," she told him. She would probably be really nervous when she did so, but she figured if Gray's relatives were even just a bit like him, they'd be alright.

"Also I have something for you," he said. "It's kind of a going away present."

Marcy was really surprised as she hadn't expected Gray to give her anything.

Let alone the really elegant jewellery box that he passed to her.

She opened it, pressing the little clasp and gasped. It was a ring, on a delicate gold chain. A sapphire blue heart set in rose gold.

Gray was looking at her, his expression intense. "I want you to know how serious I am about you, Marcy. But I also didn't want to pressure you. So it's a necklace, and if you ever want to wear it as a ring, then you can do that."

It was the most beautiful thing anyone had ever given her. Marcy put it around her neck, and while the ring was on the chain, she slipped her finger through it. "It fits perfectly. It's so beautiful, I love it. Thank you."

"I took a guess. I picked the sapphire for your eyes."

Marcy met his gaze. For a moment she sensed the years between them: how much older he was. How he was clearly ready for something that she wasn't quite ready for herself. But he was happy to wait. He loved her, and he would be patient.

And one day, just months away now, she would hopefully be permanently with him in the same city once again.

Marcy was certain her feelings for Gray would only grow. Looking at him, hearing him say how he loved her, she knew it would be the same for him.

50. Encore

Five years later

"And the nominees for Best Book of a Musical are…"

It was very strange and nerve-wracking for Marcy, hearing her name read out alongside such prestigious and well-known writers.

Beside her, Gray squeezed her hand when a few seconds of Rapunzel was shown to the audience. She knew she couldn't possibly win, but it had been such an amazing ride.

Her play, Rapunzel, had been turned into a musical and eventually became a hit show on Broadway. And now she was being nominated for a Tony award! Of course the play had gone through a lot of changes and additions, but the libretto was still nearly all Marcy. She had written or co-written the lyrics to all of the songs, and worked closely on extra dialogue and other changes. It was still essentially hers.

In the row in front, Revel turned around and winked at Marcy. She was impossibly glamorous these days, her piercings long gone, her hair like long black silk. Perfectly styled today, wearing some designer gown that had been created especially for her. Revel was fully a star in her own right now, albeit a bit of a frustrated one. Instead of the character roles she wanted she was still getting ingénue roles. Along with slews of awards and accolades, though these didn't seem to thrill her.

Addy, also still in New York, working in advertising and dating a different gorgeous guy every six months, was mystified by Revel's attitude. "Don't you like getting the leads?"

Indeed Revel had ended up cast as Rapunzel in the first, off-Broadway production of Marcy's play, not the witch as she had hoped for. What Revel wanted was character parts. She wanted to be a grande dame of the theatre, not just the winsome heroine. The Joan Crawford, not the Jeanne Crain. "You'll get there eventually," Marcy had told her. "You just need to age a few decades."

Marcy only realised she'd started daydreaming when Gray nudged her. "Go on, you'll have to go up."

What? Then she realised the reason she'd just heard her own name again was because it had been on the card drawn out from the envelope. She had won!

Feeling part dizzy, part in a trance she made her way along the row to the stage. There were people to usher her where she needed to go, so she let them lead her and ended up standing on the stage with the brilliance of the lights upon her.

Marcy had been on plenty of stages over the past year, but somehow this moment took her right back to that deer-in-the-headlight sensation of understudying for Mrs Helberg.

With one hand on the podium stand and another on her bump, which felt like it was size and shape of a pumpkin, she managed to find her voice. She listed off all the various theatre people she needed to thank, trying to speak clearly and concisely. It had been such a huge team effort after all.

"…and not forgetting Revel Holmes, our wonderful leading lady for the first run, all my dear friends and family, and most of all my husband Gray, without whose inspiration and support this would never have happened."

She looked for Gray in the audience and could make him out, smiling at her. The advantage of being nominated and married to a famous actor was that they seated you in the front rows, where the cameras were constantly on you.

Marcy returned to her seat as the applause rang out through the auditorium, clutching the heavy award. She slid in beside Gray, knowing they would be filmed in close up. He kissed her. "Congratulations, you looked beautiful up there. You totally deserved to win, I knew you could do it."

"I looked like a huge pregnant hippo," Marcy said.

Gray laughed. "You're glowing and you've never been more beautiful to me. Carrying our child." His hand lightly caressed the roundness of her stomach through her dress as he kissed her again. He was so genuinely proud of her talent, so supportive of her writing career.

On the way to the awards party Gray stopped to sign autographs for a couple of people. The past two years he had been starring in a top rating medical drama about New York heart surgeons, and it had reached the stage where he was constantly approached by fans. Fame had been a weird thing for them both to deal with.

The money had been wonderful though: they now owned a beautiful New York apartment, Marcy could fly down to see her parents whenever she wanted, and she had all the time in the world to write. She already had another play in production and one in the pipeline, and with the Tony nomination she was starting to get approached to write film screenplays.

Gray had asked her to marry him the day she graduated with honours from NYU. He had produced the most beautiful diamond ring that had belonged to his grandmother. "This is just a temporary ring, so you can choose the one you want."

But Marcy hadn't wanted another. The stone in the heirloom ring had witnessed so much love and happiness: it was such a beautiful setting and had such beautiful symbolic value, that nothing else could match it.

The wedding had been a dream. Addy had been Marcy's maid of honour with Revel as chief bridesmaid. Gray had managed to produce some devastatingly handsome groomsmen, one of whom Addy had even dated for a while.

Revel never seemed to get into any serious relationships, she was too committed to her career. She was often photographed with various male stars, some of which she confessed to Marcy were merely PR set ups. But she was happy, and determined to keep climbing the ladder. She had been a huge success at Juilliard and was clearly headed for the stars.

So Marcy was the only one hitched so far. It had been younger than she had imagined she would marry, but Gray being a few years older, it all felt right. They hadn't planned on starting a family so soon but nature had a way of deciding these things, and

Gray had been so overjoyed when Marcy told him that his reaction assuaged any fears she might have had.

She was pretty sure it was going to be a girl, and if so, they were going to call her Esme. Great Aunt Esme was very elderly these days and had moved into an old people's home. Her mind was still as sharp as ever, she just was a little too frail of body to live by herself. She had formed a strong friendship over the past years with Revel's grandmother Rowena, who visited her regularly as did Marcy's family.

Cora Helberg still reigned supreme in Springdale's theatre world. Having been the "incubator", as she liked to claim, for two hugely successful actors and now an award winning playwright, she had taken the Springdale Players from strength to strength.

Brittanny and her friends had ended up going off to different colleges, their clique finally split up. The last Marcy had heard, Brittanny had just broken off an engagement to some guy who worked in finance. Or he had broken it off. Marcy felt somewhat sorry for her, either way. Brittanny had gone from being queen of Springdale to no one in particular, forced to watch from a distance while her former enemies lived it up as celebrities in the Big Apple.

Marcy felt pretty tired as the awards after party continued. So many people approached her to congratulate her, after a while she felt like her face was aching with smiling and saying thank you to everyone.

Fortunately Gray's eagle eyes missed nothing. "We're going home," he told her.

"But the party's far from over."

"And you're already exhausted, and your wellbeing is more important than more schmoozing with showbiz people. I know you don't even enjoy it."

It was true. Marcy far preferred to be home, resting, reading a book or a play. She was thinking of doing something with The Tempest for her next project: it would definitely be a musical, she could already imagine some of the songs. And Revel as Miranda.

She lay back in the limo, Gray's arm around her. It would be nice to get out of this dress, take a shower, and just put her head down.

Reading her mind, Gray said: "it's straight to bed with you when we get back. No sitting up and writing." He knew that Marcy could write until the early hours when she got into the zone. "Besides, I have other plans for you."

"Other plans?" From the gleam in his eye, Marcy had a fair idea what they were. She was still amazed he remained so attracted to her given her condition.

"If you're not too tired. Though given how sexy you look in that dress, I may just have to keep you awake," he warned.

It was a beautiful dress. It was fitted in the bodice, and then flowed as elegantly as possible over her bump, specially adapted to do so. It also showed much more of of the swell of her breasts than she would usually have worn, but the couturier had insisted it would look best that way.

Back in their apartment, Gray drank in the sexy shape of his wife, before slowly unzipping her and carrying her to their bed.

"I love you," he told her. "You're the most beautiful woman I have ever seen. I can't believe how lucky I am to have you in my life, and our future child."

Marcy answered him with a kiss, pulling him towards her. She was tired, but Gray's mere touch still lit fires in her body. "I guess we should make the most of the time we have just the two of us," she said. As excited as she was about the baby, it was going to be a big change.

And then she was in Gray's arms, and nothing else existed. He was her world, and they were creating their own future together. The curtain might be coming down on the first act, starring Gray and Marcy, but she knew that there would be new wonders in store when the curtain rose again, and the three of them took up their new roles. Whatever dramas came their way, whatever love scenes, they were headed for a very happy ending.

About Noël Cades

Noël Cades is a British writer who currently lives in Sydney, Australia. A fan of romance from historic to erotic, some of Noël's favourite authors include Jilly Cooper, Jackie Collins, Elizabeth Rolls and Victoria Holt.

Noël is always delighted to hear from other fans, readers and writers of romance.

You can contact Noël at noelcades@gmail.com

Noël's website is at http://www.noelcades.com

Visit Noël's blog to sign up for exclusive news and the chance to receive new free book giveaways.

Excerpts from *Tempting Her Teacher* by **Noël Cades**

The punch had made Juliet feel a lot bolder. She gave a sharp rap and they waited until the door was opened. Mr Spencer stood there, wearing jeans and a casual shirt. They hadn't seen him out of the smarter slacks and tie he wore for school before, as well as at church.

Juliet smiled at him, her eyes glinting. "Trick or treat?"

He was disconcerted. "I've run out of candy, there were so many kids coming round earlier. Isn't it a bit late for you three to be out?"

"It's not midnight yet," Fhemie pointed out.

"So, trick or treat?" Juliet asked him, looking alluringly up at him.

"I guess a trick then, since I'm out of treats. Just don't destroy my car or anything."

Juliet took a step towards him and leaned towards him. She saw his eyes fall on her neckline and back to her face. He looked very uncomfortable. "Or you can have the treat," she whispered.

Mr Spencer froze as she reached up and brushed her lips against his, light as a feather, inhaling his scent. His lips were warm and dry and she wanted to kiss him more deeply but didn't dare.

She could feel the tension in him, he was wound up, tightly coiled. If the others hadn't been there she might have tried to go further. The alcohol had loosened her inhibitions and all she wanted was to be with him, making out with him, having his hands all over her body.

Juliet felt herself tingling, an ache between her legs, just from the brief contact. She was amazed that just kissing him - barely kissing him even - could turn her on so much.

As she gazed back at him, her lips parted from the embrace, his face was frozen. He didn't even speak.

She wondered if he felt anywhere near the same that she did. His body looked so hard and masculine, he was so much taller than her. Had he responded in the same way or was he in complete control, indifferent to her?

"Goodnight then," she said, smiling once more.

* * *

"Did you mind?" she asked.

"Mind what?" He was momentarily confused.

"That I kissed you."

Carl had to take a couple of seconds to steady himself. With her words Juliet had brought the whole event rushing back. It didn't help that she was once again standing in front of him with half her breasts showing, her skirt revealing most of her thighs. It took every ounce of his self control not to reach out for her.

"Were you angry?" she asked him. She had thought he was from the way he had seemed to avoid her since that night.

"No." He barely voiced it but she read his lips.

"Would you be angry if I did it again?"

The number of people and the crowd at the bar had pushed the two of them closer, nearly touching. Carl had to work on his breathing to remain still: he was a hair's breadth from being right against her. He couldn't take his eyes off her lips. "We can't, Juliet. It would be totally inappropriate."

She gave him a seductive smile. "But you want me to?" she said, her voice almost a whisper. They were so close she could smell the trace of cologne he was wearing, smell the raw maleness of his skin. She thought she had never wanted anyone so badly.

He briefly closed his eyes, trying to keep himself together. "I'm your teacher. We can't have this conversation." The rote phrases were the only thing keeping him from stepping over the precipice.

"So if you weren't my teacher...?" The question hung in the air.

"Juliet..." He couldn't answer. He couldn't lie convincingly and to admit the truth was impossible.

"Do you want me?" She was leaning even closer, millimetres from his body. Pretty much any other guy in the bar would kill to be in this position. Carl dreaded to think what Dan's reaction must be. He couldn't bring himself to look over.

"More than anything." He could hardly believe he had admitted it. She had him transfixed. "Right now, being this close to you is like torture. But it's wrong and nothing is going to happen. Even if you weren't my student, I'm far too old for you."

As he spoke he managed to get his composure back. To bring himself back down to earth.

"I'm eighteen. I'm above the age of consent."

Just this phrase nearly knocked Carl off balance again. He could only imagine the sweetness of actually taking her. But he was resolved. He picked up the drinks. "It makes no difference." His voice was firm.

234

Juliet had to get back anyway for the second half of the show. "I'll see you at school then?" She looked directly into his eyes and they held one another's gaze for a moment.

"I'll see you at school." Carl had a feeling this was far from over but he would steel himself into more careful behaviour in future. Juliet slipped off to the band and Carl return to Dan.

Dan looked at him quizzically. "That looked like a cosy chat. Do you know her?"

Carl couldn't lie, Dan might well find out anyway. "She's actually one of my students."

Dan whistled under his breath. "That's some serious jailbait. Are they all like that?"

"She's a good student." Carl found himself defensive of Juliet.

"With a serious teacher crush," Dan countered.

Despite himself Carl felt uplifted at this. After all Juliet was young and beautiful and pretty much every guy in the place would have had his eye on her that night, wearing her outrageous outfit and singing like an angel. Even though it was completely wrong, he was flattered to think that she found him attractive.

Glancing around and seeing other hungry male eyes on her, Carl had to fight his instinct to grab a coat and put it around her.

The guilt would doubtless hit him in the early hours, as he had yet another dream of her, and he would struggle to get through the weekend alternately missing her and trying not to think of her.

* * *

Juliet went up to Mr Spencer's desk. She stood there, hugging her pile of folders against her chest.

They were both lost for words. But something needed to be said. She let him take the lead, after all he was the one that had summoned her.

Mr Spencer began. "About Friday night, what I said..."

Juliet feared he was going to try and retract it.

"We both know that I shouldn't have said it," he continued.

"But it was true?"

Mr Spencer sighed. "Juliet, we can't go through this again. That's what I needed to tell you. Conversations like that are off limits."

"But you can't take it back."

"I know." He looked contrite.

"And I can't forget hearing it."

"But you need to, Juliet. We both do." His expression was serious but also sad.

She was near enough to feel the magnetism of him, drawing her in.

"I can't. And you know I feel the same," she told him.

"You're so young, it's not uncommon for someone your age…"

Juliet felt a flash of anger and broke in. "It's not because I'm young. It's not as though I'm inexperienced."

Her words hung in the air between them. She immediately regretted them: now he must be thinking that Cynthia's insults about her were true.

"I know. But these feelings, when they're not appropriate, they're sent to test us," Mr Spencer said.

"Why?"

Why? It was the question that Carl Spencer had asked himself and his God again and again. It was the question he had been agonising over. What was the purpose of him struggling with these feelings for his student? If only she were less beautiful, less intelligent, less desirable. He felt the heat rise between them again.

Juliet was weak with wanting him. Just for him to put his arms around her so she could feel the heat and strength of his body pressed against her. The smooth cotton of his shirt. The shape of the muscles beneath it.

She spoke, her voice almost a whisper.

"If you embrace me, I won't slip away."

"That's what I'm most afraid of." The spectre of her haunted him enough, the flesh and blood reality would be a devastating torment.

Juliet looked up into his face. "Could you just kiss me, once? Just to see how it feels?"

Carl knew how it would feel. He had kissed her in his dreams, in his thoughts, in his daydreams. He had amplified the memory of their brief embrace, replaying it again and again.

"I can't do that."

"But you want to."

She leant towards him, tilting her face up and closing her eyes. Carl gripped the side of the desk to steady himself. He leaned forward towards her, his face as near to her face without touching. There was barely a fraction of space between his lips and hers. He was so close, so close… he could even feel his own skin tingle. But he would not kiss her.

Feeling as though he was floating for a moment he absorbed everything he could in those few seconds: her energy, her sweet, fresh perfume, the sound of her breathing.

Then he broke away.

"You deserve better," he told her as she opened her eyes, feeling him withdraw. He saw the faint hurt and disappointment there. "You deserve better than some stolen kiss. You deserve more than I can offer you."

To find out if Mr Spencer will give into his attraction to Juliet, read Noël Cades' passionate student-teacher romance novel, Tempting Her Teacher.

www.ingramcontent.com/pod-product-compliance
Lightning Source LLC
Chambersburg PA
CBHW030515020726
47494CB00004B/1104